# SEXAHOLICS

T0385237

If you love hot and steamy erotica,
you'll also enjoy
*Erotic City* by Pynk
Available now

# SEXAHOLICS

## PYNK

**GRAND CENTRAL**
PUBLISHING

NEW YORK   BOSTON

Copyright © 2010 by Pynk

All rights reserved. Except as permitted under the U.S. Copyright Act of 1976, no part of this publication may be reproduced, distributed, or transmitted in any form or by any means, or stored in a database or retrieval system, without the prior written permission of the publisher.

Adult Sex Education Dictionary terms are reprinted from www.bettersex.com by permission of the Sinclair Institute.

Grand Central Publishing
Hachette Book Group
237 Park Avenue
New York, NY 10017

www.HachetteBookGroup.com.

Printed in the United States of America

First Edition: March 2010
10 9 8 7 6 5 4 3 2 1

Grand Central Publishing is a division of Hachette Book Group, Inc.
The Grand Central Publishing name and logo is a trademark of Hachette Book Group, Inc.

Library of Congress Cataloging-in-Publication Data
Pynk.
   Sexaholics / Pynk.—1st ed.
      p. cm.
   ISBN 978-0-446-17958-4
   I. Title.
   PS3613.O548S49 2009
   813'.6—dc22
                                        2009011212

Book design by L & G McRee

This second Pynk book is dedicated to all the sexaholics taking steps to recover and detox from obsessive lust and sex through fellowship. Here's to your successful, long-term sobriety.

# ACKNOWLEDGMENTS

Well my cherished lovelies, I lost my erotica virginity with *Erotic City*, and it was a real pleasure. It came so naturally! And so here I am again after having completed my next sex-in-the-city title, *Sexaholics*. As you hold this hot little book in your hot little hands, please know this sophomore erotica experience could not have been possible without the following cherished individuals, companies, and sites.

I'd like to offer major thankxxx to HoneyB, who has been my dear friend since 2003, and whom I call the ultimate Super Woman, for always being simply sexy, supportive, smart, and just plain old special.

And VCM, my Starbucks buddy, for giving me the great "lay it out on the floor" advice. Your suggestion about separating the individual character stories and connecting them later brought it all together.

To my loving family, as always, I am so thankful for your undying love and understanding. Your amazing support and acceptance give me the fuel to continue writing. I love you one and all!

Thankxxx to my cherished Grand Central Publishing

family—Karen Thomas (your detailed, constructive, and honest revision letters have served to enrich all aspects of my writing—love you dearly), Latoya Smith, Jamie Raab, Linda Duggins, Samantha Kelly, Miriam Parker, Renee Supriano, and others. I am so proud and honored to be part of your awesome and professional team.

Also, tender kisses to *Letters to Penthouse*, theeroticwoman.com, bettersex.com, sa.org, bastardlife.com, feministreview.blogspot.com, urban-reviews.com, book-remarks.com, Harriet Klausner, Tracey Ricks Foster, Maureen Walters, mahoganybookclub.ning.com, aalbc.com, mosaicbooks.com, sistahfriend.com, alexanderbook.com, edc-creations.com, rawsistaz.com, apooobooks.com, simply-said.net, Medu Books, Waldenbooks at CNN, Nubian Books, the Decatur Book Festival, blacksover40.org, Mocha with the NAACP Author Pavilion, author Curtis Bunn and the nationalbookclubconference.com, author S. B. Redd, all of my MySpace and Facebook Friends, Vicky Evans at Foxie105 radio, iseecolor.com, and the many online groups, bookstores, book clubs, and radio shows who supported my first erotica title, *Erotic City*. Gracias!

And a special thankxxx to you, my cherished readers, who've embraced *Erotic City*, for seeking out erotica books as a viable and very necessary form of entertainment, and for letting me know how much you enjoy my work. *Sexaholics* is set in the city of the stars, movies, women, and cars—Los Angeles. It is raw and real and racy. I love, love, love what I do and I plan to keep dishing out the spice, so hang tough. There's more to cum in 2010! Just check out the juicy chapter excerpt from my next title, *Sixty Nine*, about three sexually repressed women in Miami, born in 1969, who are about to turn the big 4-0! *Sixty Nine* is anything but missionary!

Smooches,
Pynk
xoxo

www.authorpynk.com
www.myspace.com/authorpynk
authorpynk@aol.com

# AUTHOR'S NOTE

I've written this dramatic book, *Sexaholics*, about women struggling with sex addiction. Women are rarely labeled sexaholics. Sexaholics Anonymous members are mainly men. On one end, society doesn't necessarily see women as having a problem if all we think about is sex. We're simply seen as hypersexual nymphos, and that's sometimes considered a gift to men but perhaps at the same time not seen as marriage material. On the other end, we see male addicts as Peeping Toms and perverts, as in the alleged situations involving Eric Benet and David Duchovny, so we try to fix them because having sex and conquering women is a major part of who a man is. Well, we women need help, as well. And yes, sex, be it healthy or addictive sex, is a major part of women's lives, too.

I wanted to show four examples of female sex addicts from the inside out. Four women who are flawed, just like the three-dimensional characters I would develop in a mainstream title, who struggle with the fact their lust never sleeps. I felt the need to show the lives of those who are addicted to sex, aside from just the sex act itself.

I did a lot of research into sexual addiction through

reading, interviewing, and watching numerous television specials. I also attended Sexaholics Anonymous meetings, which were extremely helpful. The level of honesty, dedication to abstinence, and uplifting support these members shared amazed me. Sexaholics rehab programs are similar to Alcoholics Anonymous, based upon the same 12-step principles, and upon faith in healing through God, because the problem is physical, emotional, and spiritual. Healing comes about once all three are dealt with.

What I've learned is that no one is born an addict, whether it be alcohol, gambling, shopping, food, or sex. We are *all* products of our upbringing. Our society is damaged and there are many perverts and predators in the world, especially—and unfortunately—in our own families.

Sexual addiction is an illness that can be overcome. Lest we judge, take a moment to think of what the ride must be like for people suffering from a sex-addiction illness—unquenched addicts dangerously driven to the brink who want more and more. They are often victims of intense trauma, sometimes sexual, usually suffered in childhood.

I ask you to free your mind and open your eyes, strap on your strap-on, and take a look inside of the world of my four girls—Miki Summers, Valencia Sanchez, Teela Raye, and Brandi Williams—as they allow us to take a voyeuristic view into their quest for sobriety in a California rehab program. I give you my sophomore title, *Sexaholics*.

WARNING

Please use caution—
this Pynk title is rated *sex*!

# CHARACTERS' MOTTOES

**Miki Summers**—*Penis variety is the true spice of life.*

**Valencia Sanchez**—*Girls just wanna have fun
and eat as much pussy as humanly possible.*

**Teela Raye**—*Take my man, please, as long as I can watch.*

**Brandi Williams**—*Hit that dick and quit it,
but never go back twice.*

# SEXAHOLICS

# 1

# *"Confessions"*

## Sexaholics

"My name is Miki, and I'm a sexaholic."

"Hi, Miki," the smiling sexaholics support group members sang in unison that warm, early-summer evening. The fading amber sun dripped its sweet honey glow upon the coastline of the city of angels. Cries of free-spirited seagulls echoed in the sexy skies above.

It was a Tuesday.

The one-story, crème brick building spanned the entire palm-tree-lined block, and was only two stop signs from the world-famous pier along the shore of the Pacific Ocean. The fresh scent and white sounds of the blue-violet ocean were constant.

The walls of the east hall meeting room of the spacious outpatient treatment facility in Santa Monica, California, were lined with framed 12-steps and Sexaholics Anonymous posters. The facility had been packed ever since a very high-profile actor had been treated there for sex addiction. The many group programs at TAC, which stood for The Addiction Center, ranged from eating disorders and codependency to alcohol, drug, and sex recovery, and were usually booked many months in advance.

Cocoa-brown Miki looked down at the folding chair. She took her seat at the same time that her best friend, Valencia, stood.

"My name is Valencia, and I'm a sexaholic." She wore a massive princess-cut rock on her ring finger.

"Hi, Valencia."

Valencia nodded and sat, crossing her legs and clasping her sweaty hands.

A woman at the other side of the circle stood and spoke. "Hi. My name is Teela, and I'm a sexaholic."

The entire newcomers group again gave their standard cheery reply. "Hi, Teela."

As she took her seat, a petite, dark-skinned woman sprang to her feet. Her voice was melodic. "Hello there, everyone. I'm happy to be here." She flashed her perfectly capped teeth. "My name is Brandi, and I'm a sexaholic and an alcoholic." Her voice said she was proud, but her eyes said she was broken.

"Hi, Brandi."

Brandi bowed her head, then scooted her backside into the chair, nodding and eyeing each member as she offered a cheery grin. She rocked back and forth and crossed her arms, embracing herself tightly.

The tall, redheaded support-group sponsor spoke from her seat. "Thank you very much, newcomers. It's rare to have four women at once. Anyone else?" She looked around, along with others who scanned the room, allowing time for anyone who might have been left out. "No? Okay." She hugged a clipboard and a small, dark blue notebook to her bosom. "Welcome to the Sexaholics Anonymous, better known as SA, program at TAC. We at SA appreciate the fact that you've shared a little bit of yourselves with the group. We want you to consider this group as your extended family." Rachel Cummings, the Sexaholics Anonymous counselor, crossed her thirty-four-inch legs and flashed a wide Colgate smile, securing a retractable pencil over her ear.

"The focus of tonight's meeting is to familiarize you with the promise of recovery. So, first of all, right off the bat, I think it would be healthy and necessary for the new members to go ahead and get your biggest sexual act out of the way now. There has to be an admission in order to have victory over any addiction, and I know it's scary. But if you wouldn't mind, please tell us the wildest thing you've ever done sexually. Preferably, the wildest act would not only be the one that possibly shamed you the most, but also one that you may have enjoyed the most. Because basically, we seek help almost always at the point when we hit rock bottom. So, let's think back and speak in truth without fear of judgment, shame, embarrassment, or shock. Give us your rock bottom. It's time to confess. And remember, we are your new recovery family."

The older members of the group of eight looked at the newer ones and offered encouraging, nudging smiles. The newer members checked each other out, each hoping someone else would step up as the first guinea pig of the night, but no one budged.

"Does anyone care to go first?" Rachel Cummings spoke encouragingly, her eyes just as friendly as her voice. "How about you, Miki, since you gave the first introduction? Would you, please?" She motioned upward, encouraging Miki to stand.

With long, straight brown hair and wide brown eyes, Miki made a weak attempt at a smile as she stood. She hung her hands at her sides and shifted her weight to her right leg. Her short jeans skirt fit like it could have been peeled like a banana. She placed her hand on her shapely hip, which curved greatly from her waist, as her mind traveled. But she lost her almost-smile just that fast.

"It was all about me. I didn't care about anything else. I remember the creaking sound of footsteps in the hallway, but our moans were like animals and seemed to drown them out. He was tall and big and heavy, and his bulging belly needed to be lifted up to find his penis. I'd already sucked his huge dick for about thirty minutes, but he didn't ejaculate. The taste and smell of his precum stuck to my tongue while he literally pounded my flesh. I remember wishing I had a stick of cinnamon gum." A woman sitting next to Miki put a familiar hand on Miki's slender arm for comfort as Miki gave a nervous giggle along with the group. She then paused, swallowed audibly as she closed her eyes, and continued:

"As much as his body repulsed me, and the smell of his sweat that dripped onto my titties was musty, my vagina throbbed faster than I thought it would or could, and I took him in like I was getting away with a crime. My pussy was wetter than it had been since I was in my teens. I was dripping slippery fluid, and I could tell he was turned on to the point of damn near having a heart attack. He breathed unsteadily. He kept grunting louder and louder, and he went deeper and deeper. I kept groaning and grinding faster and faster with an urgency I'd never known. I mean, my clit felt like it was about to burst. I felt the pressure of his powerful cum shooting deep inside me just as the bedroom door flew open. I noticed someone standing there in the broad daylight, but I didn't care.

Not even that it was Adore, my younger sister, who had just absorbed an eyeful of our fucking. Not even that the man who had just shot his sperm deep inside of me, the same sperm that had impregnated her six months earlier, was paralyzed with fear. He froze. I still didn't care.

"I didn't care enough to cease my panicky grind or downshift my pleasure-filled grunts. As I said, it was all about me . . . getting off, and the thrill of sneaking had me high. I spewed my cum while my clitoris clenched repeatedly until I slowed down to the stillness of busted reality.

"My baby sister yelled, 'Not with my husband, Miki. Not with my Tommy.' Her eyes were watery and her hands shaky. I lay there, almost giving her a look like she had some nerve to interrupt. Then I pulled the covers over my body and scooted back. She called me a bitch and a whore and ran out. He ran out after her, just as naked as he was when he was inside of me. I sat back and lay still. Maybe it was out of shame, maybe it was out of fulfillment. I ended up taking a one-hour nap and then went to work like nothing had ever happened.

"I think I'm a nympho. Or maybe worse. Whatever that is. Whatever this is. I need help to stop. I can't do it on my own."

Miki simply opened her eyes and stopped talking. Her brown skin was flushed beyond rosy. The members were silent as if maybe she wasn't quite finished. It was like the video player in her mind simply stopped. She sat down. She flashed a glimmer of her right dimple, and her chest rose and fell. Valencia caught Miki's eye. Each touched her heart with her fist.

"Very good, Miki," Rachel Cummings said. "A nympho, huh? We don't know if that's true yet. I'm sure that situation must weigh heavily on you, especially since you obviously feel as though you've betrayed your sister. We'll speak on that as we go along, and we'll help you work through the feelings involved. Very good. Next."

Tall and reddish-brown, curvy Valencia came to a stance and looked down at her friend Miki, who gave her a mini-smile. Valencia then spoke quickly with a Puerto Rican swagger. Her thick, sugar-coated lips moved fast and her neck rolled.

"I push the limits. I have always pushed limits. You know what I mean? I pushed the limits in middle school doing something as minor as ditching class, or as major as giving my math teacher a blow job for an A. I mean, I was only fourteen. I was a trip.

"I've always been bored with twosomes. I had my first threesome when I was fourteen. It was with my cousin and her boyfriend. In college I met a man who matched my freak level to a tee. We'd go online and look for adults who wanted to do group sex with strangers, we'd fuck with another man, we'd fuck with another woman, we'd go to private house parties and end up on huge beds with ten people, just swapping and swallowing cum and eating pussy and taking it up the ass. And one time I watched him suck dick. I got off on it. I'll masturbate to an exercise video, if necessary, and he'll masturbate right along with me. I love to fuck. I can't think of the wildest time because it's all been wild." Valencia now flailed her expressive hands about with urgency. Her long pearl and purple nails shimmered.

"I've fucked while smoking weed, I've tried Ecstasy while giving head, and I've drank seven shots of straight one-fifty-one rum and then had sex outside in a park in broad daylight. I love rimming, I'll screw a man in drag, I'll lick pussy till it's raw. All I know is, I can't stop thinking of new ways to push my freak button. My man has threatened to leave me if I don't stop. His curiosity has been more than satisfied. My mind is always racing to find new ways to get my rocks off. I have no limits. Piss on me, tie me up, make me bark, or slap me. Doing whatever it takes to get a rile out of me only makes me hotter.

"Today, I hate living like this. But when I'm in the middle of it, I love it." She slowed her speech and her voice cracked with exhaustion and the fragile sound of an inner shame. She spoke at a low tone. "I'm here to break my addiction to sex. I'm a freak. A sex fiend. I've had enough. And I don't want to lose my man. Thank you." She sat back down and Miki reached over to hug her. Valencia placed her head on her friend's shoulder and then wiped her left eye. A sniffle followed.

A hazel-eyed man with a low fade sitting across from Valencia gave her a wink of approval, and then glanced over at Miki's firm legs, where his eyes lived for more than a few moments. The woman next to him had a tear running down her cheek. The woman played with a balled-up tissue and looked down at her lap.

Rachel Cummings said, "Valencia, we thank you as well. I see that your addiction has caused you much frustration. I understand, and we're here for you. The good thing is that you're at your wit's end. That's the point where most need to be before they seek help. Your glass is full, and that is a major turning point. We'll get through this together, Valencia. Thanks again."

Valencia nodded and smiled and sat up straight.

Teela stood, wearing beige Capri pants and a matching vest, blushing majorly through her fair, alabaster skin from her mixture of Scottish and French. She smoothed her hand over her jet-black, pixie-cut hair and exhaled.

"My name is Teela, as I said. I am a voyeur. I love to watch, and I get turned on by being watched. Valencia, I can relate to the park thing. I do that on the regular, maybe once a week. My lowest moment was when I peeked in the room to watch my mother and father having sex when I was a teenager. I felt shame, but still, I took that curiosity into my adult life. I will peek at neighbors or simply watch my man sex up other women without even getting involved. I've never been into women, but I have no problem approaching them at clubs and persuading them to fuck my man, only I sit back and fuck myself with a dildo or a cucumber or a hot link or with my fingers or whatever until I'm satisfied. I'm not the least bit jealous. As long as I'm there.

"I'm here because two weeks ago, I went into a sex shop and sat in a booth watching an old Vanessa del Rio movie. It was one of those seedy rooms where other people can peek in and watch you like perverts. I guess that includes me, huh?" she asked the group, looking around as others shook their heads in disagreement. She blinked rapidly. "I was leaning back with my panties to my ankles and I knew two sets of peering eyes were watching me rub my clit and stick my fingers in my ass. But I still jerked myself off over and over, and then I came so hard that I squirted pee on myself. One of the men stuck his dick through the glory hole and I sucked it until he came on my lips. And when he left, I put on another movie and lay back.

"I looked up to see that I was being watched again, and I saw a set of eyes, only one pair of eyes. They were dark brown, and the lids were iced with deep-set wrinkles. The whites of the eyes were cloudy. I jumped back and pulled up my underwear, closed my blouse, and put on my pants. Turns out the eyes belonged to my uncle. Uncle Chester was always trying to hug me a little too tight when I was younger, trying to be slick by pressing against my breasts. I always had a bad feeling about him. He was always sneaky. I hadn't seen him in years, but there he was jacking off at the sight of his niece masturbating. This world is getting way too small for the type of sick problem I have. I want to be rid of this obsession. That's why I'm here."

Teela ceased her story and looked around at the room full of faces. She turned to eye her chair, and as she sat she looked over and saw Miki giving her a warm eye hug and a wink.

Teela's soft expression gave away the fact that the wink was comforting. She winked back, flashing her pale green eyes demurely.

Rachel Cummings showed no shock. She only beamed with approval. "That's very good, Teela. It sounds like your admittance is going to get you through this. Your honesty and shame can work together toward your healing. We thank you."

"Yes," a couple of members said aloud, in particular the long-legged black man next to Teela, who offered her a smile as she shifted her thick body back into her chair.

Brandi said "Yes," too, as she sprang to her feet in a prim pale yellow skirt suit. "I suppose my name suits me well, as I've been an alcoholic for the past ten years. I'm thirty-two years old and started drinking heavily in college. I never believed in AA meetings or even admitted that I had a problem. But the combination of this sexual addiction and what I know to be an alcohol addiction will surely kill me if I don't surrender. You see, I cannot bond to anyone. I guess you can say I'm a love cripple. I have never had sex with the same person more than once in my entire life. I get off on the thrill of a stranger. I have a problem.

"And I recently posed as a hooker a few times just to surround myself with men who were expecting a onetime wham-bam, without all the intros. We went to the seedy motels or fucked in the backs of cars, and when it was all over, I ended up feeling as though I'd gotten more out of it than they did. I wouldn't even take their money. But the last straw was when I got arrested for solicitation of sex. The embarrassing charges were eventually dropped, but this addiction thing is interfering with my job as an eighth-grade teacher. I'm afraid I'll run into a student's parents one day or, worse, get fired. I am a sexaholic and I'm ready. Ready to get well. I'm ill. And I admit it."

Rachel Cummings handed over a wide smile as chestnut Brandi took her seat.

Brandi looked down after smiling back.

"Wow, I must say those are some very good examples of the extreme side of lusting and being lusted over," said Rachel Cummings. "Brandi, you have a two-headed demon to tackle—sex and alcohol—but it's not unusual, and sometimes there's no need for two recovery programs. Both AA and SA cover the same principles. Some people have addictive-type personalities and some of you, like Brandi, might find that you're addicted to other things as well, like alcohol or gambling or shopping or food. Some kick one addiction and take up another in its place. It will not be easy, but the fact that you're here means that you are sick and tired of being sick and tired. Your tomorrows will not be like your past, not if you don't want them to be. Thank you, Brandi. Thanks for sharing.

"Now, unless anyone else who hasn't shared before wants to share, we'll continue on. No one?" She eyed the group. "No problem. Since we have so many new members involved tonight, the first thing I will tell you all now is that we must seek victory over lust. It's time to stop lusting and become sober. Please repeat after me: Stop lusting and become sober."

"Stop lusting and become sober," each person said as one.

"Very good. The one thing you all have in common is that you have all been driven to the point of despair. That's why you're here. I want all of you to see that each of us, each and every one of us, as sexual addicts, takes from others in a sexual way something that is somehow lacking in ourselves. But what we end up doing is giving away our power through the forbidden. At some point in our young lives, because of some event or experience, we tuned things out with fantasy and masturbation, probably because someone took away our power somewhere along the way. This is a physical, emotional, and spiritual problem, and therefore healing and sobriety must come in those three ways as well. When you lose control, you no longer have the power of choice. I want to give you back your power of choice. I want you to give yourself back your power of choice. Your stories tell me you want to gain control, and you want to live a life of making positive, healthy choices that no longer spell addiction.

"This is a twelve-step recovery program that I will tell you now is spiritual. You'll hear me talk about God as we get to know the steps of recovery. One thing you need to know for sure is that you may or may not believe in God, but even if you get to know the twelve steps inside and out, if you don't have your own source of spirituality or faith, you won't get to recovery without it.

"Sexaholism will follow you every day for the rest of your lives. It is an addiction. And addiction is the management of feelings out of control. You have to own it and be in a community of other members. Recovery takes comprehensive counseling in a safe environment. The only thing that differentiates you from the next new person who comes through that door is your sobriety. How long can you abstain from the act itself, not engaging in unhealthy sex with someone else, or with yourself in some cases? That number of days will add up to mean your anniversary. It will be part of your identity. You will be one day, or three months, or one year, or ten years sober, and you will celebrate like it is the first day of the rest of your life. And each time you fall off the wagon and engage in intercourse and sexual acts, excluding with your spouses, you start that number all over again. It's all up to you. It can be done. I won't give up on you. Will you?"

The group replied "No" all together.

The group counselor continued, "I challenge you to make a true commitment over time that becomes a part of your lives. And by the way, I am five years, two months, and six days sober and having sex only with my spouse. I could tell you the number of hours if necessary.

Years ago I had daily sex with my married neighbor while his wife was at work. Next thing I knew, his teenage son joined in to make it a threesome, so I began sleeping with both of them, the father and the son, sometimes together, sometimes not. The parents didn't know why but the son got so sprung that he tried to kill himself. My neighbor's wife confided in me that she knew her husband was fooling around on her. The final straw was when I ended up fucking the wife, too. Her husband would have no idea where she was all night long, and she would be lying in my bed right next door. She left her husband for me and is still with me today. We got married. He moved away in shame. Nothing you can say to me would shock me. My name is Rachel Cummings, and I'm a sexaholic, also. And it's time to hug a new day."

Each member of the group, an unusually equal mix of men and women, eyed each other and raised eyebrows and nodded and smiled at Rachel Cummings. Two of the men had heard it before but still wore their thoughts on their faces. Some scooted back and some uncrossed their legs, some sipped on bottled water, and some looked around the room. But a cleansing feeling of shaking off all the admissions permeated the air, and an anxiousness of knowing that it was time to learn and heal and deal, as equals, as addicts, took over.

After thirty more minutes of going over the first step in the 12-step program—admitting to being powerless over sex and that their lives were now unmanageable—the sponsor ended the session and promised to see everyone back in two weeks, same time, same place.

Valencia and Miki left hand in hand, with more pep in their steps than they had going in. Teela and Brandi exchanged new friendship farewells and exited in different directions.

Valencia dropped her hand to reach in her purse for her grape BlackBerry. She said to Miki, "I'm proud of you, *chica*."

"You too, Val. To summarize and admit all that was harder than I thought."

"You closed your eyes like you saw it happening all over again." A slight summer breeze blew Valencia's long, curly, dark brown hair away from her oval face as they stepped out of the clinic front door.

"I did see it." Miki cleared her throat. "It was wild."

"It sounded like *The Vagina Monologues*, if you ask me. It was interesting as hell."

Miki gave a soft laugh. "That it was. So, where're you headed?" she asked with keys in hand as they walked amongst the evening darkness.

Valencia looked down at her BlackBerry and touched the screen. "I'm headed to Greg's place. I see a few missed calls from him. He's so excited about the fact that I agreed to get help. I must say after this first meeting I'm getting excited, too."

Miki stopped suddenly as the hazel-eyed man who was in the group walked up.

"Hello. How are you ladies doing? You may not remember my name from the brief intros of the regulars but I'm Dwayne. Dwayne Grace." The man towered over Miki's frame. He had on a white T-shirt and jeans.

"Hi," Miki replied with an instant look of sexy flirt.

Valencia stopped, too. "Hello. Okay, I guess I'll see you later, mama." She moved in closer to her friend and gave her a lip kiss.

Miki offered a distracted half kiss back, as well as a half hug. Her eyes were stuck on big, tall Dwayne from the waist down.

Noticing her friend's visual diversion, Valencia proceeded on with her car alarm remote in hand, switching her hips in dark blue pencil jeans. "Buzz me."

Miki nodded and then yanked her eyes from Dwayne to Valencia. "Okay. I'm headed home. Drive safely."

Valencia gave an *umph* sound.

"Sorry to interrupt," he said.

Miki slid her eyes back and put out her hand. "No problem. My name is . . ."

"I know. Miki, right?" He shook her hand and kept it. "Nice to meet you, Dwayne."

He still held her hand as they began to walk toward the parking lot. "I heard your story."

Miki beamed with a marriage of embarrassment and attraction. "I feel as though you know me. But what's your story?"

"I'd actually love to share it with you."

Miki stopped, looking up at him. "Your place or mine?"

Dwayne answered without missing a beat. "Yours." He released his grip and reached into his pants pocket for his wallet, keeping his eyes on her as he handed over his business card. "My cell number is at the bottom."

She read each and every letter and number. "Oh, okay. I'm in Inglewood. I'll call you. See you in an hour."

"I'm in Ladera. Actually, would you like to come by my place?"

"Sure. I'll be there." Miki began to walk away and looked back. "And you've got a condom, right?"

"I've got a ton of them," he assured her with a naughty grin.

Miki spoke in a private tone to his wide, V-shaped back as he hurried toward his silver Corvette, walking like a stud in what she noticed to be some very big shoes. She shook her head in amazement. "Uh, uh, uh. I'll bet that's a Trojan Magnum XL there. I'm gonna fuck the shit outta his big, fine ass."

# 2

# "I Wanna Sex You Up"

## Miki

The royal blue nine o'clock nighttime skies, lukewarm evening air, sparkly diamond-like stars, and full, luminous milky moon helped to set the mood above the manicured cul-de-sac street where one particular expensive ranch-style home contained macho bachelor and long-time resident big-shoes Dwayne Grace and his guest.

Barefoot, he made his way along the Brazilian oak flooring of the art deco hallway after brushing his teeth in the grand bathroom of his lower Ladera Heights master bedroom suite. His hazel eyes met an alluring vision named Miki Summers, the tall, sexy, self-proclaimed nymphomaniac he'd known for only an hour and a half, who was seductively awaiting his return. Like him, she was a slave to the unrelenting powers of her own intense sexual urges. It was a distinct addictive need that was stronger than the both of them. She lay awaiting an exchange of anticipated mutual top-shelf sexual prowess, as though she was his female equal.

Miki was sprawled butt naked on top of the milk-chocolate sheets of Dwayne's massive, high-gloss cherry-wood sleigh bed, which matched his distinctive design colors of maroon, tan, and coffee bean. A soulful, old-school jam—"Stranger" by L.T.D.—serenaded their coming together.

Her thirty-five-inch legs were spread wide. Her body was the color of dark rum, like her curly, bushy pubic hair. Her tits were pleasingly plump, like her beautiful, bountiful ass. Her thighs were thick like her juicy, generous lips. He couldn't have asked for more if he'd personally designed her himself.

Dwayne's red-boned face and low-hanging cinnamon dick, which matched his size fourteen feet, reacted at the same time. Both smiling bigger than a fat kid with a triple dip banana split with double fudge and three fresh, red cherries and chopped pistachio nuts on top.

He removed a towel from around his neck. He smelled like amber spice soap. He stood upon the mocha rug. His six-five frame hovered over Miki's curvy body. His grand manhood pointed directly at her approving face.

He'd placed a trio of almond candles on the oversized dresser. The tiny votives flickered along the buff walls like they were blazing from a wood-burning fireplace. There was a half-empty bottle of banana red MD 20/20 on the nightstand. Both Dwayne and Miki had taken extralong swigs. The red liquid surely helped them build up the nerve, though neither really needed a spinning head to entice them to get their freak on. The problem was, it never turned off.

Miki looked up at Dwayne's long, muscular frame.

Her dark eyes said *willing to please.*

His light eyes said the same.

Even though her exposed pussy was prone, he brought his dick to her cocoa lips and inched inside her mouth. Her wide, extended tongue traced the shape of his wide shaft. She adjusted herself just so and took the oral-receiver position, slurping and sucking as he poked his lengthy penis down her throat farther and farther. It sounded like she was gargling. Her moans had depth. She obviously had no problem with him meeting her tonsils. She accommodated his size like it was her distinct pleasure to do so.

He stood with his legs apart, hands on his hips, working his happy dick into her mouth. He looked down at her deep-throating skills, while every muscle of his ass cheeks was at peak contraction, adding to the power of his pumping. "Hell yeah, you suck a mean dick. Dammit. You swallow the whole damn thing. That's how the shit should be done right there." He moved her flat-ironed hair to the side so he could get a better view of the face he fucked. Her sounds of choking on his size made his nipples hard as steel.

She flashed big, innocent bedroom eyes up at him, nodding in total agreement. All he heard were continued sounds of *gngna, gngna, gngna*. Her throat vibrated against his cock. She looked downward again and brought her mouth to meet his heavy testicles. She sucked and sucked, then eased down for a skilled tea-bag move on both balls.

He moaned and then demanded, "Let me tittie-fuck you, baby. Give me those pretty-ass titties. Now."

She placed a full kiss on his tip and stood. He lay on his back with his forever legs hanging off the bed. She straddled him in reverse, sixty-nine style, securing her chest to his hardness and her pussy to his face. From the six position, she spit just in between her breasts and slipped his penis up and back along her soaked skin.

From the nine position, he put his face in it, inserting his tongue into her creamed-up, dark pink slit and sucking her smooth pussy skin, blowing slightly and lapping her up with a long lick stroke. He did a tongue push against her skin and licked briskly from side to side.

She said like a porno star, "Oooh, you so nasty. Oooooh, that shit is so nasty." She felt him devour her pussy triangle. His wet tongue parted her drenched lips. She jumped and looked back. "Boy, you so muthafuckin nasty." She then focused on her precision tittie-fuck and asked, "You like that? That's so pretty. My tits fit just perfect around that pretty dick."

He directed her to the end of the bed, turning her around to face the headboard on her knees while he stood behind her. Her ass was propped up high for easy access.

Dwayne grabbed a Magnum XL from the headboard shelf, ripped the corner of the gold foil with his teeth and hurried to slip it on, and then entered her all the way back on the very first stroke. She gasped and began to yell, "Yeah, run that all day long. Damn. Get that. Shit. Get it." She looked back seductively, saying words that would make a prostitute blush. "Uhm, uhm, uhm. Look at you. Big dick muthafucka." She looked like she was mad at somebody, and worked him by bucking back hard and throwing much ass his way. He popped her fleshy cheeks with a "smack it up, flip it, rub it down" move. "Oh, hell yeah. Fuck that shit." Her liquidity was a voluble audible, no challenge for the next slow-fuck song in the background, "In the Mood" by the Whispers. But Miki was in the fucking mood way before they even met.

He looked impressed and continued to dig in like his dick was a tablespoon and she was seafood gumbo.

She said in a half-kidding, shit-talking voice, "Uh-oh, cavity search. Yeah, I'll take it all. Get that. Get it." She yelled like he'd made a last-second touchdown.

He watched her ass work him. "Awww, shit."

"Yeah, fuck that pussy. I'ma call you Parkay cause you on a roll, muthafucka. Slap my ass again. Slap the fuck outta that bad boy."

And slap the fuck he did.

She gave him a ride as though he was Zorro and she was Tornado, wearing a golden saddle, but her words were bordering on hood. "Ohhh, holla at cha girl. You workin that shit over, look at you. Get that shit. All up in there. Oooh, yeah, you gonna give me that fucking milk shake in a minute, ain't chu? I can tell. That shit is ready to blow. Look at you."

He stopped and almost held his breath, trying to hold out. "Here, switch up again." He grabbed his dick and pulled out fast. His words were rushed. "Get on your knees and suck this." He ripped off his rubber and threw it wherever.

She moved fast to kneel onto the carpet and he slapped her soft face with his impatient dick. She grinned, looking extrapleased by his aggressiveness. Miki spit on his fresh-from-the-pussy shaft. She looked at her own creamy saliva as it soaked his skin. "I'm markin the beast with that shit." She spit again just before she took him down her throat. The stream of excess saliva dripped onto the carpet. She kept her sights on his facial expressions, being that she saw his climbing the wall as an ego massage. Being in the driver's seat was right where Miki liked to be.

"Damn, you're messy," he said, as though it was both

a complaint and a compliment, looking up toward the
ceiling. He placed his hands on each side of her freshly
weaved hair. His jaw was tight. His eyes were tight. His
ass was tight. He looked frantic, like he was desperately
fighting to hold it. "Uuummmh yeah. Yeah. That's some
dick suckin fo yo ass."

She licked his nuts like he'd licked her pussy, and
downed him from tip to base and again growled, hob-
knobbing fanatically, twisting her right hand in a circle
from wrist to fingertips.

"Right there. Right there." His breathing grew un-
stable.

She continued to bob and bob and bob and stroke and
stroke and stroke and suck and suck and suck, like his
cock was a chocolate Tootsie Pop.

He looked down and took a half step back. Erotic
urgency took over his face. He grunted while speaking.
"Wait. Here it is. I wanna cum on your face." He choked
the throat of his platinum dick. A heavy vein sprouted
from the middle of his forehead and from the center of
his shaft.

She released his dick from her mouth and met his pee-
hole with her lips.

He cried her name, "Miki," with a baritone shrill, secured his aim, and jetted intermittent spurts onto her long
tongue runway as she stuck it out for his sperm landing.
Some hit the side of her mouth and some hit her right
cheek. She drained his dick and licked her lips and even
gave a full swallow of his salty, warm semen, as though it
would be rude not to.

She made more gargling sounds with his cum and
smacked her lips, looking up at him with her huge brown

eyes, giving him a nasty-girl face, yet she was the one to say to him, "You so fuckin nasty." As she spoke, three small drops that had landed on her throat dripped right between her tits, making a pearl necklace. She laughed. "Damn, killa. All over my fuckin mouth and throat." She looked down at the fluid facial and joked, "He painted a Picasso." She played with his droplets with her fingertips. "You a fuckin Picasso."

He laughed out loud. His eyes showed he was intoxicated from her skills.

"Let's recycle that shit," she said, as she scooped a drop with her finger and licked it off. Her porn-star performance was just her way of saying thank you.

His voice was shaky. "Damn. I could get used to this. We're gonna have to have a part two. That was a damn blow-job sandwich there. This shit is crazy." The post-orgasm hormones had him making dick promises. He looked at her with admiration for putting it on him right and took stumbling steps into his bathroom, grabbing a black washcloth and running warm water on it. He exited and then approached Miki, handed it to her, and then collapsed onto the bed, turning onto his back while his chest rose and fell.

She took the cloth. "Thanks." Miki wiped her mouth and cheeks and neck, and then held on to it, laying her head upon his stomach. "True. But don't forget. We're supposed to be reforming."

They were quiet.

His breathing was still hard. He gave a delayed response, like he'd been on a pussy trip. "Fuck reforming tonight."

She grinned.

He grinned and looked down at her round ass. "You're bad."

"I'm not bad, I'm just drawn that way." She batted her long eyelashes.

"Yes you are." His eyes stayed on her backside. "I say I eat that greasy pussy till you cum in my mouth. I mean after all, turnabout is fair play." He took her cloth and laid it upon the nightstand.

She replied by immediately turning onto her back and spreading her legs open as he maneuvered his way to what lay between her wall-to-wall thighs.

She still tasted as sweet as she smelled and he noticed. He inhaled even deeper and his head swam. The smell of pussy had him going. It was his drug.

Her thighs were now his earmuffs and he was all hers. The touch of his tongue upon her clit had her squirming in ecstasy. She let him examine her every nook and cranny, and closed her eyes to focus on his oral travels.

Ten minutes later, Miki's legs tightened and she came in Dwayne's mouth. He lapped it up, feeling her clit dance. He ended with a soft, subtle kiss against her opening and looked up at her with an inkling of wonder. And then he mounted her again.

And for the next hour, they fucked again and again, using two more man-sized condoms.

Once the last bit of their erotic screwing was un-screwed, they lay back side by side, coated with each other's sweat, with looks of pure-dee satisfaction, even though they'd already fallen off the no-fucking wagon on the very same day of their first rehab meeting. And even though he had a bevy of beautiful and willing women at his disposal each and every night, women who came into the popular nightclub he owned, for some reason aside from her booty of life and heavenly pussy, Miki had his full attention.

For Miki, it was routine. It was just a fuck. The rest was only a fantasy. Dwayne was definitely Dr. Feelgood, but it was just another lustful need fulfilled. Just an everyday thing, the variety she craved. Her tank was again temporarily full.

Miki's mind momentarily slipped away from the intense, high-powered lay she'd just experienced. She sat up in the bed and came to a naked stance, fingering the tousled strands of her long hair. She never was one to lounge in the booty-call afterglow and hang around unless there was a commitment. Though because of her impossible sexual desires, she really didn't know the true meaning of the word *commitment*, anyway.

She began to gather her clothes so she could head home for a quick shower and change. Her six-year-old son, T.J., would be at his father's house until the next morning, and right now all she could think about was how much pussy-fun she was going to have at her favorite place, the place that had employed her for three years awhile back. The tittie bar.

She got dressed and approached the bed where Dwayne lay upon his back. She leaned down to kiss him on the cheek. He then rose to a slow stance and took delayed steps, following her to the front door, eyeing every inch of her shapely frame from behind.

Miki's platinum phone rang, and she took it from her green Coach satchel to eye the screen. It was her boyfriend, Tariq. It was his third call. She pressed Ignore.

She noticed Dwayne as he stood in the doorway, looking like the bomb-ass pussy of his life was about to head out to Afghanistan and never return. She turned her sights toward her car after he watched her step from the front door to the driveway of his cul-de-sac home. She slammed her hips on purpose from left to right.

She hopped in her black cherry Mitsubishi Montero and sped off.

Sexual sobriety would be a stranger to them both for at least another day. Lust, just as it was before their impulsive sexual encounter, was their closest friend.

They had the exact same libidos.

They were lushes. Sex drunks.

Their sex drives were in overdrive.

Perfect for the moment.

# 3

# *"How Does It Feel?"*

## Teela

Short and thick with a sister-girl rear end, Teela Raye rode in her cloud-white 300Z through the predictably slow-moving evening traffic of the 405 North, taking the short drive after stopping by her mom's place in Westwood near Wilshire Boulevard. It had been an unheard-of three-hour visit. She was now headed to the townhome she shared with her man, Austin Henderson, in the beautiful Fox Hills area of Culver City, mainly inhabited by younger African American professionals.

Most of the handsome neighborhood consisted of large apartment communities, but a few of the buildings had been converted into condos. Teela bought her unit over six years ago and was saving up to buy a new home in Baldwin Hills. Austin moved in with her three months after they met, and they split the bills in half.

She rested her left elbow along the soft leather-lined door of her sports car, with the gentle nighttime breeze spiraling along the strands of her spiky hair. She struggled to eject the mental video of the conversation playback she'd just had with her mom. *You need to leave Austin. You need to tell him to move out. He'll be the death*

*of you or the death of himself. Believe me. You can abso-*
*lutely do better.*

Teela thought to herself, *She's disliked him ever since he*
*moved in with me. Said no real man would do that. And now*
*that I admitted to her that I'm a sexaholic, in her opinion it's*
*all Austin's fault. Funny.*

She called Austin, using the speakerphone. "Hey Austin. I'm on my way. Once the meeting was over, I did end
up spending more time at Mom's than I thought."

"Oh, okay, cool. So how'd it go? The meeting, I mean,"
he inquired, with an excited depth to his voice just as she
prepared to hang up.

She readjusted her elbow along the door and smoothed
a few strands of short hair behind her ear. "I don't know. I
guess it's too early to say. The lady who's the group sponsor seems cool. Everyone in there has issues just as deep
as the next one."

His voice was deep. "Well, hell, you know how I feel.
What you seem to call issues really aren't issues at all. You
must be the most normal one in there."

Her voice was soft. "I don't think so. If you ask me,
my shit is right up there with the rest of em. Mainly it
was men, but there were four of us women, the newbies.
This cool girl named Brandi and a couple of other girls. I
think their names are Valencia and Miki, all confessing
the worst. Basically admitting what put them over the
edge."

"Oh yeah? What kinda shit did they have?" His in-
quiring mind wanted to know.

She clicked her tongue. "I can't tell you. Everywhere
you look, the signs say nothing goes beyond those walls.

And we all vowed that what happens at Sexaholics, stays at Sexaholics."

"Oh yeah, right. Like most of those folks aren't at home telling everything they heard by now."

"Well, I sure won't." She exited at Centinela and proceeded to Bristol Parkway.

"I'll bet I can get it out of you."

She turned on Green Valley Circle. "Your ass needs to be sitting in there right along with me, confessing. With your kinky self."

"I beg to differ. No need to detox on my end. You and me, we do what we do, and that's cool. You know how I feel about that. I say you're wasting your time. Being a voyeur is not that serious."

Teela made a left along Buckingham Parkway, past the southwest portion of the elevated and green, ten-acre Fox Hills Park. A few late p.m. joggers walked the workout trail, and one lone woman did a fast walk with a large, protective-looking golden retriever. As Teela spoke, she was reminded of the time she and Austin had sex in the park, right on top of a picnic bench. "Maybe not to you, but it's serious to me. This turn-on-by-watching crap, these fantasies, are ruining my life."

"I say whatever floats your damn boat."

"I'm here to tell you that one day my boat is gonna sink with my big ass in it and yours, too. This shit is an addiction. And like the group sponsor said, I have to stop lusting and become sober. Period."

"Okay. You say so." He gave a small laugh as Teela pressed the garage door opener. "Damn, I hear the garage. Are you home already?"

"Yes, I am."

"Perfect. Listen. Come on upstairs. But on the way up, take your clothes off, every stitch, because as soon as you hit the door, I'll be on my knees waiting to eat your pretty pussy from the outside in."

"Oh really?"

"Really. And Teela?" His tone was teasing.

"Yes." The feeling of anticipation was knocking at her chest. She took a deep breath.

His voice was suddenly even deeper. "At this very moment, my dick is deep inside of Payshun's mouth. She's young, has the velvet face of an angel and the flawless body of a stripper. And she's on her back on the floor. I'm on my knees straddling her fine-ass face, fucking her wide mouth like I fuck your deep pussy. And you're about to have the time of your life. Now get your hot ass on up here."

Teela put the car in park and turned off the ignition. She sat. Speaking of wide-open mouths, hers was so wide her chin was hitting her chest. The image in her mind was an unwelcomed turn-on. She gave a loud exhale and shook her head. "Austin, there's no way. I just told you I'm trying to . . ." Another moment of mental hesitation rolled, along with an even louder, deeper sigh. And then her words flowed clearly: "I'll be right up."

Teela's suddenly seductive voice growled long and teasingly. She was naked as instructed. Their bedroom smelled of a seductive mix of Issey Miyake cologne for men and Perry Ellis perfume for women. Teela's nipples were at full attention. Her vagina was totally fired up. All at the sight of her man's dick being swallowed alive. Expertly.

Teela examined the mad head skills of her man's young lover. "Oh yeah, suck that dick. Every damn inch of it. Suck my man's dick until you choke on that shit. Damn, she's all the way down to the balls." Teela took a more up-close-and-personal look.

Payshun had moved her long, burgundy hair to the side and away from her face, and then focused on taking all of Austin's anatomy as completely as she could possibly throat him. She looked up at Austin's face with big, willing, "your wish is my command" eyes. She rotated her head from side to side while going up and down to accommodate his size. The meat of her generous lips shellacked his black dick-skin up and down, in and out, over and over.

Austin pumped her face with his magnificent hooked penis as he reached back to pet the skin of Payshun's pussy. Payshun's waxed vagina was nutmeg colored, with a sterling silver stud gracing the hood of her clit.

She continued to devour all of Austin's angled cock with ease, smiling the whole time.

When he moaned, she moaned, and Austin inserted his middle finger deep inside her, probing her tightness. She ground back on his hand in a slow, circular motion. Teela stayed quiet and was all eyes.

Austin continued to look back as he finger-fucked her from juicy wall to juicy wall. "Hold up, I've gotta taste me some a that. Talk about peaches and cream," he said, as a silky flow of slippery juices escaped from her split. He removed his drenched fingers at the same time he backed out his fully grown dick from her mouth. He eased himself down from her face to between her legs and took a long sniff of her glazed opening. His dick jumped beneath him.

He pointed his tongue to catch every bit of her secretions. He licked his lips and groaned, going back closer toward the heat, inserting his tongue deep inside fast. She raised her ass and arched her back upward. She noticed Teela standing over her, rubbing her own engorged clit.

"Bring that bushy pussy over here and sit on my face," the young woman said, as though she had no problem pleasing Teela with just as much skill as Austin had.

"I'll just watch. You two get it good," Teela told her. She found a spot on the end of the bed where she leaned back on the pale blue comforter and opened her legs wide. She eagerly played with herself, squeezing her breasts and adding spit to her clitoris, continuing to massage herself at the sight of her dread-wearing man eating the obviously delicious stranger's pussy.

Payshun hungrily checked out Teela, from her perky, peachy titties to her thick, shapely legs. Payshun moaned and then closed her eyes, grooving her hips while Austin made sure to press her legs all the way back so he could really get to work.

Teela warned her, "You're about to find out for real that real men do eat pussy."

Austin's actions were precise. One long middle finger inside just a little, and then upward just a bit, just enough to find the rough meat of her G-spot, another finger circling her rectum. His wide biceps muscles contracted as his fingers did the skilled pussy walking. His bottom lip resided right at the top of her opening, and he shifted his tongue and top lip from a flicking motion upon her clit to a tongue insertion just barely inside, while he continued to press inside just so, and then he heard her make . . . that sound.

"Aaaaahhhh, ooooooooohhhhh, uuuuuummmmmmh, yes, what the fuck? Shit. Wait, wait," she begged, and panted and tried to scoot. "What are you doing? Oh shit. I can't take it. What are you doing to me?" He held her in place and she bore down. Her grip tightened. "Damn, I'm cumming. I'm cumming." She stiffened and made a gurgling sound, then shouted like someone had swallowed her whole: "Ayyyyyyyyyyy, awwww, yes, yes, yes." Each yes was louder than the previous.

Teela's volume matched. "Shit. Suck all that cum outta that black pussy." She watched Payshun's orgasm erupt and then sucked her teeth hard. "Get it like you do me, baby. Suck it all." Her own squirting steam started to roll. There was a squish sound and she howled. "Ahhhhhhhhh, uuugghh."

Again and again, Austin gave moans of agreement from down there.

Payshun and Teela came hard at the same time. Payshun's spill was due to getting the mustache ride of her life from an ebony man who was built like an Adonis. And ivory Teela's liquid spill was due to the ultimate visual. Her greatest pleasure. A man she loved making another woman cum while she watched. She would always spill when her fantasy was lived out. Usually within two minutes. Watching was her thing. She was addicted to it.

Teela squeezed the last bit of her prolonged nut and flexed her legs while tightening her ass. Juice seeped from her opening onto the drenched covers beneath her. She took a deep breath and gave a long exhale. Her hand moved from her pussy to her forehead. She brushed back her drenched black bangs. "That's as much as I've squirted in a long-ass time." And then she simply said, "Now fuck her." Her eyes were greedy.

Teela stood and got behind Austin while he secured a condom onto the mass of his curved dick. She put her hands on his back while Payshun cooperatively got up on all fours and braced her wide, plump, but firm ass for his penetration. He let his finger tell him exactly where it was, then inserted himself little by little while Teela massaged his back, pressing her pale frame along his contrasting skin, moving with his exact motions, slow and nasty, until he engulfed Payshun's pussy cave completely.

Payshun grunted and held her breath, trying her best not to scoot again.

"Oh no, girl, you gotta stay still and take all that big dick. Go ahead, Austin, fuck her like that's my big dick inside of that pussy. Fuck her so good I can feel it from behind you. Fuck her for me." She spoke to his other woman. "My man knows just where to aim when he's in there. His dick is strategically designed to hit just the right spot, as you see. He has a PhD in B-E-D. His shit is brief but scientific. You just watch." Her voice sounded comical but her face looked serious.

Payshun moaned her words like her head was in the clouds. She looked back at Teela. Her eyes were begging. "You really do need to have your pussy in my face while he cums." She smacked her thick brown lips and grunted deep.

"I'm good, baby. I get off just like this. And so will you."

Payshun wailed, "Oh shit. What's that he's hitting?" She turned back to eye Austin with a look of temporary love. "Oh fuck, baby, what're you doing? What the hell is that? Uhhh. Oh no. Damn, that shit feels good like a muthafucka."

"Take that. Take that," Austin said, encouraged by the fact that this was Payshun's indoctrination to his hooked magic stick. He grinned and continued to get his long stroke on, smacking Payshun's overgrown cheeks, first her left and then her right. *Pop. Pop. Pop. Pop.* The roll of her crimson ass wave was dynamic. She had a dark purple tramp-stamp that read, *Puuuurfect,* and three tiny paw prints that led down the meat of her ass.

"I told you, girl. Don't be scared. Back that shit up and fuck him back. Buck those hips and take all that dick."

"Like this?" Payshun's voice sounded innocent, but her ass worked like a hooker.

"That's a good girl. Milk it. Feel the length and fuck it," Teela insisted, sounding bossy.

"Oh fuck," said Austin, extraloud.

Teela spoke just as loud. "Oh *fuck* is right. We're deep in that tight-ass pussy now."

Payshun's breaths grew shorter. Her grind moved quicker. "Yeah. Yeah. Ooohh, yeah. This shit feels so muthafuckin good. I'm gonna cum again. Dammit."

Teela assured her. "Me too, baby." She asked her man from behind, "How about you?"

He replied as though in another zone, and he looked like he was losing the fight of making this one last. "Aaahh, ahhhh, it's, aaahhhhh, shit, she's moving like, damn. Here it is."

And at that very moment, Payshun bucked one time hard, meowed a long meow like a lost prairie cat, and then was completely still while she wailed an authentic feline purr, throwing her head back and upward, trying to handle the roll of her pussycat thunder. Her eyes were wet, and when she closed and reopened them, a tear rolled down the young skin of her face.

Austin pulled out and yanked off his condom, turning toward Teela while she suddenly brought her mouth down to take in his ejaculate, swallowing each fast-moving shot, then inserted her finger deep inside her own drenched pussy to bring on her expulsion, gulping cum while secreting cum simultaneously.

Teela's eyes looked sultry while she unraveled. "Ooooohhhhhhhhh, uhhhmmmmm." She backed away and licked her lips, shaking her head while looking at her man's new, turned-out fan. Her breaths were unsteady. "Yes, that's the shit. Watching you get off on that big dick."

Payshun rolled over onto her side. She put her hand over her chest and fought to steady her heartbeat, wiping her tear. "You guys are amazing. Austin, you were right. I didn't even get to touch her and she made this shit hot as hell."

Teela nodded. "I'm just the cheerleader, girl. And can I just tell you that your mama gave you the right damn name? Cause passion is what you are for real."

"You're one to talk." Payshun spoke like she had much respect. "I didn't know white girls rocked it like this. Fuck."

Teela spoke right up. "Okay, so now you know then. Now how about you stay for the night and we do the damn thing again in the morning? We'll make a sandwich out of him while we sleep." Teela flashed a playful half smile as she sat on the edge of the bed.

"I'm down." Payshun's smile flashed back.

Austin grinned at their feminine mutual admiration that kept his dick hard.

They watched him while he tried his best to stand with his weak knees, his dark chocolate dick pointing straight out like he could have hung his coat on it.

Teela laughed and asked, "Is that okay with you, baby?"

He nodded as he stumbled to the bathroom. He reached over his shoulder to scratch his upper back. "Hell yeah. Hell fucking yeah. After all, she lives two floors down." He stood in the doorway for a second, looking like an ebony stud, and then closed the door.

Teela admired his manly design, and then darted her eyes back to Payshun. "What? You do?"

Payshun replied with extrarosy cheeks, "Yeah. Austin was kind enough to come by this morning after I called the office to have my garbage disposal fixed. But wow, I got so much more than I bargained for. I guess this is my lucky day." She sounded as though she'd won a year's free rent.

Teela cut her eyes toward the bathroom door again and then looked back at her bedroom guest. "Yeah. That's Austin for you. A real nice guy. Always willing to please. Always willing to go the extra mile. That's why they voted him top maintenance supervisor of all the communities last month."

"He *is* good. A damn bully in bed though." Payshun looked forever convinced.

"That he is. A real true Mr. Fix-It."

Teela stared at Payshun as she stood and carefully stepped into her purple panties. The sight of her sturdy, long brown frame made Teela's clit hard. Again, she began to lay back and get comfortable, masturbating at the sight.

"Just stand there for a minute, baby. Let me look at you," she told Payshun, who batted her eyes and gave a sexy smirk while turning around to purposely flash her ass, making her round cheeks bounce like two basketballs.

Teela Raye was in visual heaven.

Her hungry green eyes were completely satisfied as Payshun joined her in the oversized bed, facing her as they continued to talk.

For now, Teela's obsession was fed just enough to cure her ills.

Thanks to her equally freaky handyman of a boyfriend, Austin Henderson.

And to their new girl-toy, their hooked neighbor, Payshun.

# 4

## "I Love My Sex"

### Valencia

After stopping back by the restaurant she managed, spending time there to make sure everything was closed down and secure, Valencia Sanchez, soon to be Valencia Sanchez Hooks, eased her SUV down a winding street of manicured lawns, sturdy mahogany trees, and blossoming, multicolored rosebushes. The Mediterranean style homes were secluded, tucked away far beyond the well-paved sidewalks. She pressed the garage opener and the door trundled upward, exposing her own personal parking space in the three-car garage. She stepped her hot body from her ride in her pink and pewter platform pumps, sporting her tight jeans.

Valencia slid her gold key back into her wallet and locked the beveled glass and distressed wood front door behind her as she entered her fiancé's massive, three-bedroom, three-and-a-half-bath Brentwood home on Country Club Drive. The thirty-five-hundred-square-foot, blond brick home with a clay terracotta roof sat on the seventh hole of the Brentwood Country Club. With eggshell crown molding, butterscotch walls, and bay windows framed by custom white leather treatments, the split-level house had a media room, a large backyard, a family room, and an executive office, as well as an oversized master with a circular sitting area, and most every piece of contemporary furniture was off-white.

She desired to add some color to the place. A bit of red or yellow to make it pop. But it wasn't time for Valencia to move in just yet. That would happen soon enough. They were set to be married in the spring.

For Valencia, the only child of parents who had been brutally murdered after their restaurant was burglarized when she was twenty-one, the fantasy of arriving home to a husband and family had been put off long enough. Now twenty-nine, she had recently decided she was ready to slow down and tame almost all her wild oats. After all, she now had a great position as a restaurant manager in Redondo Beach and a great man, an ex–football player who owned his own home and had a job as a high-six-figure executive with UPS, whom she could share the good life with. She made up her mind that she was ready to be a wife and mother so she could do it all over again. Do what her mother and father could not do: raise a child the right way. That was her ultimate desire.

She walked into the sprawling residence that was soon to be hers, then headed past the oval entryway and to the rear of the house with the soaring vaulted ceilings above her, noticing the man she'd been with for seven years sitting in his home office.

She was sure he would be the perfect father to their future children. Gregory Hooks was on the computer as usual. At five foot five, three inches shorter than she, he was known in the college ranks as the shortest star running back ever to play at USC.

"What's up? Sorry I missed your calls," she told him with a kiss on the top of his bald, caramel head, as he sat at his desk in a rust leather executive chair. He was barefoot, wearing blue boxers and a white tee. His fragrance was his usual white musk.

He turned from the computer and leaned back, extending his chiseled arms toward her, also stretching out his short, muscular, hairy legs from sitting so long. "I assumed you were at the meeting," he said, as she received his hug and kissed the side of his unshaven face. "Please tell me you went."

"Yeah, I went." She stepped back and placed her pale pink bucket bag on the sofa table.

"Good. And?"

She shrugged her shoulders and folded her arms. "And what?"

"You know what, Valencia. Don't play games with me."

"What, Greg? What you wanna know? You want me to say they fixed me with one meeting? Okay. I'm all better now, just like that." She handed him a sarcastic look and snapped her eyes as though they were fingers.

He gave her a look. "Don't be a smart-ass. I want you to tell me what it was like."

She sighed and stepped to the snow-white leather love seat, plopping down on the oversized arm. She twisted her more-than-sizable diamond bling along her ring finger, then took a deep breath and exhaled. Her arched eyebrows sank as she spoke. "It was a meeting. It was a meeting of confessions. It was embarrassing, okay? It was wack. I felt like I killed someone. The people seemed broken and fucked up. But hell, it was like looking in the mirror. They were me. How's that?"

"Your attitude will definitely not be helpful in the long run, and you know it." He folded his arms.

"Well, hell, like you told me last week, attitude is my middle name, right?"

"Anyway." He sat up straight. "Did Miki go?"

"Yeah."

"Did you two talk about the two of you?"

"About the fact that every now and then we fuck? That we're bi? You can say the word, Greg. Bi. Bi. Bi." Her neck tilted with each two-letter word.

If looks could kill, Gregory would have been on death row for first-degree, unadulterated, premeditated murder. "You know what I mean."

"It was only one meeting. And I'm not so sure that's an issue anyway."

"Obviously I think it is."

"No, duh. Listen, me playing with Miki every now and then has nothing to do with my addiction. It's just plain old fucking without feelings. Nothing more."

"Well, with you about to be my wife, I say that adds up to infidelity. Nothing more."

She gave a long blink. "Greg, please. We talked about this before, not long ago. You said were cool with it then."

"Well, now I'm not."

She cut her eyes from him to the tray ceiling and waited, tapping her foot. She then returned her squinting sights to his frowning face. "So you're just gonna change your mind now that I'm wearing your ring? You know I want a family. I want you and I want children. But I also wanna do all that with you because you said you were cool with me having my fun. I had fun the night I met

Miki at the strip club when she was dancing a few years ago, and I have fun now. No harm. She and I are close friends. I'm not prepared to give up the option of experiencing her as my part-time lover. It's just a little icing on the cake. I love my cake. But sometimes the frosting is sweeter." She stood, walked to him, and bumped his knee with her leg. "Greg, come on now. You of all people should know what I mean. You've hit every crevice of her pussy and counted da pimples on da booty enough times yourself, so stop trippin. I surely don't know why you're complaining now."

"Well, I am." His arms remained crossed.

"Look, I already cut out Ferrari for you. But I'm not cutting out Miki. So you think about that and let me know what the deal is." She walked over to the window and pushed up a horizontal wooden slat, peeking outside at the upscale neighborhood.

He said to her back, "Hell, you'd just throw us away so you can be with some woman every now and then. What's up with you?"

She faced him. "I need to be asking what's up with you? You'd throw away being husband and wife because I'm with a woman every now and then? You? The man who won freak of the year in college?"

He twisted his chair left to right and back, again and again. "That was then. I got all that nonsense out of my system, and now that I'm thirty, I'm good. But you need to ask yourself how you'd handle it if the shoe were on the other foot. What if we'd had a threesome with some guy and now I want to creep with him just for fucking fun. You'd lose your damn mind. I'll bet you'd throw away being husband and wife if that happened, if I left the house to go have sex with some dude and asked you to understand."

"That's not the same thing."

"That's exactly the same thing."

She again sat on the soft arm of the love seat, gave a long exhale, and crossed her legs. "First of all, you know as well as I do that a woman being with a woman is not seen as the same as a man being with a man. I can deal with a little same-sex action between men, but the whole thought of a man letting another man penetrate his ass is way different. Second of all, you're the one who convinced me to join a detox group to shake my addictions, and I admitted I needed to. And not because you threatened to end this, but because I knew I had a problem. But now it sounds like you're holding this thing with Miki over my head and threatening to leave anyway. I mean, damn, Greg. What's the deal?"

"The deal is I just can't understand why this is so important to you. We've had our fun. It's time to get serious and get ready to act right. But, damn, I just have to ask you. Are you in love with Miki, or what?" He ceased twisting.

She uncrossed her legs and spoke a notch louder. "Oh, hell no, of course not. I don't want a relationship with her. It's just recreational. My goodness. Most men would be happy to have a woman who had a chick on the side." She talked with her hands. "I'm bisexual. I can't just shake that like you treat a cold. I mean, I just can't help it. And making people stop being attracted to the same sex is not what Sexaholics is about. And besides, if it's not Miki, it'll be someone else. You said you'd rather it be her, and now you sound like you're threatening to leave again after almost eight years, like it's an ultimatum. Damn. I'm trying to shake this addiction shit first, and you won't even let me get through that part. It wasn't that long ago you and me were trying out our open-relationship thing. But please, Greg. Wow. Give me a break." She took a breath, eyeing him down. "I know we're not your everyday, average couple. But I mean, just because you shook the freak in you so easily doesn't mean I can do the same at the same pace. It's like you won't even wait until I get through a few meetings without acting like I should be Polly Purebred when I walk in the door. This is serious, honey. I need your patience. But I have to tell you that if you can't deal with this, then let me know now. Don't waste my time. Please. Hell, I am not getting any younger, *mijo*."

Upon her last word he looked down at the floor, then eyed his desk and turned toward the computer screen. "Valencia, you know I want you. That's why this is so important to me." He clicked the mouse.

"Then give me a break. Please." She took in the object of his sudden focus. "And what the hell are you doing? Are you on MySpace?"

"No." He cleared his throat. "I was looking on the Home Depot site so I can get those low-flow toilets this weekend."

"All right, now." She cautiously stood and grabbed her purse. "Anyway, I'm gonna go home and change. I'm going out."

He glanced up at the oversized iron wall clock over his desk. "This late? Out where?"

"Over to Purple for a minute."

"You're kidding, right?" He spoke with his back still turned.

"No. I'm not. Where would you prefer I go?"

"You know, go on ahead." His voice told on his frustrated thoughts.

She stepped to him and again kissed the top of his head. "And hey. Get off that computer. Even if that shit *is* MySpace. You know how your ass is, Gregorio." She walked away and exited his office.

"I'm not on MySpace. Besides, I don't think Home Depot has a webcam link, so relax."

Moments later, her heels could be heard clicking along the crème travertine floor of his living room as she stepped. She yelled while opening the front door, "Okay now. I'll call you later."

"You do that," he said extraloudly.

She left and locked the door with her key.

And Greg instantly logged into www.jackoffcam.com, sat back as the smooth leather cushioned his gluteus maximus, and then pulled down his boxers, taking his nearly raw shaft into his left hand.

He scooted down and leaned back with his legs open, assuming his regular position.

The webcam was on.

And Greg was braced and ready to go.

As usual.

# 5

## "*Creep*"

### Brandi

With her medium height, medium build, medium complexion, and medium-length hair, medium Brandi Williams had been home for hours, relaxing after a long day of teaching her beloved eighth graders and attending her first Sexaholics meeting. She'd also stopped by Gelson's Market for some bananas, her regular breakfast of choice.

She lived on the west side of Hollywood on a narrow street just south of the Sunset Strip. Her neighbors' quaint homes ranged from French chateau and Venetian villa–looking houses to newly remodeled, California stuccoes. And Brandi's one-bedroom, eclectic-looking Spanish bungalow resembled a Hansel and Gretel–like cottage, though life inside was far from that of a fairy tale.

Along her lush lawn, a large nectarine tree sprouted its growth from west to east, enough to shield her small front yard. A brief wind had kicked up, and even after the midnight hour, a sparrow could be heard singing along one of the slightly swaying branches. Small jasmine vines crawled along the front stained-glass window, giving off a sweet smell.

West Hollywood, also known as Gay Village due to its large gay population, resembled the French Quarter. It was also known for its trendy, well-known shops and restaurants, its never-ending extravagant nightlife that looked as if it were Halloween on any given evening, and for its amazing view from the top, near the Sunset Strip. The magical view of the city was breathtaking.

Overall, the area was one of busy sounds, bustling happenings, and a constantly hurried feel. Yet inside of Brandi's home, it was none of that.

Her comfortable residence was her safety zone. It was her isolation sanctuary when she wasn't spending her daytime hours as an English teacher at Harcourt Middle School, in the upscale neighborhood of View Park.

Her perky and energetic public side was the side her students knew and loved. But her private side consistently made its usual appearance once she stepped in from the moonlit, outside world and double-locked her front door. The door that safely separated her from the surefire cruelness that lurked out there.

Her average-sized home with crisp celery-colored walls always smelled of the citrus FreshMatic scent that intermittently chased away any evidence of stale gloom, just in case the scent of jasmine from the outside hadn't been able to permeate the premises. It was always dark. The only illumination was from the overhead stove light. And that was just the way she liked it. She stepped through the arched doorway into her vintage small, tiled kitchen, and grabbed a tall drinking glass and a bottle of Patrón, pouring the clear liquid to the rim. She was not one to sip nor drink from a shot glass. She drank tequila head-on. No fear.

Actually, anything strong and anything straight would do. But tequila had been her desired liquor since her days at UCLA, where she earned a degree in education. Back then she drank Cuervo, guzzling shots that raced down her throat like Mexican moonshine, doing the lick-it-and-stick-it move. The firewater brought about many a morning filled with headaches and hangovers, lying upon stench-filled sheets spotted with lingering remnants of her upchuck. Though now she seemed immune after having learned to imbibe only the premium brands.

Alcohol was the perfect fit back in the good old days of college, when she'd party most of the time, skip class, sleep the day away, and cram for tests with whatever time of the day was left. Even so, her knack for making the grades brought her much attention, even scholarships. But not the kind of attention the other girls got. She was, after all, nothing to write home about. Or at least that's what the one guy who took her out the one time in college told her. And it wasn't the first time she'd heard that. The thing was, without question, she agreed.

She was, after all, very average.

Plain-as-paper average.

Average at everything but the books. Brandi overcompensated her downsides by having an overly exuberant public personality and an inherited high level of intelligence, though she also inherited her love of booze. Her favorite pastimes were her greatest escapes . . . crooked sex and straight liquor. Both always seemed to fill in the blanks once she shielded herself from the world by being . . . at home.

Home facing herself.

And her demons.

Just like those before her, who had passed it on down like a cursed baton.

But recently she admitted to herself that even the sex and booze weren't enough to fill in the blanks.

Brandi had kicked off her low heels and stripped down to all but her brown boy shorts. She'd stepped, bare feet against the cool, mahogany hardwood strips, while shutting down her Motorola phone. With drink in hand, she took a seat on the black leather sofa, turned on the volumeless TV, and drank her liquor, swallowing the strength of the silver petroleum liquid as though it were water. As with all the other nights alone, the intention was to feel numb.

A porno movie that she'd neglected to finish watching from the night before shone before her, called *Monster Booty Meets Monster Dick*. Actually, she'd neglected to watch it the night before that and the night before that.

She leaned back and opened her legs to allow freedom to her greedy, needy vagina. She put her hand down into her panties like Al Bundy would do on *Married . . . with Children*, and began fiddling with her curly pussy hairs, petting herself with long strokes as though she were a cat. She poked the tip of her middle finger inside and she was wet. She was ripe and ready like always.

Her thoughts momentarily shifted from the light-skinned young woman who was giving deep throat with her amazing soup-cooler lips, heading down further to lick the lucky man's balls. Brandi thought back to her meeting. Rachel Cummings had talked about abstaining from unhealthy sex. She remembered the one sentence more than the many others. *Stop lusting and become sober.*

But as usual, the alone time with nothing to do but produce thoughts from her addicted mind brought out her other half. And thirty minutes later, even with the success that getting liquored up brought toward reaching her numbness, she'd transformed herself into the fast side she'd given a nickname.

She stood in her bedroom feeling a little dizzy, but that was usually how she felt when her mind shifted from worried teacher to not-a-care-in-the-world sexpot. She gave long blinks as her head began to swim, then she shook it off. Having learned to deal with it, she squared her shoulders and stared at her reflection in the full-length mirror before her.

She was now a vixen of a woman, wearing a low-cut, sheer-back jumpsuit and high heels, a ruby-red curly wig, hazel-blue contacts, false eyelashes, and heavy makeup. Brandi snatched her keys and a credit card, driver's license, cell phone, three orange condoms, and a can of Mace, and locked the door behind her. She jumped into her bright red Chevy Camaro, red for the world to see, and headed out under the nighttime skies to be all she needed to be. She drove the short distance over near Sunset and La Cienega, listening to her radio. The song was "Naughty Girl" by Beyoncé.

She parked her bright car in the nearly packed, dark lot of a closed gasoline station and began to walk through the night with a sweet, sticky stroll. A stroll she had mastered. She shifted her hips in a way that the sun would never see. It was a sight only for the moon and stars, and for sore, horny eyes.

Immediately she heard a honk, and then a holler and a hoot, and then a catcall, and then a whistle. She knew she had the look. And she worked it even harder as she kept on strolling.

"What's a nice girl like you doing on a street like this?" a thirty-something woman with blond hair asked as she pulled up in her dark blue SUV, going one mile per hour.

Brandi looked on but kept her stroll on. "I'm just taking a walk. Why?"

"How much?"

Brandi stopped. "For who?"

The woman stopped. "For me."

Brandi chuckled. "I think maybe you might be missing the right equipment for me to answer that question."

The woman leaned over to her right and opened the passenger-side door just enough. She reached down and lifted her pleated skirt, exposing that she was not wearing panties, and showing Brandi the eight inches of manhood she was working with. "Now, can you give me a price?" the chick with a dick asked, now with a voice that had slipped into baritone.

Recalling that Valencia's sexaholic confession involved a similar freaky lay, Brandi said assuredly, "This is your lucky night. No charge."

"No charge? What? You just fuck guys indiscriminately just for kicks?"

Brandi came closer and closer as she spoke. Her eyes showed odd pleasure. She could clearly see the throat with a well-defined Adam's apple and a chin tainted with razor stubble. "I'd hardly call this haphazard or by accident. I'm here for a reason. And you, my dear, are just what the doctor ordered. So are you down with it or not? Cause I am."

"Hell yeah, I'm down."

"Perfect." And Brandi hopped in.

"What's your name?" the woman-slash-man asked as he pulled off. The inside of the messy truck smelled like old, musty sweat socks.

Brandi rolled down the window and looked over to notice the strands of forearm hair as he kept hold of the chrome gearshift. "I'm Camaro. I'll just call you John. Or Johnetta, which one?" Brandi giggled inside.

"Johnetta will work for tonight. Pleased to meet you, Camaro."

"The pleasure is mine. All mine. Don't tell me, you're the stereotypical man who looks for women on the street . . . the giant in the corporate world and your wife isn't into what you're into, right?"

He smirked, focusing on her chest. "No comment."

With a leer like she knew the deal anyway, Brandi sat back in the passenger seat as the kinky driver headed the few blocks to the seedy Astro motel.

The Hollywood air met Brandi's curious face while she reached into her bra and turned on her phone. She had two missed calls, one from her mother and one from her new friend, Teela. They wouldn't get a call back, even if she wasn't playing free hooker for the evening. They shouldn't feel slighted, though. She shut her phone as the driver put the car in Park and adjusted his stiffness under his skirt as he stepped out.

Camaro's pussy was on fire.

The anticipation of the unknown had her all worked up.

He came around and opened her door as she stepped out and followed his lead. He towered over her, wearing a long blond wig, parochial skirt, white midriff top, and bobby socks with bright pink stilettos.

Fast-ass Camaro couldn't wait for her first taste of the cross-dresser with the sexy, brown muscular legs in four-inch heels.

Or transvestite he-she.

Or whatever the hell it was.

# 6

# *"I Kissed a Girl"*

## Miki

Miki's girl, Valencia, pulled up along the curb on Pico Boulevard in L.A. and rolled to a stop, placing the platinum Infiniti FX in park as the hustling, well-mannered valet opened her door. Another fast-moving valet approached and opened the passenger side.

Miki stepped out. "Thanks," she said, speaking softly with a head nod, while adjusting the strap of her zebra barrel purse along her shoulder.

Valencia and Miki strutted up to the purple door wearing tight jeans and tighter braless tees, both with ruby red pumps.

A burly-looking bouncer who wore all black greeted them. "Ladies. Go right in. Good to see you, Valencia."

"You, too, Miguel. Gracias," she said, as he held the door open for their more-than-welcome entry.

The song was Gorilla Zoe's "Pole." Miki sang along, "She drops it down low, she mix it up slow, she's workin that pole," bobbing her head as they made their way inside with an energy that smelled of estrogen.

The strip club's crowd of testosterone was thick. Some of the gentlemen, who made up 90 percent of the patrons, held dollar bills in hand. Most sat around the stage with their mouths open, lost in a mental fantasy, comparing the young ladies who danced before them to some woman they wished could be so limber, or so damn fine, and so willing to fulfill their every lustful eye-need.

The room smelled like an urban honky-tonk spot, with day-old cigarette smoke and lingering cheap perfume. The guys made sure to steal glimpses of Valencia and Miki, like they hoped the ladies would be down for anything, being freaky enough to even show up. Or that maybe after a little while they'd be juiced up and ready to take home once the dancers did their preliminary jobs of foreplay. Miki and Valencia had other plans.

Miki took a moment to eye a girl on the main stage. She was a tall Brazilian dancer with much yellow ass. She hung upside down with six-inch clear platforms, expertly spreading her legs and bouncing her bare cheeks. "Damn. I remember when I used to be that damn flexible."

Valencia took a quick peek but kept focused on claiming a spot at a large bar table. She stepped to it and adjusted two leather stools, moving them closer together. Her reply to Miki was a delayed half smile.

Miki noticed her reserve as they took their seats. "I keep forgetting you're about to get married, girl. I know Greg's trippin out about this girls-only stop of ours."

"He is, with his insecure, narcissistic ass. But you know I don't give a damn."

"Oh, girl, stop playin it off. You know you care."

"No, really. I don't. He can just move on if he can't handle it."

"Oh please." Miki crossed her legs and placed her purse on the table. "He's not going anywhere and neither are you. You two have been together far too long."

"True. That's my point. If he doesn't know me by now, he'll never know me. We both fucked anything that moved for years, but hell, his ass went cold turkey so damn fast, it's like he's a different person. But now he's replaced fucking other people with choking his chicken all damn day. Chronic masturbation is one fetish he'll never kick. And I don't beat him up for beating himself up, now do I?" Valencia tilted her head and gave a sly-looking smirk.

Miki shook the thought out of her mind and flashed her eyes as a stop sign. "How long has he been doing that shit?"

Valencia only eyed their surroundings. "Greg has been addicted to Internet porn ever since he gave up swinging. You know how that shit is. People replace one craving with another. Thinks he can get over it on his own. Not. I'm not trying to air his dirty laundry, but his own poppa left his mamma after he fell in love with a hooker he almost stalked. I've heard of she's gotta have it, but damn, he's really gotta have it in the Hooks family. The men are truly hooked on something. Even Greg's brother was a crack addict. Folks just turn to something to cover up for what's missing, kind of a distraction. Yeah, his poppa and brother are a trip. But his mamma's cool. Whatever."

Miki's expression downshifted. "Val, I had no idea his family has been through all of that. His mom looks so conservative, so Claire Huxtable–like."

"Yeah, well, I guess you can't tell a book by its cover.

Gotta open it up and read it." Valencia suddenly caught a glimpse of a major, wagon-draggin, ba-donk-a-donk working overtime on the stage. Her train of thought went from pissed off to turned on no time flat. She bounced her head to the beat of the T.I. song "Big Things Poppin'." "All I know is, that there is da body of life, for real."

Miki followed Valencia's stare. Her sympathetic thoughts were immediately stolen. "Oh heck yeah. She is fit and fine. Sure looks a whole lot better than I ever did on that stage, I'll tell you that."

Valencia glanced down and gave an eye-check to make sure she had cash in her two-tone croc clutch. "Have you ever thought about coming back and dancing like you did when we first met? I mean just to make some extra money." She looked at Miki. "I'll never forget you giving me that private dance in the VIP room when I came in here with my girl Ferrari that night. You had me lying flat on my back and you went to town. That was the shit, there."

"That was a bed dance, Val. Hell, that seems like a lifetime ago. What was it, like almost ten years?"

"Something like that."

"That's a long time. But no, I had my day. This place served its purpose." Miki looked around at another stage. "I made a lot of money, but the best thing is if I hadn't worked here, I wouldn't have met T.J.'s dad, with his foolish ass. Up in here after he got his deal with Island Def Jam, throwin all his money around. After I got with him, he got into some shit and got his ass fired, then his money got funny. Just my luck I ended up getting pregnant by a deadbeat."

"Girl, all those ball players and actors you met in here and dated, and you ended up with Anthony. That boy can't even keep up with his child support payments."

"That's exactly why I have my friends with benefits."

"What you have is a sugar daddy in Robert, you're still messin with your baby daddy, you have a man, and you met a rehab fuck at the meeting tonight. That's four friends with benefits." She held up one finger for each man. "My girl is a stone freak."

Miki shot her eyes at Valencia and jerked her head back. "Excuse you? I wouldn't talk, Miss Equal Opportunity Love. Not after you admitted to pushing the limits and licking a pussy till its raw in that meeting. And yes, I do say, penis variety is the true spice of life. But I also say, since your ass is engaged, you're one to talk."

Valencia nodded. "True. True. I admit if it ain't freaky, it ain't right. Twosomes do bore my ass to death, unless it's with someone who looks like that." She aimed her index finger at another extra curvy silhouette approaching.

"Hey baby. How are you?" a woman wearing bright orange asked Valencia.

They hugged and Valencia patted the girl's meaty backside. "I'm good. This is my girl Miki. Miki, this is Tangerine. She's the best."

Tangerine spoke first. A smile curved her lips. "Hello." Her mandarin color lipstick was a beautiful contrast to her dark cocoa skin.

Miki offered a smile. "Pleased to meet you. Nice name."

"Thanks. It's kinda my trademark now. Everyone expects me to live up to the orange thing."

"It's workin."

Tangerine looked at Miki somewhere around her belly button. "I've never seen you here before."

Valencia explained. "Tangerine, Miki used to work here. She's a mamma now, so she doesn't get out like she did before."

Miki replied, "Well, I do every now and then. But I think it's been a few months since I've been here."

"I've only been here a couple of months myself."

Now Miki eyed Tangerine right around her crotch. "I see. Looks to me like they hired the right person."

Tangerine gave a flirtatious wink. "That's a compliment, coming from you."

Miki blushed, flashing her deep-set dimples. "Believe me, that was a while back."

"You say so."

Valencia touched the arm of a waitress who then stopped at their table. "*Hola, mami.* Can I have a Guinness, *por favor?* And what'll you have, Miki?"

"A Long Island."

Tangerine interjected quickly, "So can I get a drink, too?"

Valencia looked at Tangerine like she'd grown to expect the request. "Of course."

She asked, "Can I get an apple martini?"

"Fasho," Valencia replied, also looking at the waitress.

"Okay," the waitress said, making a mental note while wiping off the bar table with a wet towel and then stepping away.

Valencia joked, but with serious eyes, "Girl, you're gonna have to work for that damn drink."

"I'm down," Tangerine said, while bending over to pull down her sunburst-colored thong. She gave a wide smile to Valencia, exposing her perfect, bleached teeth and gold tongue stud. She removed her skimpy, orange satin peek-a-boo bra. Her firm, brown-sugar breasts were topped off by pointy nipples.

Valencia said sultrily, "Dance for my girl. Make her hot for me."

"My pleasure." Tangerine's eyes agreed.

"Do her like you do me," Valencia told her erotic-dancer friend.

Miki eyeballed her buddy with a look of appreciation and positioned herself so Tangerine could go straight to work.

"No, baby. No lap dance tonight. Stand up, baby. You're about to get the girlie grind of your life."

Miki raised her eyebrows as the suggestive words spilled from Tangerine's grapefruit-scented glossy lips. As she stood, her glance skimmed downward to the Playboy Bunny tattoo on the left side of Tangerine's flat belly.

Tangerine eased closer to Miki and pressed right up against Miki's pubic area in full circles. She moved mostly with her hips, like she was a professional belly dancer, also making sure to swirl her breasts to Miki's, nipple to nipple. Against Miki's tight blue jeans, Tangerine held handfuls of Miki's overly developed butt cheeks, as though her hands were a booty brazier.

"Damn, you got a nice booty." Tangerine spoke slowly and deeply into Miki's ear. "A coconut *derrière*."

The warm words sent a shiver down Miki's spine. Her eyes closed as if commanded to do so.

Tangerine continued to lead the seductive body dance.

And they ground.

The waitress brought their drinks but none of the three noticed.

Eric Benet's song "Chocolate Legs" did the honors, escorting their sways and bumps while the two moved as one, as if they'd done a naked lambada before.

Valencia simply sat back and watched while the heat rushed wall-to-wall between her thighs. She opened her legs and leaned forward, resting her elbows on her knees. She grabbed her own breast and squeezed it, then leaned all the way back to make room for the heated rush of blood that flowed from her head to her toe. She rubbed her own nipple back and forth through the fabric of her black T-shirt, as if only the three of them were in the room.

With Miki being taller, Tangerine made sure to press her body right along the shape of Valencia's pee-bone. She pressed forward and back, adding more pressure with each slow roll of body contact.

Tangerine held Miki tight. The long colorful nails of her left hand fanned across the arch of Miki's back. Her right hand spanned the line of Miki's body. She was providing enough X-rated contact to send Miki's head spinning and to send her erect clitoris into an extra-engorged stage that spoke loud and clear throughout her body.

Tangerine bent down just so and gained a more forceful stance, massaging Miki's ass cheeks and kissing her neck. The warm, sweet breaths from Tangerine's sweet mouth sent waves of tingles down Miki's back. Her breathing grew more and more shallow. Miki's eyes rolled back in her head, and she abruptly jerked her orgasmic pussy against Tangerine's bare body, scrolling her clit along as it swelled in spurts.

By the time the one song wound down, Miki opened her eyes as Tangerine kissed her on the lips. Miki kissed back.

Valencia asked, "You okay, baby?" She swigged two gulps of her cold beer.

Miki shook her head and opened her eyes wide. "Ahhh, yeah. Where the fuck was I?"

Tangerine replied, "I know where you were. You were in cum-candy land with Tangerine. There's more where that came from if you guys are down. It's up to you. There's a VIP room available where we could all have some real privacy." Tangerine reached over to pick up her martini and gave two fast swallows, licking her lips and batting her eyes.

Valencia said, "Oh no, not tonight. You already took my girl to another level. Now it's my turn to finish the job." She downed her brew again.

Miki eyed her Long Island, but didn't touch it. "No, thanks. I already had mine. It's Val's turn."

"Okay. Okay, either way. But can I watch?" Tangerine asked, half serious and half joking.

"No." Valencia stood up, handed Tangerine two twenties, and grabbed Miki by the hand. "We got this."

Miki again eyed her drink, gave a lingering wink good-bye to her not-so-private dancer, grabbed her purse, and let Valencia lead the way to girl-on-girl.

*　　*　　*

Minutes after pulling off into the late-night traffic, Miki had Valencia's right tittie released from her top and was sucking her nipple like it was an overgrown clitoris. Valencia's skin was scented with Lick Me All Over, one of her many trademark body oils, and it was doing a serious number on Miki's head.

In the blink of a horny eye, the drive was done and they were at Miki's place. Miki was kneeling on her silver carpeted floor as she brought naked Valencia's wide hips to the edge of her queen bed, positioning her just far enough upon her back. She placed a foam pillow under her ass and went to work, just as Valencia had taught her.

She approached Valencia's vagina ever so gently, placing her hands along each side of Valencia's waist. She lightly brushed her lips along the collection of V-shaped pubic hairs and then circled the shape of Valencia's labia majora with a light blowing technique. She found a cranny between her vagina and thigh and nibbled. Miki ran her fingers along Valencia's thigh just as she liked, which evoked a feminine moan that was as soft as her pecan skin. Her response to the light fingertip touches made her squirm in anticipation.

Miki looked up at her friend and took in her sensual expression of pleasure. Valencia looked back down at her, then leaned her head back, placing her hand on Miki's head. She sighed in total surrender and trust.

In tune to Valencia's melodic responses, Miki pointed her tongue and penetrated her insides with a rolling point and narrow motion. She moved up from the entrance of her red-honey vagina to the bottom of her hood and swept her tongue upward, curling the tip and then sweeping back downward.

Miki circled her prey, sucking both the labia and the clit hood.

Valencia's pussy lips grew redder and bigger, engorged with a rush of hot blood. Her womanly hips begged for more. Miki was teasing and withholding, provoking a desire to take her all the way.

"Spread your lips for me," Miki demanded.

Valencia complied in an instant, bringing her hands down to expose her heated opening. Miki squinted her eyes and plunged her tongue as far as it would travel, and at the same time she grabbed Valencia's ass.

Miki backed away and smacked her lips. "Tastes so damn good."

She brought her mouth to the skin that surrounded Valencia's opening and gave a tugging kiss, offering broad, fast, and then slow licks up and down, like it was cherry ice cream.

Valencia's hands were now on her own breasts, squeezing and kneading her skin, and she ground her hips.

And then Miki went straight to Valencia's tender clit and gave a kiss and lick on the outer skin. She used her thumb to pull back the hood, seeing that her bud was expanded, emerging in anticipation for what was to come.

Miki focused on her girl's breathing and grooved her tongue across Valencia's clit, clockwise and counterclockwise, squeezing her clit with her lips, sucking it into her mouth, tickling it with lavish strokes. She then used her mouth as a vacuum, using up-and-down tongue moves similar to sucking a dick. Her head bobbed as she kept her rhythms exact. She sucked the clit to the roof of her mouth, gave a tongue push and flick, and held it. She then inserted one finger into Valencia's greasy vagina and one finger against her perineal skin, all while making up-and-down tongue motions.

Valencia ground like she was face-fucking and revved up in response, giving a bucking jerk, then she became motionless.

Miki did not back away but kept at it with the same intensity, keeping the rhythm going, feeling the pulsating of Valencia's tiny red penis in her mouth, and she held on. Knowing her friend as well as she did, she waited, then continued as another rolling orgasm burst into her mouth. Miki let it take its journey to full effect and then unravel little by little as it subsided. She removed her mouth from Valencia's smiling clitoris and couldn't help but smile herself.

Valencia had her wrist over her forehead with her eyes closed. "Damn. I seen spots. I'm trippin, yo!"

Miki grinned.

"Chronic. I'm telling you. Your tongue is like chronic."

Miki giggled childlike and playfully popped Valencia on her thigh. "Ooooh, yeah. Your shit is so damn sexy." She came up to lie upon her, kissing her neck and then coming mouth to mouth. They kissed each other squarely.

Valencia backed away. *"Gracias."*

"You're welcome." Miki climbed off and lay next to her.

Valencia caught a glimpse of the digital clock. "Dammit. I have to go, otherwise Greg is gonna have a damn fit." Valencia looked reluctant. Her BlackBerry rang from inside her purse, which was on the chair next to Miki's sleigh bed. She ignored it and swung her feet off the bed. "Speaking of the devil."

Ten seconds later, Miki's iPhone rang. She reached over to the pine nightstand to read the display. "It's Tariq." She didn't answer.

Valencia took in a long breath and forced herself to stand, preparing to leave. A beep tone sounded on her phone, signaling a text message.

At the same time Miki's phone beeped to signal a voice message.

Both from the same number.

# 7

———— ∞ ————

# "Turn Me On"

## Teela

The following day, even though Teela's thick but muscular frame was far from the stereotypical weight trainer's body, as usual she managed to squeeze her five-foot-two, one-hundred-fifty-pound self into tight black leggings and a gold and black form-fitting top.

Part of her job was to greet prospective members of the brand-new Olympic Gym and Spa in West Los Angeles. The gym was so swanky they had valet parking. The rest of her responsibilities included handling prospective member tours and supervising the early-shift employees, as well as serving as personal trainer to certain clients who could afford the star-treatment level of individual attention.

Her 11 a.m. appointment, the local wife of a rich businessman, was listed on the day's log as Falon Fox. Teela scrolled through the log, then exited her shared management office and headed toward the front counter to make sure she was waiting for her VIP client the moment she walked through the door.

The health-club lobby was contemporary, with chocolate leather sofas, accented by beet red throw pillows, and oil paintings. The random knickknacks along the oval glass tables had an African theme. A large crested OGS was carved into the enormous, snow-white tray ceiling above. And a magnificent, hand-cut crystal chandelier was perched overhead.

"How are you?" asked a tall black man with a finely trimmed beard and a buzz cut. He'd just walked in and scanned his membership card through the magnetic stripe reader.

Teela nodded, looking up at him. "I'm good. Welcome to the Olympic."

"Thanks. It's good to be here this morning. Wouldn't have wanted to have missed out on seeing you standing there looking all good, like you're God's gift to mankind." His eyes spoke to her body.

Teela blinked and blushed from the sheer force of her body wanting to speak back. "That's nice of you. You have a good workout now." She wasn't trying to be obvious by biting his flirtatious vibe too hard, even though she did take a second to check out his well-defined ass as he turned to walk away, admiring the fruits of his obvious long-term weightlifting labor. He turned back and caught the not-so-sly ending to her molesting glance. She tried to be slick and rubbed the back of her neck, focusing on her coworker who was on the other side of the counter. Anything but lick his ass with her eyes.

"So, Jennifer, did you work yesterday?"

"I did." The young lady's face said she didn't miss a second of the booty fantasizing taking place before her.

"I heard it was quiet. Usual hump-day crowd, huh?" Teela asked, fingering through a stack of papers, straightening things along the granite countertop.

"Yeah, you could say that," her coworker chuckled.

Teela turned back toward the door and saw a brown-skinned, slender woman with wide hips approaching, carrying a small canvas gym bag over her shoulder. She was looking down at her smart phone as she walked. Her long hair was red, and so were her scarlet nails. Teela said, "Hello."

"Hi. I'm here to see Teela. Teela Raye, I believe."

"I'm Teela. You must be Falon." Teela extended her hand.

Falon extended her hand as well, both offering firm shakes. "I am." Falon dropped her hand and, without looking down, placed her phone in her bag.

Teela asked, "You joined yesterday and already had your tour, right?"

"Correct."

Teela gave her a once-over. Twice. She had obvious breasts that gave new meaning to the term *double-breasted*. "It looks like you work out quite a bit."

Falon smoothed the fabric of her tight sweat jacket. "No, not really. I haven't belonged to a gym in years. I guess you could say I have a high metabolism. It's hard for me to gain weight, so that's good. I'll admit that." She placed her bag down between her feet and began to unzip her jacket. "But I have absolutely no muscle tone whatsoever. I'm very soft, actually."

"Well, if that's what no muscle tone looks like, I'll trade with you. You look like you should be training me."

Falon smiled and examined Teela from head to toe. "Oh no. I think you look great."

"Thanks. I will say I've learned to love my body. I've had no choice. I come from a long line of short and thick women."

"Thick sounds good to me. They always say we tend to want the opposite of what we are." Falon bent down and placed her jacket in her bag. She came to a stance.

"I've heard that before. So, do you want to head off to the lockers and I'll meet you back here when you're done?" Teela pointed to their right.

"I can do that."

"Good. I'll be waiting."

"Cool. Thanks, Teela. Love that name, by the way." Falon stepped away, looking back at Teela. She smelled of a whisper of sweet melon oil.

And Teela noticed. "Love yours, too," Teela replied. Unbeknownst to Falon, she was imagining Austin fucking her doggie style. Teela's clit got hard. "Uh, uh, uh," she said in a low tone, looking down at her tennis shoes, crossing her arms. *Stop, Teela. Stop.*

"Pardon me?" Jennifer asked from the other side of the counter. Her expression said she could again read Teela's dirty mind word for word.

"Oh, nothing. Nothing at all. Just thinking out loud."

As was always the case, to make her members feel more at ease Teela put herself through the same regimen that she did them as she went through the training.

After thirty minutes on the elliptical and thirty minutes on the treadmill, Falon was panting hard. Her breasts jiggled as she stepped. She picked up her Evian water bottle and sucked from it hard. From beneath her green midriff top, sweat dripped under her heavy breasts and under her arms. She wiped her forehead with the back of her forearm and said, "Whew. I think I'm about done."

Teela said cheerily, "We're almost at the end of the cardio. We just have a half hour or so of weight training and then a cool-down on the bike."

Falon inhaled and exhaled big. "Teela, I'm telling you. I am spent. This is more than I've done at one time in years."

"Okay, okay. I can see that." Teela stopped her own machine and looked over at Falon. "Your heart rate is really elevated." She pressed the button on Falon's machine. "Let's take a break then until you cool down some."

Falon's steps slowed to a stop. "Let's." She grinned at Teela. "Wow. You haven't even broken a sweat."

They both stepped down from the machines.

"Hey, there you are." It was the tall black man Teela had greeted before. His towel was draped around his neck.

"Hi," Teela replied.

"Hello." Falon said, using her white hand towel to dab down her wet forehead.

He said to Teela, "I'm Reggie. And you are?"

"Teela." She examined the powerful shape of his ripped biceps.

"And?"

Falon wiped the beads of sweat from her drenched hairline. "Falon." She gave a few short breaths as she used her hand to blow air toward her face.

"Hello, Falon. Are you okay?"

"Just a little winded."

Teela said, "She'll be fine."

Falon gave a quick check of her diamond-encrusted wristwatch. "Teela, I need to make a call soon to my daughter's teacher, so I'm going to head out if it's okay."

"Oh, sure. Let me know when you're ready to finish the circuit I've designed for you."

Reggie spoke right up. His eyes were stuck on Falon's healthy chest. "Hey, I'm about to leave. How about if I walk over to the locker rooms with you?" He extended his arm to her.

"That'd be nice," Falon said to Reggie. She then said to Teela, "And maybe you can meet me by the front desk in a few minutes? Do you think?"

"Oh, sure."

"Good," Falon told her. She took Reggie's arm. "So Reggie, are you headed back to work?"

"Not today."

"What do you say we meet up at Starbucks after I make this call?"

"I can do that." His pleasure showed in his deep-set smile as they walked.

Falon turned back. "Teela, you wanna join us? It is around the lunch hour."

Teela nodded after looking at the wall clock. "Actually, I think maybe I can."

"Good."

And after a couple of hours rolled by, it was obvious the ménage would not make a Ladera Shopping Center Starbucks appearance anytime soon. Reggie, Teela, and Falon were three deep in room 333 at the Holiday Inn Airport on Century. The three cars were parked right next to each other, with Reggie's smoky gray BMW seven-series smack dab in the middle, in the very corner, in the very back in the shade. And all three cars were backed in.

Reggie, the hunk with hard-earned muscles, who had dark brown skin and big brown eyes, stood at the end of the full-sized bed, wearing a super-thin Durex condom, with ass cheeks pumping like he was drilling for gold. The golden pussy he occupied, owned by foxy Falon, was hairy and plump and wet and filled to its maximum capacity with his heat-seeking dick at full tilt. His girth had widened her out, and his length had bottomed her out.

He had Falon flat on her back, with his ass providing all the power. He stood tall and placed his feet firm, slightly bending his defined legs. She was getting fucked like he was Big Punisher, and her large breasts, one of them pierced, were rolling from side to side. She looked like she was holding her breath, gritting her teeth and grunting each time he plunged his overgrown cock to meet her cervix.

"Uhph, umph, umph," she said again and again with each forward pump motion. "I ain't never squirted in my life, but hell, if there ever was a time, this is it. Either that or I'm about to piss on myself. Shit." Her face looked both worried and satisfied. Her soft hips were at the very edge of the bed, allowing for the deepest penetration. His massive arms were hooked under her legs, making sure to hold her up at just the right height for his dick-sploration.

Teela lay on her back next to Falon, finger-fucking herself with an urgency, breathing at an intense rate, spreading her own slippery lips. Three of her fingers slid across her clit while she watched the first-time couple fuck.

The sound of Falon's slapping flesh and the squeaking of overworked bedsprings was obvious. It sounded like somebody was fucking somebody. It smelled like somebody was fucking somebody. Intensely.

"He's fucking the shit outta me," Falon yelled for dear life.

Yep. Somebody was indeed fucking somebody.

"Yeah, you're taking all this dick. All the way back to the uterus."

"Teela, baby, you gotta help me with this man. This is enough dick-dinner for two."

Teela smirked. "You look like you've got it handled. Just relax. Take deep breaths and then exhale slowly. You can handle it."

"Oh hell. I didn't know what I was getting into." Falon's face showed her pleasurable dilemma.

Reggie said, breathing hard, "Or what *we* were getting into you, huh? I'm a big boy, but damn, this is my lucky big day. This is the bomb ass pussy here." He went at breakneck speed. Or breakpussy speed. His forehead was laced with sweat.

Teela watched and instructed with a calming voice, "Fuck her slower, Reggie. Fuck her slower and grind on her. Lean down a bit and grind like you love her."

"Grind?" He looked as though his mind was working as hard as his libido. He readjusted Falon's legs and Teela reached in, placing her left hand on Falon's supple thigh, moving her leg to the side.

Teela told Falon, "Spread your legs out straight, on each side of him. Reggie, hold her up from underneath her hips, along her butt."

"My fuckin pleasure." His colossal hands still weren't big enough to cover the meaty flesh of her soft yellow backside. Loose booty spilled between his manicured fingers.

"No, grind. Slow. And try to hit the top of her pussy.

Try to hit it halfway, not all the way," Teela said, watching his every move.

He did.

And then Falon's tone and moan changed. "Oh yeah. Ahh, yes. Ahhhh, ahhhh. Uh-huh." She ground counterclockwise back like she was milking every inch of his slow-moving, smooth dick. "Oh yeah, that shit feels good." She gave a deep tongue roll.

Teela came to a stance and got on the floor behind Reggie. She knelt down upon the dark green, soft-pile carpet and watched Reggie's long dick enter Falon's accommodating pussy, slowly and deeply. The sight brought a rush to Teela's cunt and her lips swelled. Her clit had a hard-on. She knew the feeling all too well that Falon had, the feeling of peeing, but she knew the truth of what that sensation meant. Teela was feeling it herself. But she knew that instead of fighting it, she needed to contract her pussy muscles for a moment and hold it while rubbing her clit button in circles. Getting a close-up of dick meets pussy, she said, "Fuck her nice. Make her cum. Make *me* cum." Her voice was deeper. Teela was gearing up.

Falon spoke sultrily. "Oooh, oooh, oooh, baby, your dick is making me wanna pass out. Tell me your name again baby?"

"Reggie." He looked down at her soft, sexy face.

"Reggie what?" She looked up at his fine, chiseled face.

"Walker. Reggie Walker." He got a groove going and an angle going and a stroke going.

"Ohhh, yeah. God damn, Reggie Walker, whatcha do to me?" She revved up even more. "Reggie Walker, whatcha do to me? Reggie fucking Walker, what the fuck?" Her voice shook. "I'm cuming, baby. I'm cumming."

Falon cocked her head to the side and squeezed her eyes shut, taking it all in and letting it all out. She squeezed her own nipple while she yelled to free her pent-up release of girlie ejaculate, pushed like she was giving birth, and then there was a *squish*.

At the same time, Teela bore down like she knew she should, and immediately pressed her sweet clover fluid from her Skene's gland, squirting from her pussy straight out down her leg, his leg, and onto the floor. Reggie felt Falon's warm wetness run down his balls, and Teela's warm wetness on his calf. He grunted like a caveman. "Ugggggh, shit. Fuck. Fuck. Uuugg, hell. Awwwwwwwww, yeah. This shit is cumming hard. *Fuck!*" He shouted like it was the first and the last pussy he'd ever have in life.

"Damn," yelled Falon, feeling his dick expand even more and then explode, releasing his seed into the condom.

"Oh yes!" yelled Teela, continuing to rub herself. "That is some of the prettiest shit I've ever seen. That is some pretty ass fucking, Reggie Walker. Reggie Walker, whatcha do to me, too?"

Within ten minutes, Reggie Walker had left the building on cloud nine. Teela hurried around to get herself together, having just taken a more-than-two-hour lunch.

Falon lay still in the middle of the bed, on cloud ten. Her wide, round breasts separated left and right, sliding near her armpits. Her tawny nipples sprouted from her wide areolas and were still at attention from watching Teela's thickness.

She proceeded to suck her own tittie, putting it to her

lips with one hand and sucking on the nipple ring, and played with the hairs of her vagina with her other hand as she spoke softly: "Listen, Teela. My husband and I have parties sometimes if you wanna come by and play. He's a bit of geek just looking at him, but he knows his way around the bedroom. He's one of those nerdy IT executives at Compaq in El Segundo, so he does pretty well for himself. And I think he'd like you."

Teela looked her over while clasping her underwire bra. "Sexy Falon, you know, I have a man and I don't really explore other men too much. But to be honest with you, I was thinking the same thing about you and my man. I think he'd really, really like you. And he knows how to please like no man I've ever met."

"Well, we just might have to hook that up, the three of us. As long as you can promise to come to one of our parties soon."

"Agreed."

"So Teela, you mean to tell me you don't play with the girls?" Falon flicked her nipple with her stiff tongue.

"No. I just like to watch, as you can tell."

"I see. I understand. I was like that for a while. I do love me some dick, though." She continued to watch Teela and gave up on her own molestation job. "So, what's his name? Your man, I mean."

"Austin."

"Austin, huh? Is he black?"

"Yes, he is. And a good-looking black man at that."

"I see." Falon gave a moan like she figured as much. "Not that it would matter if he wasn't. Good-looking or black, I mean, it's all good. And what does he do?"

"He's a maintenance supervisor at the community we live in."

"Ahhhh, blue-collar, huh?"

"Yeah, girl. He works hard."

"I see. Well, how about if you set something up and let me know? Maybe I can even meet you at work one day when you get off."

"Okay. I'll let him know."

"And do I get to watch him with you?" Falon's eyes shifted to even more devilish.

"*You* like to watch, too?"

Falon said, "I do. I always say, take my man, please, as long as I can watch."

"That's my very motto. I think we can make that work. With your sexy ass." Teela winked.

"Takes one to know one."

Now fully dressed and with car keys in hand, Teela stepped to the bed as Falon positioned her lips for a kiss. Instead Teela tapped her on the leg and said, "I hope to see you later."

Falon played off the shining on. "You will, foxy vanilla. I had fun."

Teela paused and then simply said, "Me, too." She headed toward the door, opened it and stepped out, closed it and walked down the hall, down the stairs, and past the front door, then walked to her car, got inside, started the engine, and began the drive back to work, all the while feeling satisfied about her sexual thrill, but also feeling a little bit of a downshift.

Part of it was the usual guilt she felt coming down from her love high. Also guilt for giving in to an attraction and having sex so impulsively without her man. The closer she got to her normal life at work, the more she felt the frustration. And as much as she wanted Austin to experience saucy Falon's sexy flavor, she also wondered what was up with the "foxy vanilla" comment. And the question about Austin being black.

She made a call on her cell. "Hi. It's Teela Raye. I had a personal situation to tend to but I'm on my way back. I'll see you in a minute. Bye."

Still, the hairs on the back of her neck were at attention.

# 8

# *"Let's Get It On"*

## Valencia

That evening, as the final hours of the long day wound down at Cravings Restaurant on the beach next to the Portofino Yacht Club, Valencia's thoughts drifted to the reality that in eight months she would be a wife for life.

After dialing Gregory's number from the landline phone in the narrow hallway near the kitchen, Valencia watched her assistant manager, along with two hardworking busboys and an overworked waitress, wind down from cleaning up the main portion of the elegant restaurant. Decorated in hunter green and white, Cravings was known for its signature steak and shrimp, and international cuisine. The head chef and his assistant were shutting down the state-of-the-art kitchen area.

"How are you?" Gregory greeted her.

"I'm good," she replied, leaning against the festive papered wall. She was wearing black pants and a fitted top, with a black, pocketed apron. Her hair was tied into a scrunchie that she kept readjusting. She smoothed her long ponytail as it fell along her back.

"You want to come by for a drink or something?" The sound of muffled traffic backed up Gregory's voice.

"No, I'm cool."

"Are you sure?"

"Yeah, I'm just tired." She looked down at her feet as the busboy walked by. Her black, round-toed flats were spotted with stains from the many beverages and cuisine that had splattered on them throughout the day.

"You can spend the night if you want."

She thought to herself, *I don't know why. It's not like anything's gonna happen.* "No. I think I'll just go home. Plus I made a list on the computer for some things I need to start doing to get ready for the wedding. I mean, the hotels in Vegas book up way ahead of time. I haven't even done that yet."

"We haven't even decided on Vegas yet, have we?"

"I know. Just doing research."

"Sounds like you do need help. You can't do everything yourself, Valencia. Can't you ask somebody for help?"

"Like who?"

"Like my mom, maybe?"

"Greg, your mamma is having a hard enough time after having hip surgery. I'll let her recuperate for a while."

"While she's recuperating, she's available to help. It'll give her something to do."

She crossed her arm over her stomach. "I know. You're right. But to be honest with you, I just wish I had my own mamma to call. That's what the mamma of the bride is for."

"True. But like my mom told you, she's there in your mom's absence."

"She did say that. But my own mamma and poppa

should be around to see their only child finally getting married."

"Finally? You make it sound like you're forty."

"Sometimes it feels like I'm way past forty. Almost like I'm an old maid with no kids. My mamma had me at the age of eighteen. The Sanchezes come from a long line of big families. My grandmamma had ten kids. But my mamma only had me, and then they came to the States and never had more babies. They were way too busy with the Sanchez restaurants." She watched her employees hustle in the main room.

"Valencia, you'll grow up with our kids just fine. You've been busy with your career for a while, but not like they were. You've got time."

"I know, but that was my parents' problem. I wanna make sure I'm not like them. That restaurant was their first love, if you ask me. They didn't take the time to keep an eye out and give the attention where it was needed. That time is irreplaceable. You won't catch me doing that when we have kids."

"That's good to know. Look, I know all of this brings up those deep-down feelings. But I'm here for you. You got that?"

She stood up straight. "Thanks. I've got it. I'm good. You know what? Yeah, come on by, baby."

"Okay. When?"

She checked the gold Movado watch Gregory had bought her. "How about in a couple of hours? I need to take care of some stuff here. You know, go over the books once everyone leaves."

"That'll be midnight."

"Is that okay?"

"I guess in the morning I could just head to my staff meeting from your house. I'll see you in a little while, then."

"Okay."

"Bye, baby. Love you."

"Love you." Valencia hung up and went into her small office near the back door. Taking hold of her satchel and sweater, she spoke to her assistant manager, who was walking by. "Hey, listen, I'm headed out. You got this?"

"I do," the fifty-something woman said. "No problem."

Valencia told her, "Cool. See you tomorrow." She darted out of the back door and hopped into her truck. She pressed Miki's name and waited, then had a horny conversation with Miki's voice mail in her best feline tone.

> Ay, Mami. I'm calling to see if I can come over tonight and slide underneath your covers and suck on your clit a little bit, ummmmh. Lickie-lickie, suckie-suckie. Hssssssh, ummmmh, I can taste you now. I've been feenin for you. I just wanna bury my face between those juicy thighs and just lick your fat, wet, kitty kitty. Umm-mmh, it tastes so good. I wanna wrap my tongue around that clit and just pull on it softly until you moan uncontrollably, ummmmh, and suck your sweet juice right outta you, every bit of it. Uummmh. And then I'll stick my finger inside until you come on my finger like it's a dick—and nut on my face at the same time. Then I'll start all over, turn you over, and suck the front of that pussy from the back a ya. Yes. Call me.

Valencia hung up with an impatient clit erection in her damp panties, and dialed again. And again. And again. And again. Finally she heard, "Hello."

"Hey."

Miki said, talking fast, "What's up? You called like four times?"

"Yeah. Whatchu doing?" Valencia said, still sounding lustful as she pulled onto Sepulveda Boulevard.

"I'm getting dressed. I'm at the gym in my complex, about to leave. My phone was in my locker. Why?"

"Oh, I just left you a message."

"Okay. Yeah, I see it says I have a message."

"Can I come by?"

"When?"

"Now."

"You sound rushed, Val. What's up with you?"

"Nothin. I just wanna see you."

Miki sounded winded. "Excuse me, girl. I'm trying to put these tight-ass jeans on all these hips. Anyway, Anthony picked up T.J. earlier, and I'm about to stop by Dwayne's house. You wanna come with me?"

"Dwayne from our group, Dwayne?"

"Yeah. I have a strong feeling he'd be cool with that."

Valencia seemed surprised. "You're doing him again? He sure as hell must know his way around a chocha," she joked but didn't laugh.

"Ha ha. He does. But not like you, of course," Miki joked back. "Come on. Where are you?"

"I'm just leaving work."

"Come on over here, then. You're not far."

"No. I need to get back home by midnight. Greg's coming by."

"Oh, this won't take long, believe me. Plus, I'm not staying over."

Valencia heaved a sigh but said, "I'll be right there."

She hung up and aimed her ride toward Miki's side of town. Her panties were unusually wet from the message she'd left, and she was actually ripe for the prospect of a threesome with Miki and Dwayne, who she knew was the epitome of tall and handsome—and Miki did say he was tall all over. After all, Gregory didn't seem to have the energy to fuck her all night like he used to. When they did get down, he'd cum in five minutes flat, always without tending to her needs.

Suddenly, she received a call from a number she knew, though she hadn't programmed it into her contact list yet.

She greeted the caller. "Hey."

"Hey, fox. How's it going?"

She smiled. "Fine."

"What's going on with you, Ms. Tease a Brotha Forever?"

"Oh, I'm not teasing at all, Tariq."

"I can't tell. So where're you and your girl going tonight?"

"What? How'd you know that?"

"She just sent me a text that said you two were gonna hang out. Where? Must be Purple, right?"

Valencia sounded cautious. "Oh yeah. Well, I think so. I didn't, umh, know we were going there. We might go some other place. Maybe a friend's house or somethin."

"Who?"

"Her friend. I mean my friend. Just someone we met in the group."

"Oh. Why are you guys going so late?"

She waited at the red light and thought, then spoke slowly. "Not sure. Maybe you need to ask your woman that, Tariq?"

"No. She's good. You two have fun."

"Where are you?"

"I'm out. Just cruising," he said.

"Cruising. Cruising what?"

"Just driving. Needed to get out of the house. Thought you might wanna make good on your promises. Besides, those high school recruits drove me crazy today. You can't tell em a damn thing. They know it all. I'll just head over somewhere for a drink. Nowhere in particular."

"Okay," she said, proceeding toward Inglewood.

"One day you'll tell me when you're going to stop being so stingy and end this curiosity thing. It's sexy but damn, you're cutting it close, don't you think?"

"Me cutting it close?" she asked.

"I mean, close to the cuff of your girl. Guess it's the thrill of getting caught, huh? That risk factor."

"Maybe. But don't put it on me like that. I mean, *you're* the one who called *me* tonight, smarty."

"True, oh feisty one. I can't help but be attracted to what I see. Just don't think anyone can get hurt if they don't know."

"I guess that's true."

"So let's keep it that way," he said, as though it was a requirement.

"I will if you will, *mijo*."

"I will. You two have fun. And maybe from this point on we should block our numbers."

"Okay. But it's kind of hard to do that when you text me, don't you think?"

"I won't, then."

"Good."

He said, "But I guarantee you by this time next week, I'm gonna know what that sexy pussy's like. One way or another. I'm out. Yo." He hung up before she did.

She was even closer to Miki's place and began thinking. She made a U-turn toward her house so she could change, and called her friend again. "*Mira*, Miki, I'd better not go over there with you tonight."

"What? But I already told him you're coming."

"I know. I'm sorry. You two go ahead and have at it. It's just that I've got a lot on my mind. I just need to get stuff lined up for Greg's and my wedding. Plus, he'll probably show up early tonight. He usually does."

Miki's voice downshifted. "Aww. Okay. No problem. But, don't think you're fooling me. I know your bad ass is headed to Platinum or Purple, or some place that involves a pole so you can get your freak on."

"Maybe. And maybe I wouldn't be if I could just get some alone time with someone tonight." She cleared her throat.

"I wonder who. And I got your phone-sex-operator message. That shit was hot. I wish I'd known ahead of time. Even more reason for you to come with me, but for tonight you do your thang. I understand. And have fun."

"You too. By the way, tell little T.J. when he comes back home that I said hello. I love you."

"Bye, Val," Miki said, hanging up fast.

With a blue, low-cut, belted-waist top, pencil-leg black jeans, and Oxford ankle boots, Valencia walked around the familiar strip club to the song by Plies featuring Jamie

Foxx called "Please Excuse My Hands," with a nearly empty bottle of Killian's Red in hand, eyeing all the cotton-candy girls that strutted before her. She passed by an occupied table for two when a man who was sitting down slapped her on the butt. She stopped.

"That's gonna cost you, now, *papi*," she kidded, trying to look offended.

"I got money," a blue-black muscular man said. He looked certain.

"Well save it for the *muchachas* who work here. I'm here for the same reason you are."

His yellow woman who looked like she had ten years on him, spoke like a female rapper: "Girl, if looks were a minute this would be a long-ass day. You should be right up there working that." Obvious admiration dripped from her eyes. Her vision was stuck on Valencia's cleavage.

Valencia told her, "Well, aren't you flattering." Her eyes were playful.

The man replied, "Deservedly so. My girl is a smart lady. She knows what I like."

"And what does she like?"

He said, "She likes you. She pointed you out when you first walked in."

"Really? Is that true?" Valencia asked the fiftyish-looking, light-skinned woman with a short, curly Afro.

"That's true. Are you Spanish?"

"Puerto Rican."

He joined in, "Sexy-ass Puerto Rican, *mami*."

"*Gracias*." She asked the lady, "So, is this your man or your escort for the evening?"

"He's my husband."

"Uh-huh." Valencia glared at him, examining his face,

giving a sweet look. "He is fine, I'll say that. Even though his busy hands need to be cuffed, if you ask me. He ain't Jamie Foxx." She offered a sexy giggle.

He spoke right up and placed his hands up in surrender. "True. True. But if Jamie Foxx was right here, he wouldn't be apologizing." He grinned with a devilish look. "So, why don't you see to that? We've got another one of my girls at home. We live the life of a threesome."

"You have two women?"

His lady said, "He does. But I like to say I'm the lucky one. I have a husband and a wife."

"Wow, I think I could do that shit. That would be the life."

"You wanna meet her?" he asked, looking hopeful. "My girl at home, that is."

Valencia nodded. "That I do."

"Let's go, *mami*," he said as he stood.

Both the yellow lady and Valencia said together, "I'm ready."

Less than an hour later, the blue-black man held up a specially prepared blunt. They were all together in a cluttered one-bedroom apartment in Hawthorne. The room was dark, the furniture was dark, and the mood was dark, but it was a horny kind of lustful, freaky dark. A high-energy dark.

"You wanna hit this?" he asked Valencia. He lit it up with a blue lighter. The leafy, strong smell was enough to give off a mighty contact high.

Valencia's reply was, "Puff, puff, pass. Wouldn't wanna mess up the rotation."

"Here," he said, passing the funny cigarette to Valencia, who took a long, slow drag with her right hand, and then she passed it back to him.

Valencia allowed the smoke to do its seduction thing in her head. She inhaled while laying back upon a huge brown sectional in the threesome's living room, with the man's black dick in her left hand. She was getting eaten out through the slit of her panties by the gifted girlie lips of the yellow woman, as a red woman stepped up with a big butt and a smile. Valencia's eyes devoured her from head to toe. "Damn. Aren't you a whole lotta woman?"

"More to love, *mami*."

Valencia wore only her frilly, lime-green crotchless panties. She said, "Bring that right on over here. I've got just the place for you to sit. Put that pussy right under my nose."

The red woman approached, taking sensual steps, and crawled onto the sofa at just the right position to sit upon Valencia's face. "Like this?" she asked, looking down to get her angle right.

"Uh huh. That's it." Valencia inhaled her hairy sugar cookie. Her spine shivered at the lovely scent. "Pussy heaven. I always say, girls just wanna have fun and eat as much pussy as humanly possible."

Valencia still had one hand on the man's dick while getting her pussy eaten while eating pussy herself. Her thoughts concentrated on the yellow woman who was sticking her lengthy tongue deep into her vagina. Then Valencia focused upon the size and shape and color of the man's hard, dark penis. "Your man has a pretty dick."

The red woman said, "Yes, he does. His pretty dick and your pretty pussy. I think the two should meet."

"Bring it on down, Mister."

The red woman rose up from Valencia's face. The yellow woman backed away from her sloppy, wet pussy. Valencia's juices dripped like egg whites.

Valencia ripped off her panties and got up on her knees. The man got up right behind her. He snatched her arms and pulled them back toward him with a jerk, grabbing onto her wrists so he could hold on.

Valencia squinted her eyes and smiled. Her buzz was on.

He told the yellow lady, "Put my dick in her. Now."

As he scooted his hips into fuck position right up to Valencia's opening, the yellow woman took a two-handed hold of all of him, wrapping her palms around his penis, shoving it inside. Valencia's juicy insides gripped him like a glove.

"Yeah," he yelled. "Can the church keep it funky one time, or what? My God." He growled like a caged lion.

Valencia told the red woman, "Slap this ass as fucking hard as you can."

She popped Valencia's cheek like she was bitch-slapping her face.

Valencia told the yellow woman, "And you, eat her pussy while I eat yours. Get over here so I can go down like you went down on me. I'm gonna devour your pussy like Dracula." She looked back at Mr. Big Stuff and told him firmly, using seductive eyes to point at his face, "And you. Don't you cum till all three of us cum. This is ladies' night here. You got that?"

He replied like a good soldier, "Ladies first. I hear you."

"I hear you, too," said the yellow woman, who slid her vagina under Valencia's face as the red woman sat upon her face. The red woman had a large tattoo on her stomach of a black and pink tiger. And the tiger had a woman's vagina.

Valencia grinned nastily and shouted before she did her hands-free pussy eating, "You got anybody else in the house that might wanna fuck?"

"Just the three of us," the man said, giving her a man-sized dick-running thrust.

"Uhgh, ugh, shit. Cause I can handle all that." Valencia licked her lips, flicked the up-close clit, and took it into her mouth with suction, then went to work tearing up the fresh, older pussy from top to bottom, trying her best to not be too distracted by the deep dick fuck their man was serving her but good.

Eleven o'clock turned into midnight turned into one, and then into two. Before long, it was four in the morning, and Valencia pried open her eyes. She was in a strange, dark room, in a strange home, on a strange playpen sofa, with three strangers spooned up against her. One in front of her, one behind her, and another with her head on Valencia's thigh.

"Where the fuck am I?" she asked groggily, trying her best to focus. Now sober.

The man barely opened his eyes and said, "Huh? Oh. Go back to sleep."

"What time is it?"

No one replied. It was like she had put them all to bed. She saw from the cable box display that it was 4:17.

Valencia immediately sat up and pushed the woman's head from her lap, swung her legs over, and stood. "Where are my clothes? Where's my purse?" All the colorful threesome did was readjust their positions without her.

"Ay *dios mio.* Greg is gonna kill me." Valencia's head was doing flip-flops. Her breath smelled like beer and weed and pussy and cum. "My ass is grass now," were the last words she spoke before leaving in a shoeless rush.

Within two minutes she was in her car dialing Gregory's number in a hurry. He hadn't called even once, which made her dial even faster.

He answered the phone with "I came by and you weren't home. I waited. Who were you with?"

"I was with Miki. I fell asleep. We hung out after you and I talked, and I ended up at her house and we dozed off. I'm sorry, *papi.*"

"Are you telling me the truth?" He sounded distant and drained and angry.

"Yeah."

The sound of keystrokes upon a keyboard could be heard under his voice. "Valencia, I'm asking you. What the hell is up with you two? You and I had plans. We agreed I would come by."

"Nothing. We just had a drink or two and I was tired anyway. I told you, I'm sorry."

"Valencia, one more time. I give you one more time. You keep it up, okay?" His throat sounded like a guarantee.

"I won't, baby. I promise. Where are you?"

"I'm at home." Along with his keystrokes, the faint audio of someone breathing and mumbling was detectable.

"What are you doing? And what are you doing up?"

"I couldn't sleep worrying about you. Call me later. I'm

gonna try and get some sleep. Bye." He simply hung up in her face.

She looked at the display on her phone screen that said, Call ended.

Valencia took a deep breath.

She wore a vertical frown line between her eyes the entire way home.

All the while, her heart beat fast like something bad was bound to happen.

Her untamed desires were getting harder to handle.

She sighed. *Yes, something is bound to happen. And soon.*

# 9

## "Candy Shop"

### Brandi

Two of the words spoken by her newfound friend, Teela, banged around in Brandi's usually curious head. *Glory hole.*

Yes, curiosity had its usual stronghold on Brandi while she strolled inside her local sex shop on Hollywood Boulevard the next evening. The stand-alone building was black and white inside, with pink and blue rows of track lighting. It resembled a small strip club. Chains and whips and handcuffs hung from the ceiling. Black and white photos of nudes in bondage graced the walls all around. The store was called Kinky. And Brandi was a regular.

It was late afternoon after a long day at her middle school. The sun had almost made its descent. Brandi had decided to make the visit that her unrelenting voice of wonder insisted she make. Her bad side dared her to check out what it was that was so ultrasatisfying about a glory hole that Teela knew about so intensely, but Brandi didn't.

"How are you, lady?" asked the middle-aged worker behind the counter. He had cryptic tattoos on his forehead and neck.

Brandi was upbeat. "I'm good, thanks for asking. And you?"

"Good. Good. Nice to see you again. Can I help you find anything?"

"No. Just looking, that's all."

"No problem."

"Thanks, though. I appreciate it." Brandi's wide smile was for him, even though she aimed her sights at the many devilish products displayed along the glass shelves.

She examined the multicolored bottles of scented lube, the jet-black King Kong dildos, the vibrating clit stimulators and pocket pussies, then headed over to the video rental section, picking up and eyeing the orgy movies in particular. She browsed and browsed subjects ranging from hairy vaginas to Asian honeys, then saw a machine labeled *Upstairs Video Tokens*. Her smile dropped.

She pulled a bill from her ivory purse. Just when the man behind the counter stepped up to assist a customer, she stepped to the token machine, inserted a five-dollar bill, grabbed the large coin, and darted up the short flight of creaky and worn wooden stairs.

Brandi stood at the very top step, wearing her conservative pumps, and peeked to the left and then to the right and then to the left again. Stale and musty was the smell. She fought to ignore it.

With enough curiosity to kill her cat, she took a slow-moving step to the left. The first stall was occupied and the door was locked. The lock on the second stall was broken. The third was the charm. It had a shiny new brass lock, a functioning TV monitor and a nice, large hole in the wall. She entered with caution and flicked the sliding lock behind her.

She hung her purse on the doorknob and removed her lavender wrap dress, hanging it on a rusty door hook. She stepped up to the monitor, inserted the token and pressed play. It was an old movie with nothing but close-up fuck scenes. She then took a couple of steps to the wall and peeked through the hole. It was about the size of a saucer. She took a deep breath. Her rush started to take over at what she saw.

A skinny, hairy man stood before his own video screen with his pants to his ankles. His stiff dick was in both hands. He stroked his Johnson with his right hand with his legs apart, jerking himself for dear life while lusting over the woman on the TV screen, who was receiving anal sex from a woman with a major strap-on.

His face showed his turn-on. He eyed down the movie as he panted, and then his gaze shifted to the hole, which was shared by the occupant from stall number three. He sped up his jack-off pace even more now that he knew he had an audience. His face remained serious and his hand movements remained vigorous.

Brandi took a small step back as he took a big step forward and placed his penis into the hole, dropping one hand to his side. Brandi's hand took hold of his white shaft; she brought her mouth to his dick, opening wide, and began to blow him hard. She placed her right hand between her own legs and gave a wetness check, flicking the juices that seeped from her opening. As she sucked the thin stranger's tall dick, she finger-fucked herself deeper and faster while he flexed his ass muscles, pumping deeper into and out of her mouth with a fury. She licked him and placed short sucks to his tip. His moans grew louder than the volume of his porno movie.

She slipped into a quiet, slow-moving orgasm that spilled from inside her pussy like a melting ice cube. His pumping ceased, and the thick veins of his ashen dick visibly throbbed. Brandi backed her head away, and he removed his dick from the hole and spewed his sperm onto his hand, grunting like he was trying to lift a five-hundred-pound barbell.

Five minutes later, Brandi was in her red Camaro and on her way home.

Now she knew the glory behind the hole.

Her curiosity was kinkily contented.

Again.

# 10

## "Your Sweetness Is My Weakness"

### Miki

Miki, the elder of two daughters, born to parents who'd now been married forty long years, was thirty-four years old, even though she looked an entire generation younger. She met her boyfriend, Tariq Thomas, two years ago at the hotel where she worked, when he and his team were in town for a play-off game. The team had booked a block of rooms for a few days. He slept with Miki the second day they were in town. She spent her lunch hour in his room and worked him like he was running up and down the football field.

He played arena football in Atlanta, but a few months after they met, he moved to Los Angeles to work as a sports agent, and Miki couldn't have been happier. By then her son was four and she and her son's dad, Anthony, had long ago ended their relationship due to Miki's infidelities. He blamed it on the fact that he met her at a strip club. She blamed it on the fact that he couldn't handle what she called the boomerang.

Tariq knew when he laid eyes on Miki in the hotel

lobby that fall that he had found the one. He was hooked at first glance. And she was good in the sack. To him, his mission to find a good woman was accomplished.

It was a clear and sunny Friday morning, as smog free as it had been in a while in L.A. The slick sun slid through the thick slats of the natural shutters. The large blades of the Casablanca kitchen fan spun through the air, on guard to fight off the day's upcoming heat.

Miki spoke into her cell. "Hey baby. What's up?" she asked, after sipping her morning orange juice from a small carton in her tiny kitchen. She sat upon the suede bar stool at the caramel Corian counter. She'd just taken a long shower. A large, sunny-yellow towel was all she wore; it was tucked just under her arms, ending at the level of her sepia upper thighs. Her hair was in a banana clip.

"Not much. Just about to head to the office."

"Already? You just left here an hour ago," she told Tariq.

"Hey, I'm showered and changed, and already in the car."

"Wow, Mister. You move fast."

"Shoot. I got that Miki energy boost. I think we ought to get you a deal with a beverage company and name an energy drink after you called Good-Good, and make some damn money. Well, not literally, but hell, you know what I mean," he kidded. "Holy shit!"

"Very funny. But if that's the case, you should do the same." She heard a call-waiting tone. "Hey, can you hold on a minute?"

"Sure," he replied.

She pressed Answer. "Hello."

"Hello back. Good morning, beautiful," Robert said. His voice was slow yet upbeat.

"Hi, Bob. When can I meet you?"

"Well, Rose isn't staying in Santa Barbara with our daughter anymore. I think my daughter's in denial. Rose is now here in the Venice Beach house, so I want to stay nearby and keep an eye on her. I can't leave her alone for too long unless a nurse is here. I can meet you somewhere around here. Even within the hour if you can."

"I can't. I've gotta wait here until Anthony brings T.J. home. He's had him since Sunday, so he's bringing him home in a minute."

"Oh. Don't you have to go to work today?"

"No. I took the day off. I've just got a few things to do. And T.J.'s off, so I want to spend some time with him."

"I see. Listen, maybe I can just come by there later on tonight once he's gone to sleep."

She readjusted her towel under her arms. "No. How about if T.J. and I meet you for lunch today in your area? Maybe over on Washington, like at Killer Shrimp. Is that okay?"

"Okay, our old spot. That'll work. I can run out for an hour or so. Maybe around one o'clock. How's that?"

"That's good. How much do you have, anyway? Money I mean," she asked.

"You said three thousand, right."

She corrected him. "I said thirty-five hundred."

"Oh. Well, maybe I can give you the rest later on. I'm pretty sure I can sneak by late."

"No. Like I said, not tonight. But three thousand is fine." She remembered her other call and spoke quickly.

"Listen, I almost forgot. I'm on the other line. I'll see you at one."

"See you then."

"Bye." She exhaled a sigh and then clicked back over, talking slower. "Hello."

"I'm here."

She shifted her tone by a notch. "Okay. Sorry about that."

"Who was that?"

"Oh that was just Anthony. Remember I told you he's bringing T.J. back today?"

"Oh yeah. What time is he coming?" Tariq asked.

"Actually, they'll be here in a minute."

"All right. Well, you enjoy your day off. Tell T.J. I said hey."

"I will. Are you still coming by tonight?"

"You know it," he confirmed.

"Good."

"I love you, baby."

"I love you too, baby."

She disconnected the call and placed her iPhone on the bar when another call rang. It read *Front Gate*. She pressed 9.

She stood barefoot upon the off-white level-loop carpeting and rushed around to toss the empty bottles of Corona she and Tariq had devoured until the wee hours of the morning, and then hurried to the bathroom to brush her teeth.

Moments later she heard *Knock, knock.*

Miki sprinted to the front door, toothbrush still in her mouth, undid the latch, and turned the knob.

With excitement filling his eyes, the voice of little T.J.—short for Tony Jr.—leapt before she could fully get the door open. "Hey, Mom. Guess what? Dad bought me a SpongeBob SquarePants watch. Look." He burst inside, holding up his wrist and opening and closing the yellow flip top. Then he removed his tennis shoes, tossing them upon the blond bamboo entryway floor. His blue soccer-team shirt had his last name on the back—his father's last name, Santonio.

Anthony Santonio watched his elated son, who was his spitting image from his wavy hair to his red skin, and stepped inside, closing the door behind himself. He pulled off his shoes as well.

"That's nice," Miki said with a mixture of saliva and toothpaste in her mouth. She did not fully eye Anthony, and stepped away. "No need to take your shoes off," she said while giving him her back. She reentered the bathroom, leaning over the black marble vessel sink, where she rinsed and spit. She turned on the brass faucet, rinsing again and brushing her tongue.

She heard his deep voice behind her. "So, what's up with you?"

"Nothing, Anthony. Why?"

"Just wondering what you guys are doing today since T.J. doesn't have school and you're off work."

"I don't know. We'll probably head to lunch and maybe the park. Why?"

"Just asking," he said, as he closed the door and slowly locked it.

Miki grabbed the bottle of cocoa butter lotion from the sink and sat upon the side of the roman tub.

Anthony sniffed slowly, taking in the scent that soaked

the air as she rubbed the cream over her bare legs. He crossed his arms and watched. "You sure smell good. I love the way that smells on you. Always have."

"Thanks."

"You need help with that?" he asked. His eyes looked pathetically willing to accommodate.

She put one hand up and cut her eyes. "No, Anthony, I don't. Now don't start."

"Don't start what? I just wanna help you out."

"Well, I don't need any help."

"Are you sure?" he asked, sounding half-sexy as he leaned down and rested his knees upon the warm russet ceramic tile, smack dab in front of her. "You usually do."

"Anthony." She took a deep breath, dropping her shoulders.

"Anthony, what?"

She shook her head. "Not today."

"Why not today?"

"I'm tired. That's all. Just . . ."

He kissed her eyelid softly and she closed both eyes for two seconds. But she opened them as he retreated from her face. She just looked at him.

"Just what?" he asked. He undid the towel from her chest, and it fell behind her. He stared at her full breasts as they hung free. With one hand he strummed her large nipple with his thumb, rolling it along the hardening tip, and with his other hand he rubbed her elongated calf, moving his hand up to massage the shape of her curvy thigh. He leaned in toward her hair-line and kissed her forehead. Her damp hair smelled of garden rain shampoo. He moved his head back and simply stared.

Miki stared at him as well. He was good looking, like a shorter version of Rick Fox. He wore dark blue Enyce jeans and a white and blue T-shirt. She was six inches away from his face and he was eyeing her down. She could smell his spearmint breath as his hand found her pussy lips. She leaned her head back and sighed.

She felt him lower himself down more and heard him say, "Relax."

"Anthony."

This time he replied with his tongue.

His tongue upon her middle.

His lips upon her juicy split.

Her legs separated involuntarily as though giving permission for him to continue.

She shut her eyes again and leaned back even more against the tub's ceramic surface.

T.J.'s voice sounded from the other side of the bathroom door. "Mommy. Mommy can I have some ice cream?"

"Huh?" she asked, half-concentrating.

"Mommy, I want some ice cream, please."

"It's too early for ice cream. Go in your room and wait."

"Where's Daddy?"

"Tony, go," she yelled insistently, trying not to sound breathless, while Anthony didn't miss a beat.

T.J.'s footsteps could be heard stomping away, along with a grunt and a whimper.

And Miki made a sound of a whimper herself. Whimpering because her baby's daddy always knew just how to find her clit and bring her to a climax in record time. And whimpering for the fact that for the life of her, she couldn't resist what he was still willing to do to her.

Her legs quaked and she came in his mouth as usual, always harder than she had with other men. His face departed upon her last throb. Her legs trembled for another second.

He allowed her to catch her breath and then stood up, wiping his mouth with the back of his hand. He poked his chest out farther than before he'd walked in.

Miki shook her head, as if to shake herself from his pussy powers, and sat forward, putting her towel back around her chest. "Damn, your dumb ass does know your way around a vagina."

"Unlike any other you will ever meet. Bank it."

She scooted forward and continued lotioning herself. "Maybe. Maybe not. But I'll tell you one thing. Your significant other's gonna kick your ass one day if she ever finds out. You need to stop fucking around on that girl."

"You need to stop fucking around on that boy."

"Good-bye, Anthony."

Miki's eyes shifted to his crotch as he adjusted his obvious hard-on beyond his jeans. He simply walked out, closed the bathroom door, said his good-bye to his son, and left.

Anthony always had been able to bring on the millisecond orgasms. And she knew she would probably always let him do his thing.

It wasn't hurting her.

It was on him.

He was the one who violated his marriage vows.

Not her.

She hadn't made any vows, and as far as she was concerned she never would.

*     *     *

Miki pulled up to the concrete building on the corner near Venice Beach with the bright red capital letters that read *Killer Shrimp*. Little T.J. was strapped in the backseat. It was just before 12:55 p.m. and the heat of the day was at its height.

Robert Levine was already sitting in his bloodred Ferrari Enzo talking on the phone. The new sports car was just one of his many high-end automobiles. His Ferrari vanity plate read 24KGOLD, which was appropriate, being that he made a ton as the owner of a chain of very successful jewelry stores. His other cars had 14KGOLD and 18KGOLD on their plates.

He waved and smiled as Miki pulled up next to him, then he disconnected his call, stepping out in a hurry.

He opened her door before she could even prepare to exit and stood with the bright sun shining upon the top of his salt-and-pepper head. Miki took his hand as she exited, coming close to his tall, thin, but muscular body and meeting his puckered lips with a peck. He wore rust dress shoes and brown matching shirt and slacks.

"You look beautiful," he said as their faces parted. He eyed her from head to toe as she stood before him in jeans shorts, a white tank top, and sage Marc Jacob flip-flops.

"Thanks, Bob." She adjusted her Louis Vuitton tote over her shoulder. One that he'd given her.

Robert peeked into the backseat. "You need help getting T.J. out?"

Miki opened the back door and reached in as she spoke. "No, thanks. I've got him." She unstrapped him and he slowly stepped out. He wore shorts and a Batman T-shirt, and looked as if he was two seconds from falling asleep.

Robert extended his hand. "Hey big man. How are you?" He closed both the driver's side and back doors.

"Good." T.J. gave a weak shake and fidgeted with his digital SpongeBob watch, like he really needed to know the time.

"Are you hungry?" Robert placed his hand on T.J.'s back, and they stepped away from the car while Miki set the alarm.

"Yes," T.J. said, looking up at the big red sign. He began to show a smile.

Robert said, rubbing his own flat tummy, "Good. So am I."

They proceeded inside and were escorted to an outside table, where they sat in dark green plastic chairs under an umbrella.

Both Miki and Robert removed their sunglasses and looked over the brief menu. He wore his wedding band proudly as usual.

Robert was nearly twice Miki's age, as he was in his sixties. His face showed that his skin hadn't aged well. He had deep lines around his icy blue eyes and his mouth, his cheeks had lost their firmness, and his neck was wrinkled, all mainly from too much sun. He was a true outdoorsman. But he had a trim and firm body. He'd always worked out from the time he was a baseball player in college. Robert was also an avid swimmer and mountain climber. And he cycled ten miles every other day no matter what the weather, no matter what city he was in.

Today, the skin on his angular face, neck, and arms was extra golden brown. As usual, he wore a twenty-four-karat gold-and-diamond-encrusted Star of David charm, which hung just above the few graying chest hairs that sprouted from between his tanned pectorals.

Miki noticed as she closed the menu. "Your skin looks good. Very golden."

"Thanks. You know I bought my own tanning bed, right?"

"No, I didn't."

He looked proud of himself. "Oh, I didn't tell you? Yeah. Just a few months ago."

"Looks natural. Like you've been in the sun." Robert smiled wide and Miki added, "And you look happy."

Robert closed his menu and smiled at T.J., who sat forward, coloring with the four crayons he was given. "I'm okay." He looked at Miki and continued at a lower notch: "Things could be better. You know. Just still dealing with caring for Rose." He blinked fast as he talked, speaking as though love and the word *Rose* were one. "My wife's Alzheimer's is so bad now that she's bedridden. She can barely talk and she's on a feeding tube. It's just hard to see her like this. And my daughter is not dealing with it well at all."

Miki placed the napkin on her lap. "Wow." As the waitress approached, Miki asked her son, "T.J., do you want lemonade?"

"Yes please," he said without looking up.

Robert did the honors. "One lemonade, please. And two killer shrimp and pasta, and one with what, rice, right, T.J.?"

T.J. replied, shuffling his feet under the table while still coloring. "No, just bread, please."

Robert said to the waitress, "Okay, make that one killer shrimp with bread. And two waters."

She took their menus and said with a smile, "Coming right up."

Robert reached in his shirt pocket, pulled out a thick, folded envelope, and handed it to Miki. "By the way, this is for you. I'll have the rest soon."

"Okay, thanks." She smiled and nodded, reaching over to the empty chair where she'd placed her tote. She put the envelope inside.

Robert continued, leaning his forearms along the glass table. "Yeah, so my wife is gonna need a twenty-four-hour nurse. It's getting harder for my daughter and me to manage. Taking turns just isn't working."

Miki's eyes were plain. She leaned in closer to him. "Bob, I can only imagine how it must be. But do you mind? I just can't. I mean, I'd rather not."

"Oh, okay, sorry. I know."

She went on to say, "It's just that it makes it too personal, and well, especially with T.J. here, I mean, I know you've met him before and all, and well, I just want to keep it casual and, I guess the less I know, the better."

He shook his head. "No, really, no problem. Just wanted you to know what's going on. Why it's changed the amount of time that I'm free. You know. Just friend talk."

Miki kept her eyes on Robert's face. "I know. We *are* friends, but not really like that. It's complicated, Bob. I think I've been able to keep things simple all these years by not knowing. And, well, I'd just rather keep it that way."

"No problem. It won't happen again." He shifted his focus to T.J. "So, how's school been?"

"Okay."

"Which do you like best? Spelling? Art? Math?"

T.J. turned a page in the coloring book and said, "Ummmm, I guess math. Like my dad. My dad is a banker. He said he works with numbers. I wanna be just like him when I grow up."

"Oh, really." Robert grinned.

Miki smiled.

T.J. said, "Yeah." He used his left hand to escort his young words. "And my mom, I mean stepmom, is a banker too. That's how they met."

"I see."

T.J. looked up at Miki and said, "He still likes my mom, though."

Robert's eyebrows lifted. "Really?"

Miki took over and spoke, just as the waitress approached again. "Ahh, T.J., the waitress is bringing your lemonade." The teenage girl carefully placed the lemonade and water glasses down before them.

Robert told the girl, "Thanks," as she stepped away.

Miki looked at T.J.'s tall glass of lemonade with ice. "That looks good. Can I try it?"

"Yeah." He nodded as he spoke.

Miki's sip was small and she smacked her lips. "It's perfect. Nice and sweet, just the way you like it."

Robert watched Miki's mouth, "Beautiful. Just the way I like it."

A different waitress brought a tray with their steaming hot bowls of food and stepped away.

Miki didn't miss Robert's focused, almost-sexy look at her mouth. She took a peek at her wristwatch and changed the direction of the conversation again. "They're fast. Another reason why I like this place."

Robert broke his stare. "True. Good food, good company. This is a good day. I really need this time with you two."

Miki moved T.J.'s plate closer to him.

T.J. looked up at Robert's face when Robert wasn't looking. "You're nice."

Robert smiled at him, then at Miki, then at T.J. again. "Well, thanks, T.J."

Miki picked up her fork. Noticing Robert blush, she said, "Yes, you are. We'll have to get together again soon, you and me."

Robert replied, "The sooner the better. I could use it."

"It'll happen."

"When?" he asked.

"Soon." Miki knew it was time to pay up. It was her turn to reciprocate for the cash, and he would hold her to it as usual.

After all, she'd understood the sugar-daddy deal with Robert for years . . . it was what it was.

# 11

## *"Sexy Can I?"*

### Teela

It was early evening that same Friday, the end of a long workweek. Teela arrived home wearing dark-colored workout clothes. She'd gone grocery shopping after work. She received a hug from Austin as he took the bags from her and placed them on the kitchen counter.

"Baby, I got a call from a friend of mine named Falon. She was gonna come by my job when I got off but I'd left early. I invited her by tonight though."

Austin opened a bag and began putting things away. "Falon? How come I've never heard her name before?"

"I just met her recently at work." She saw him put away the ground turkey. "Oh, you can leave that out."

He placed it on the counter. "Okay. So, you met her at the gym. She's a member?"

"Yes. A new member."

"I see. So you're inviting her over for dinner, or what?" He took a bag of Chili Cheese Fritos from one bag and broke it open.

"She's coming over to see you."

"Me?" He smiled after chomping down on a mouthful.

"Look at you, grinning. Greedy ass. But, yes. And it's

okay if you don't want to. I'd understand." She looked at him like she was humoring him, just knowing he wasn't going to pass up a chance to fuck some new pussy.

He chewed fast. "Are you shittin me?"

"No, Austin. I'm not."

"You told her about me?"

"I did. See, she's married. She told me that she and her husband have these couples' parties, and that we should go to one. But it's not for a few weeks, so she called today and asked if we wanted to have fun before then, but without him. Just her. She knows the deal. That I rarely, if ever, do other men, and if I do, you have to be there. And that you don't do other women unless I'm there. But that I'm the one who likes to watch. She's cool with it all, believe me. And she's ready."

"Damn. What does she look like?" He leaned against the counter and put another handful in his mouth. He was all ears.

"She's black. Kinda light brown. Tall. Slender. Big tits. She looks like she's rich as hell. Just classy and sophisticated. She even looks stuck up. But, believe me, she's a freak."

He ceased his chewing for a second. "How do you know?"

"I'm just saying. She told me."

He chewed again and then swallowed. "Well hell, have her come on by."

"She'll be here at nine."

"Hell, I'll be ready at eight." Austin closed the bag and placed it on top of the refrigerator.

"Silly. I'll start cooking." Teela opened the lower cabinet, bent down, and pulled out a large pot.

He watched every move her heavyweight booty made. "This is the fucking life."

"Yes. It sure is," she said, filling the pot with water for her award-winning spaghetti.

Falon dabbed her full red lips with a paper napkin. Her dress was short and bright red. Her legs were bare. Her heels were high. "You're a great cook, Teela. Austin, you're a very lucky man."

"That, I am," Austin said. Falon and Teela sat on either side of him at the formal dining table.

"Thanks. Austin cooks, too, sometimes. I think he cooks even better than me." Teela sipped on her last bit of Pinot Grigio.

"I'm gonna have to come by and try that." Falon eyed Austin and gently touched his arm right where the sleeve of his golf shirt ended along his buffed biceps. She looked impressed.

"Anytime," he replied, looking like his dick agreed.

"I'm not very good at cooking, I'll admit it. I have a woman who comes over once a week and makes meals for all of us. She makes enough for seven nights. I admit I'm a little spoiled."

Teela stood up and said, "I wish. That must be heaven." She took her and Austin's plates and headed to the sink.

"It is. I'm thankful. But sometimes I think the old-fashioned ways are the best," Falon explained.

Austin stood, took Falon's plate, and said, "How about if I clear the table and you two ladies head off into the family room? I've got a movie all set up to play. And there's a decanter of cognac on the table. I'll be right in."

Teela took the plate from him. "Better yet, how about

if you two go ahead and *I'll* clear the table? I'd planned on it anyway. I always prefer to clean up when I cook. It just kind of completes the whole act of making a meal. I've got it." She kissed his cheek and shooed him away with her eyes.

"You sure?" he asked.

"I am," Teela said, opening the dishwasher and bending over.

"Okay. Thanks," he said in complete surrender. This time he missed the view of his wife's backside. "Hurry up, baby. We'll be waiting."

Austin led the way, and Falon, taking his hand, looked back at Teela. She blew a small kiss Teela's way and then said to Austin, "You smell so good. Is that Nautica?"

"Why yes, it is."

"I knew it. And by the way, Teela was right. You are a very good-looking man. Much more handsome than my husband," Falon told him.

Teela could see him grinning from ear to ear, like he stole something, even though his back was to her.

He replied, "Thanks. You're pretty fine yourself."

Less than fifteen minutes later, after closing the dishwasher and turning it on, underneath the sound of the jets from the machine shooting streams of heated water, and amongst the melody of a Johnny Gill CD, changing from "Let's Get the Mood Right" to "My, My, My," Teela heard a soft moan. And then another.

She switched off the light in the kitchen and passed through the hallway, entering a dimly lit family room where the few vanilla amber candles burned, giving off their scented flicker, along with a low volume of a brown-sugar big-booty-girl porno on the fifty-two-inch plasma screen. Austin was sitting on the brown pile carpet beneath Falon's wide-open legs. His face was deep diving into her muff. With her oversized titties hanging, her left nipple pierced by a silver hoop, Falon looked over at Teela as she approached. Her face was coated with a look of sheer ecstasy. "We've been waiting for you."

Teela stepped closer and said, "My, my, my. Don't you look comfortable?"

"I am, baby girl. I am. Your man eats pussy real good." Falon moaned twice. Her hands were on each side of Austin's head.

"Tell me about it. I call him a lesbian trapped in a man's body."

"Oooh, hell, yeah," Falon agreed.

Teela gradually unbuttoned her silk blouse and undid the front snap of her underwire bra, freeing her breasts from their confinement. She stripped down to nothing.

Falon's voice began to sound dizzy as though the cognac suddenly hit. "Pretty titties. Your girl has pretty titties, Austin."

"Uh-huh," he said from between her legs.

Austin held on to Falon, grabbing her wide hips, interspersing his oral actions with equal time on the clit, equal time penetrating with his tongue, and equal time lightly kissing her magical inner thighs.

Teela began squeezing her own breasts. "That looks so good. I love that shit." She stepped to the side to grab the end of the round coffee table and pushed it over just enough. She got on her knees and then lay on her back, scooting herself closer to Austin's knees.

"Straddle my face, honey," she told her busy man. "Let me suck your dick."

Austin did not miss an oral beat, but lifted his right leg.

Teela ducked her head to meet his elongated dick, which protruded along the end of the mocha sofa. She was on her back upon the floor.

She reached under him, grabbed his smiling dick with her hand, and opened her mouth wide. Upside down, she tightened her lips around his honey-colored shaft and began an up-and-down motion with her head, positioning the taste-bud side of her tongue on his underskin. His erect shaft curved down her throat perfectly. She offered twisting, deliberate licks, like her tongue was a swirling ribbon. He backed his face from between Falon's legs with a groan, and looked down to admire Teela's talents.

Falon said softly, "Wow, baby girl must be going to work down there. Let me see what she's doing." He moved his arms and Falon slid off the sofa and stood, then lowered her body to the floor to give full eyes to Teela's dicksucking skills. She then brought her head to Austin's balls and began to lick, serving as Teela's assistant—first with the tip of her tongue, then curving it, then flattening it, as though licking an ice cream cone. She pleased his testicles while adjusting her body to straddle Teela. Falon's vagina rested right on top of Teela's vagina and Falon began to squirm. Austin kept taking in his double treatment and pumped his penis just enough to get the movement of penetrating a mouth pussy while receiving a tea-bag move at the same time.

Teela could taste his precum. She could also feel Falon's wetness upon her peebone. Teela took his dick from her mouth and said from between his legs, "Baby, let her sit on you. Let her ride that good dick."

After a realignment of all three bodies, Austin was lying on his back on the sofa, with his legs opened wide. He was in a perfect position to watch the porno but never did. Falon climbed on top, facing him. She began rubbing her vulva against his thighs. The soft feel of her silky skin made him say, "Umh, umh, umh. Your body is beautiful." He ran his fingers through her long, coconut-smelling hair, and she tossed it about.

Teela noticed their two brown-skinned bodies meshing together. Falon was more statuesque than she. Her frame and Austin's frame looked good together. Teela took a condom from the coffee table and gave it to Austin.

"Thanks, baby," Falon said. She watched him stretch it over himself. "Wow, his dick is curved so nice."

Teela watched Falon lift her hips so that Austin's penis barely touched her entrance, teasing him while she wiggled upon his tip; then she finally lowered herself on his fully loaded shaft, taking him all in. Her body shook as the feeling of his hooked wonder grew within her. She leaned all the way forward and began to kiss him. Her titties rested upon his chest. Their tongues danced as they exchanged saliva, moaning together. She rocked her hips forward and sideways as they both thrusted.

Falon backed her mouth away and said, with a lust-filled expression, "Ummh, how does that black pussy feel, Mr. Big Stuff? You know you love it. You know you do."

He took her pierced breast into his mouth and licked it softly and then said, "Yeah. I'm feelin that black pussy choking my dick. I'm feelin that shit."

Teela watched them, feeling their passion with her eyes.

Falon fucked Austin like she'd pay his bills, riding him

like she was a cowgirl. Like Cat Ballou. And he bucked into her tight pussy with a fury, kneading her backside with his hands. The heavy part of her ass bounced along his upper thighs.

Teela stood behind them and watched. At first Teela had rubbed Falon's back with her fingertips, assisting her movements by leaning against her lower back. And then she took two steps back. And another. And another. She eyed them from across the room as they fucked in equal measure. His penis slid in and out, and she purred. Her pussy enveloped him, and he grunted. He now had his hand firmly on her breasts, and again she leaned down just enough for him to suck her titties. She yelled. "Yes, baby. Suck those big titties while you fuck this pussy, with your fine ass. Gimme that dick like you can't live without this black pussy. Like you need it. Like you've been missing it. Like you can't breathe without more of this pussy. Dammit. Fuck me like you want me. Fuck me like I'm your woman." Falon dug into his firm skin with her ruby fingernails like she needed to hold on, and then ran her fingers through his dreadlocks, panting like she was starving. He also again ran his fingers through her flowing red hair and lightly kissed her face. Their hands were all over each other.

Falon and Austin made inaudible sounds together.

By now, Teela only heard the erotic sounds with her tender ears. She no longer had the visual. She'd turned her back and quietly headed all the way upstairs and through the bedroom door, and closed it.

She stood over the bed and braced her body as she sat down upon the pillowtop mattress and leaned forward with her elbows to her knees. She began to cry, still hearing the intense wailing of Falon and her man, fucking downstairs.

As much as Teela fought to tune out the lustful sound, she heard Falon hit the big O like a firecracker.

And Austin yelled his usual "Fuck," while Falon made a sprung sound.

All without Teela watching.

Yet and still, they simultaneously got off on each other.

And Teela had no one to thank but herself.

This time, Teela didn't get off.

Not even a little bit.

For once, the green-eyed monster now lived in her green eyes, ruining everything.

# 12

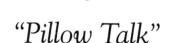

# "Pillow Talk"

## Valencia

The weekend wound down fast and an extrawarm Sunday evening had arrived. The central air conditioner was working overtime, even late in the day.

Valencia successfully fought off the urge to go out. She'd just hung up from talking to Gregory. He had wanted her to come over, but she put him off until the next night. She'd wanted to turn in early because she had a meeting first thing in the morning. But, with her bedsheets kicked all the way down to the foot of the bed, she took the time to talk to him for over two hours.

However, by the time she dozed off, her home phone rang. She snatched it in a murky daze. Her greeting voice was groggy and slow. "Hello."

"Val."

Valencia yawned and looked over at the alarm clock. It was 1:52 a.m. "Yeah." She wiped her forehead and her eyes.

"Whatcha doin?" Miki asked softly.

"I'm sleeping."

"This early?"

"Early? Baby, it's two in the morning."

"I know. I'm sorry to wake you, but. Val. Well, we were just thinking about you."

"We?"

"Yeah. Me and Tariq."

Valencia's eyes opened fully. "You and Tariq?"

"Tariq just asked about you. And it's not the first time."

"Fa real?"

Miki said in a seductive, throaty whisper, "Like, he asked me what your pussy tastes like."

"Honey. Come on now." Valencia heard Miki's quick-paced breathing. "What are you doing?"

"We're lying here. His mouth is between my legs. And we're talking about you." Miki's voice grew sexy.

Valencia shook her brain to make sure she wasn't dreaming. "Ay dios mio, mija."

"I know. My sexy baby was sleeping. Just listen." There was a sound of a slight muffle, and then a sloshing, smacking sound of wetness.

Valencia's eyes were now wide open. She turned onto her back and switched the phone to her left hand.

The sound grew louder and louder, and female moans of pleasure backed up the earful of intense slobber. And then a male voice, simmering in an erotic marinade asked, "Ya hear this? Is this what it's like when you eat my baby's pussy? Is that how you make her sound?"

"Yeah," Valencia replied. Her voice showed turn-on.

"Isn't my baby's pussy pretty? Full lips. All hairy. Isn't it sweet?"

"You know that."

His questions kept coming. "Doesn't she cream so good? She cums like a river. My baby cums good, doesn't she?"

"Ay sí." Valencia's lids shut in surrender. The visual behind her eyelids was X-rated.

"And how about you? Does my baby suck that pussy just right? Does she know how to make you cum in her mouth?"

"Ay sí." She slipped her hand down her panties.

"Like this?" And his voice turned from words to a revving, deep moan, and the sloshing liquid sounds grew in her ear until, suddenly, Miki's tigress voice spoke: "Oh yes, Val, he eats my pussy so good. Just like you. Just like you. Listen to me cum, girl. Listen to what Tariq does to me." She paused and then spoke while groaning. "I'm about to fuckin rip a good one." She paused again and screamed her short sentences. "Oh yeah. Oh yeah. It's cumming. Val. Oh, damn. It's cumming."

As Miki's cries revved, Valencia already had two fingers deep inside of her own wet vagina, probing herself, and using her thumb to flick her clit as she spread her slippery wetness from side to side and top to bottom. She cheered on her friend, "Get that good nut, Miki. Get that shit." She sucked saliva through her teeth.

"Ahhhhh, dammit. Ungggghhhh, yes. Fuck. Fuck, yeah! Ummmhhh."

Valencia could hear Tariq's pussy-eating groans with his *uh-huh, uh-huh* encouragement, even with his mouth full.

And then he took the phone and said, "Valencia, I'm about to finish what I just started. You know your girl is laying here drenched with her own cum, and I'm about to finish the job. I'm climbing on top of all this body right now, with my stiff dick in my hand, about to fuck your friend's pussy the way she likes to be fucked."

"Ay sí, papi." Valencia's pussy contracted over and over. She licked her lips.

"Listen. Listen to her as I stick this big-ass dick in her fat pussy. Listen."

And Miki made the sound of a tribal sexual grunt, and held her breath, shifting into a prolonged exhale. Her breaths then became short and deep. "Ahhh, ahhh, ahh, ahh, ah, ah," she yelled, as though being stroked for dear life.

Valencia said, "Ay sí, coño. Fuck that pussy, mijo. Make her cum again, papi."

"Oh I'ma fuck it. And I want you to think about what it would be like if you were right here, getting fucked right along with her. All that pussy-eating shit you two do. You need a big, long, hard dick after all that damn licking. Miki's getting fucked deep and hard and I can feel her pussy grip my dick, squeezing me while I slide in and out. I know every damn nook and cranny of this greasy pussy. And I know the spots way down deep. That's the place I hit that make her hit this high-pitched sound like she's fuckin crying. Like this."

"Oooohh, uhhhh, ohhhhh, ohhhhh, uuum, uuum."

"Hear that? You know you want me to fuck you. We've had you as a fantasy in our bed for months now. I know she already told you what I do. Now it's time for you to hear what I do."

Valencia groaned her words, "Let me hear that, baby."

"Take this dick. This is your dick. This good-ass pussy makes me hard every damn time it's within a mile of my ass. Kiss me, shit. Got all your pussy juices on my lips. I can still taste you when I swallow. Kiss me."

Valencia listened to the smacking sounds of the hot

and heavy couple on the other end and cradled the phone between her chin and shoulder. She kept up her finger-fucking, also squeezing her left nipple.

Tariq's moans were deep. His breathing pattern accelerated. "See, this shit is about to make me cum."

"Cum, *papi*. Cum for us both."

The phone suddenly sounded muffled again, and Valencia could hear the frantic sounds of the mattress squeaking and a headboard banging.

Miki let out a burst of mixed sounds that resembled a foreign language. She screamed as though she was being pussy-stabbed, and then her wails were plaintive. Her moans dripped with eroticism.

Tariq yelled, "That's the shit. Cum for me. Cum all over that dick. Oh hell. Oh shit. I'm cumming. Uggghhhhhggh. Ugh. Ugh."

Miki and Tariq's grunts were twins. Then Valencia spoke up as if she were their triplet, as she ground onto her own hand job, "Ay, *siiiiiiii*. Uhhhhhm, shit." And she sucked saliva through her teeth again while she squeezed her eyes shut and panted in response to her own pulsating clit-throb, pinching her nipple even harder. "Ayyyy. Fuck!"

She popped her eyes open and again focused on the phone call, when her best friend said, "I heard you baby. I just picked up the phone and I heard you."

"Damn, Miki," Valencia said, trying to control her breaths. "Girl, that was some sexy, crazy-ass shit."

"I know. I'm sorry. He dared me."

"Oh hell no. Don't be sorry. Not even." She still breathed fast.

"Did you cum good?" Miki asked.

"Hell yeah."

"Good. I owe you one for this."

"You do, *mami*." She pursed her lips and blew her breath from her mouth slowly. "Where's Tariq?"

"He's in the bathroom. He was shaking his head from the moment he stood up, still wearing a hard-on."

"Damn, he be doin it like that? He was fucking the shit outta you. Sounds like he knows how to throw that dick." Valencia managed a chuckle.

"That he does."

"Damn. I wish Greg and me were still this freaky. I miss the days when we were both acting like damn fools in bed. But his ass is a damn nerd now."

"Shit, girl. Tariq is square, too, believe it or not."

"Hell. Doesn't sound like it to me."

"Well, he's no sexaholic, if that's what you're thinking."

"You say so. But anyway, Greg's ass is pissed at me for not coming home in time to meet him the other night."

"What? What'd you get into? You went to Purple, right?"

"That, and I got with two women and a guy afterwards."

"Good Lord. You know what? Good night, Val. I'll talk to your hot booty later."

"Good night. And tell that nonsexaholic stud of a man I said, finally."

Miki snickered. "I will. Bye."

"Adios, 'ma."

Miki and Valencia hung up, both smiling.

\*     \*     \*

The next night, as promised, Valencia had shown up to spend time with her fiancé. While watching *Devil in a Blue Dress* together for the fourth time, they shared a frozen garlic chicken pizza and Skyy with cranberry, then turned in. But sleeping this particular night had to wait.

Gregory had Valencia prone in the missionary position. He looked her dead in the eyes and had her long legs bent back to the headboard of his rosewood California King.

He was talking shit. He liked to scoot all the way up, nearly hovering over her pubic area so he could hit it directly. Her body was longer than his and he didn't really prefer doggie style, as her legs were so long that he couldn't reach her hole without propping pillows under his knees. But this position was his favorite. He could tuck his legs near her ass and pump in and out as fast and furious as he wanted to. Only sometimes, she wanted him to slow down and find the right spots for the size of his dick to hit. "You've been running from this dick, huh? I'm about sick of your ass hitting the streets and not taking care of home."

She did her assorted grind moves, trying to slow him down by reversing in a slow circle for a second. But he fucked like he was too eager to downshift. She said sexily, "Baby, it hasn't been on purpose, I promise you. I love my dick."

He leaned in and smacked a big pucker of a kiss on the bridge of her nose. His breathing was deep and loud. He'd been at it for only five minutes but had worked up a sweat along his forehead from all his humping like a K-9. "How bad? How bad do you love it?"

Valencia pressed her hand to his hairy chest and could

feel his heart race. She looked up at him and then down at her pubic area, watching him pound her silly with his less-than-average-sized dick. It was short and thick, just like him. "Bad enough." His sweat dripped upon her cheek.

"Bad enough to let me fuck you in the ass?"

"Bad enough for that, too. But baby, you know you gotta at least try to eat me out. You know the ass fuck doesn't make me cum like eating my pussy does."

"I know." He continued his fast grind. "I just got so excited tonight when you hopped your fine ass in bed with no clothes on. My bed doesn't even know what it's like to have you in it anymore. Let alone, butt naked, and ready to fuck."

She gave him big eyes. "But baby, just for a minute." She took a deep breath and said, "Eat me. Please."

"Come on," he said, pulling his penis from her pussy. "I'm ready. You're about to get really wet on this one. Then I'm gonna hop in that tight ass and fuck you like a muthafucka on death row. Like Mr. Marcus be fuckin his bitches in the movies." Gregory was definitely not talking like a nerd tonight.

Valencia gave him a look like he need not be trying to sound gangster, yet grinned like she was at least impressed by his goals and opened her legs for him. At first she watched his teasing approach and then she turned her head to the side, bringing her forearm to cover her face so that she could simply feel him eat her out. And so she could also imagine whatever she wanted to. Whatever would help her to get off, she was ready to do. She was used to fantasizing as necessary. He could be whomever she wanted him to be.

Gregory moved down her body and crept his tongue to her belly button.

She squirmed.

And then he met her hairline.

She wiggled.

And then right down to her split, licking around it, up and down and side to side. He looked up at her and she looked down at him. His eyes were wide like quarters. She watched him watch her like he was waiting for her face to tell him he'd hit the right spot.

It did not.

His tongue grazed over her opening and she longed for him to penetrate her with the tip, using a scooping motion like she'd taught him before. She scooted her pussy closer to his face, hoping to refresh his memory.

"Yeah, you like that don't you?" he asked.

"Uh-huh."

"You gonna cum for me. Come on my face now."

She still squirmed, almost as if trying to make her pussy find his tongue and handle the movement for him. She moved her vagina down, hoping his mouth would rest near her clitoris and elicit a butterfly lashing.

But it did not.

He lowered his mouth in exact measure to her lowering. He shook his face and made a growling noise and managed to say, "Cum for me. That's it. Cum for Daddy."

Valencia waited for a moment, trying to allow him to go through his motions as usual. Sometimes, he could bring her to climax, but it took awhile. Tonight though, she had no patience whatsoever.

She began to recite her fake-mode script. "Ooooh, baby. Yes, that's it. That's it. I'm cumming for my baby.

You're so damn good. Yes. It's cuming. It's, oh Greg. That's it. Yes." The zero sensation from her pussy was in direct opposition to her words. She performed as though it was a mercy fuck.

He stopped, immediately backing away from what he was doing and took on the spectator role, watching her facial expressions as she moaned. His eyes said he loved her and he had a look on his face like he was the man. "Yeah. Get that. Uh-huh. See. See what you've been missing." He had both hands on his own dick and had been strumming his meat like it was a banjo.

He arranged himself to mount her. She took long, bogus panting breaths to signal the end of her orgasm. He pinned her legs back and lay upon her. She noticed that his chest was slightly flabby, almost to the point of getting man-boobs. But he didn't notice her noticing. He spit on his hand and rubbed it along her asshole, finding his way by touch. He pressed one finger inside. "Oh yeah. There it is. That's all mine there." Greg placed the tip of his dick at the opening of her tight ass and darted inside with a look on his face like he was high on Hennessey when he hadn't had a drop.

She flinched for one quick second, tightened her eyes, and then was still.

He lowered his chest upon her and buried his face deep into the nape of her musk-oil-scented neck. "Umh. Umh. Umh. Aww shit. Uhghhhh!" He paused, froze, pumped, froze, and then rose up. As she unzipped her eyes, he looked down at her face and said, "That was the shit."

He was done.

He had shot his wad in her ass already.

Valencia never even moved. She never ground back.

Never had a chance to get the feeling of his penis inside of her backside long enough to spark the thrill of a flame.

He never hit that spot or any spot.

She barely even felt him.

He maneuvered himself to a stance and held on to his soft dick. He shook his head and said, "Damn, girl. I almost forgot how good you are. I'm gonna go ahead and take a shower. And then I need to send an e-mail."

She lowered her legs and lay flat on her back. "Okay."

He headed to the bathroom, saying, "You can go ahead and get some sleep. I know how you are when you get in that postorgasm mood after I work it. You'll be asleep in no time."

She said nothing, but he didn't notice anyway. She went to the guest bathroom.

An hour later, Valencia tossed and turned in the large, empty bed, still naked. Gregory was still on his computer, sending e-mails or surfing or working or playing or whatever it was he did, still naked.

Valencia lay on her back looking up at the black cherry blades of the ceiling fan. *Is that all there is? I guess this could be a good life. A man. A house. Money. Maybe a child or two. But so-so sex.* She nodded and looked over at him. *Yes. Security is enough to keep me right where I am. Whether or not I get great dick from my future husband isn't the thing that matters. I love him. And he loves me.* She glanced over at him with groggy eyes. *What in the hell is he doing, anyway? Oh Lord.* The screen was facing the other wall. All she saw upon the side of his face was the reflective light from the screen's grayish-blue illumination.

Within minutes of her own ongoing reflections running through her head, from her wedding to her sex life, Valencia quietly snuck her hand under the covers, turned her back to her fiancé, and rubbed her stiff clitoris on the slide. In her mind, she thought about Miki's premier clit-sucking skills, pretending Miki's mouth was under the covers. Valencia tightened her ass and burst a smooth cum against her hand. She held it in with an internal grunt. And Gregory was none the wiser.

A minute later, with dick in hand, Gregory took a quick glance at her back and darted his eyes back to the screen, back to her, and back to the screen, while he busted a quiet webcam nut of his own.

She sighed.

He sighed.

He had his woman in his bed.

She had a man who loved her.

Valencia fell fast asleep.

Satisfied.

Gregory stayed up just a little while longer.

# 13

※

# "Magic Stick"

## Brandi

In the middle of the following week, Brandi's eighth-grade class arrived for the start of the school day at the retro-looking Harcourt Middle School, a one-hundred-thousand-square-foot, newer magnet school with sixty prototype classrooms for students grades six through eight.

The bell was to ring at 7:50 a.m. It was 7:40.

Some backpack-wearing students walked far too slowly and some rushed about. Most were in groups, chatting. A few walked alone. A few were hugged up as couples. But none were with their parents. Except one.

"Hello, Miss Williams," said a female student with long ponytails, sounding cheery as she said good-bye to her father, who had walked her to class.

Brandi, standing beneath the long, covered breezeway, said to her, "Hello, Asia. How's it going?"

"Good, thanks, ma'am."

"Did you study for your test today?"

"Yes, ma'am."

"Good." Brandi looked at Asia's dad. "Hi, Mr. Turner."

"Hey, Ms. Williams. You can call me Harold."

Brandi looked at his daughter as she entered the class-room. "Thanks, but we don't call parents by their first names."

"I see. Any rule against a parent calling a teacher by her first name?"

"My name is Miss Williams."

"Miss, huh? I see." He sounded let down.

"That's my name at school." Brandi met his eyes. "But away from school, my name is Brandi. Maybe we can meet at seven tonight at the bar on Olympic called Francisco's."

His face beamed as well as his voice. "I'll be there."

"Tell me your number. I'll remember it," Brandi promised, leaning her ear toward his mouth and looking around.

He whispered his digits slowly.

She turned her back to him, thumbing her earlobe. "Drive safely and have a good day."

"I will. Oh, it's good already." He walked away, stepping like he was on cloud nine.

Brandi placed her hand on the back of a young man who'd rushed down the hall and turned on a dime to enter the classroom. "Hello, Keyshaun. I see you barely made it."

"I know, Miss Williams." His voice was deeper than middle-school deep but not quite grown.

"How are you?"

"Good." He looked at Brandi's legs, which extended from beneath her peach-colored sheath dress.

She told him, "You look nice today."

"Thanks, Miss Williams. So do you." He focused on her hip area.

His height dwarfed her as she stepped in after him and closed the door, "Come on now, class. Let's settle down." She headed toward her desk when the door opened.

"Hi, Miss Williams," said the school principal.

"Hello, Mrs. Ross."

"Can I talk to you for a minute?" Mrs. Ross asked, holding the door open. She gave Brandi the come-hither motion with her index finger.

"Sure." Brandi said to her students, "Class, I'll be right back." She exited the room and shut the door behind her. Standing inches from the quartz tile wall in the quiet hallway, she crossed her arms and said, "Yes?"

"Brandi, your mom called me this morning. Said she's been looking for you. She asked me to have you call her," her boss said. She looked conservative, with a slightly graying flip hairstyle and an all-beige skirt suit.

Brandi spoke softly, "Oh, okay. I will. Thanks." She offered a wide smile.

"Aren't you wondering what's going on with her? I mean, the fact that she's looking for you like this."

"No. I know she's okay. I know she's just checking on me."

"I see." Mrs. Ross frowned. The vertical line between her eyes and the crow's-feet beneath her eyes indicated her years of wisdom. "Brandi, look. I've known you since you and your mom moved next door to me on Verdun Avenue when you were the very same age as these kids here. Now, I'm going to tell you this. One of the parents mentioned that they thought you smelled of alcohol early in the morning yesterday. I dismissed it. Now, while I can't say I've ever noticed that myself, I have to tell you that if another parent or teacher or child or anyone else says they noticed something, too, I'm going to have to look into it further. You know I love you, but if I find there's merit to this, I will have to let you go. I cannot have the possibility of these types of violations while teachers are on school grounds. Not around our students."

"Oh, I totally understand, Mrs. Ross. And I would never put you in a position like that by doing something so stupid. Never."

Mrs. Ross's maternal stare spoke of cautioned inquisitiveness. "Okay now. So, you're telling me this is not the case? You've never come to this school after having something to drink?"

Brandi shook her head. "No. I'm telling you the truth." Her eyes begged Mrs. Ross to believe her.

"All right. Have a nice day." Mrs. Ross walked away and then looked back, speaking louder. "And make sure you call your mom. I don't want her getting on me thinking I didn't tell you." She aimed her finger Brandi's way. "I'm telling you, Brandi, don't make me look bad."

"I won't. I'll call her."

"Good." Mrs. Ross walked away fast, without saying good-bye.

Brandi said "Thanks" to her from behind and reentered the classroom, "Okay class. Let's discuss your book of the month, *Fallen Angels* by Walter Dean Myers. I'm quite sure everyone has read it and is ready to discuss it in detail."

The students ruffled around, some reaching into their backpacks and some flipping open their notebooks.

Brandi took a deep inhale and a long exhale. She counted to ten and then told her students, "Excuse me one second. I need to go to the ladies' room for a quick minute. I want all of you to please be prepared to debate the period of time, in the sixties during the Vietnam War, and how that same story would have been told today."

She exited the room with her purse in hand and reached inside for her cell phone, darting into the restroom two doors down. She pressed *67 before she dialed and didn't bother programming the name into her list of contacts.

"Hello. Yes, this is Miss Williams. Brandi Williams. Asia's English teacher . . . Yes. Good. . . . Oh really? Well, thanks. . . . Listen, I'm sure you're on your way to work, but I just wanted to tell you that I go to lunch at 11:30. There's a place right down the street called the Best Western, right off La Tijera. Can you meet me there? . . . You can? . . . Good. Okay. Sure. Bye."

And before she could get her phone back into her purse, she snuck her other hand inside and took hold of a silver flask, uncapped it, and brought it to her mouth, tossing her head back and taking two long gulps of clear lightning. She clicked her tongue and wiped her mouth with her wrist, running her tongue over her bottom lip. She twisted the cap back on and replaced the flask in her bag. Brandi took a look at her reflected image in the scuffed-up mirror, then removed a stick of Big Red from the side zipper of her bag. She rolled it into her mouth, chomped on it, and silently said, *Eleven-thirty can't get here soon enough* as she headed back to her classroom. She closed the door tightly to instruct her education-hungry students, doing her good-side thing.

The burgundy blackout drapes were pulled.

At 11:42, Brandi's flask rested upon the walnut nightstand next to the full-sized bed in the tiny, dingy, dark, and drab hotel room while she gave a major blowjob to a tall, dark-haired man with curly hair, who was built like a boxer. Brandi, hot and horny and talented, lay between his long legs, looking up at him with her big brown eyes as she devoured his penis. She crafted a vacuum pressure on his dick, wrapping her lips around his cock and sucking in air so that her cheeks inflated and deflated. She made fast up-and-down movements and fluttered her tongue in her mouth. She went down as far as she could and opened as far as she could, then she sucked in as much air as her lungs would allow, and blew. She let her mouth travel up and just as she reached the head, and then went back down again.

"Oh damn. Hold up. Not yet. Shit." He choked the white cotton sheet beneath him and curled his toes.

"Yeah, you're right," she said at a low, soft pace as she released her mouth grip. "I'm going to save that sucker because I want you to have the time of your life on your lunch hour. I want you to live out your dreams, baby. What's your ultimate afternoon delight?" She looked up at him while resting her head along his thigh. Her eyes looked drunk, either on gin or on sex.

"My ultimate?"

"Yes, what's your fantasy?"

He looked around the room and then at her. "This is it right here. I've been watching you for a while. No one would believe the phone call I got today. I had no idea when I woke up and took my daughter to school that I'd be alone with you a few hours later. Never."

"Oh please, you can dream bigger than that. What is it that you've always wanted to do sexually?"

"I don't know."

"You can't think of anything?"

"No. I haven't had that much of an unusual sex life, but I've been okay. I guess. Except have sex on an elevator or get head under the table at a restaurant, maybe."

"Kinky. Though we can't do either of those right now."

"True. I guess one thing I've never done, that I think most men have definitely done my age, is have anal sex?"

"Anal sex? That's not as big as I want to give you. Unless you want *me* to give it to *you*. That might be big."

His forehead creased. "Oh, no. I mean me as the giver, thank you."

"Okay, that's what I thought. Not big enough. Bigger."

"Two women at once, maybe?"

"That's common. Wow, as much as you think you have, you really haven't done much. Come on. Think bigger."

"Well, I did see a porno flick where this girl choked this dude, and before he came he shot his cum in her mouth, and then she kissed him so he could swallow it himself."

"Oh, recycling it, huh? That's called snowballing, my love."

"Yeah, that."

"You'd want to do that?"

"I guess so."

She looked over at the digital clock on the nightstand and moved from her position. "We'd better get started. We don't have long."

He braced himself by laying his head upon two propped-up pillows. His face showed that he was trying to ease his mind. "You don't even remember my name, do you?"

"I do. But it doesn't matter." Brandi stood on top of the hard mattress next to him, balancing herself. She parted her Southern lips and began rubbing her clitoris with her index and middle fingers, flicking the slippery skin and pressing her hips forward toward him.

He took his already ripe dick in hand and stroked himself. She spread her lips open for him to examine every inch of what her pussy was drawn like, as she gave more brisk stroking to her clit. She started moaning and grinding in the air, then stood over him, straddling his torso while he slid his hand up and down his shaft.

"That's a pretty pussy there."

"Uh-huh."

"I wish I could fuck that."

"Maybe."

His voice grew deeper. "Oh yeah, that's a pretty-ass pussy. My God."

She looked down at her own vagina. "Yep. That's the prettiest part of me all right."

"It's all pretty. And I'll bet it's tight."

"It is."

"I can tell. That slit is just begging to be ran through. God damn, I like that. Oh yeah. I'm about to tear that up."

"Are you ready to cum in my mouth?"

"Hell yeah."

"You need me to squeeze your throat first, right?"

"I do."

"Come here," she said. She knelt down on top of him and placed her hands around his wide neck, squeezing hard and then harder, pressing her thumbs into the front of his throat. He closed his eyes and she could feel him beating up his honey-nut dick from behind her even faster. She squeezed harder and harder. His face began to turn a dark red. Her hands began to hurt. She jerked his neck like she was wringing a washcloth until the grip she gave could not squeeze any tighter.

His toes curled. "I'm cumming," he gasped, fighting for air. She let go of her grip, rushed downtown to his tip after missing one half shot, and took the rest of the hot cum that spit from his tip to her tongue. She quickly moved up to approach his face and he opened his mouth wide as she exchanged the fluid to him while they kissed. He sucked her tongue and she carefully backed her head away. He gulped "Ahhhhh," as though satisfied with the sensation, the texture, and the taste.

She smacked her lips and ran the tip of her tongue over her teeth. "Is that how you wanted it to be?"

His face became less flushed. He shook his head to aid his scratchy words. "Oh yeah."

"Ever tasted your own cum before?"

His breaths were short. "A little from masturbating. That shit was sexy." He rubbed his throat.

She played tug and pull with the fine hairs on his chest. "You know you're going to grow more hair on this chest of yours. That's what happens on a sperm diet."

He brushed away the stray hairs from her forehead. "Funny."

She massaged the muscular definition of his pectorals and traced his hard nipple with her finger while he put his hand on her shoulder and slipped his arm around her.

He held her and she stayed put in his arms. But then

ten seconds later, she jumped to her feet, noticing that it was 12:22. She sipped a fast swallow from her flask and gathered her clothes, which rested along the back of the desk chair.

"What about you?" he asked as he watched her, still lying on his back.

"What about me, what?"

"What about you? You didn't get yours."

"Oh, I'm good."

"Maybe next time?"

"No. Next times don't exist. No second chances here."

"Why's that?"

"That's just the way it is."

He sat up a bit. "Can I call you?"

"No," she said simply and exited the room, leaving him lying there naked with his dick, and his mouth, coated with cum.

Brandi headed back in her Mustang to the middle school that employed her. The pep in her step was a tad bit peppier. She felt the rush for the short drive, but by the time she stepped out of her car and headed down the walkway to her classroom, the high had downshifted a notch.

Her body had its way again.

Her head said, *Stop lusting and become sober.*

But being sex drunk truly had its freaky hold on Miss Williams.

# 14

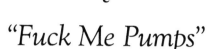

# "Fuck Me Pumps"

## Miki

**H**ave a good day, sweetie." The next Monday, Miki sat in the short line of cars in the circular driveway at the all brick, two-story Westwood Elementary School. The sun had not yet shared its heat with the early-morning air.

"Mom. I don't wanna go to Mrs. Johnson's class anymore." T.J. sat in the backseat wearing his gray sweatshirt and jeans. His eyes showed six-year-old misery.

"Why?" Miki asked, as she put the car in park.

He spoke with a sleepy whine. "Because I wanna go to Mr. White's class. He has all the *Star Wars* things."

"*Star Wars* things?"

"Yeah. I wanna be in his class." He pouted like he was purposely trying to break her heart.

Miki hid that she was tickled and spoke sympathetically while reaching in the backseat and smoothing the side of his thick hair. She unbelted his seat. "T.J., I'm sure all the kids get excited about Mr. White's collection, but you have to go today. We'll get you a *Star Wars* toy, and you can take it to school on share day. Now go on before you're late." She took his arm to pull him up for a kiss.

T.J. scooted up and gave a silent, weak peck, and his lip

stuck out even further. "Bye." He took hold of his Sponge-Bob backpack.

"Bye, baby. Mommy loves you."

"Love you, too," he said, nearly inaudibly and with no eye contact whatsoever as the teacher's aide opened his door and helped him out, giving Miki a wave, then he pushed the door closed.

Miki watched her first-grader son. Just that quickly, he flung the straps of his backpack over his shoulders and spotted his best friend, Travon. The two darted off past the teacher's aide and through the gate, and disappeared.

As she pulled off, Miki wore her full-on smile, grabbed her hot pink travel mug and sipped her chocolate silk coffee, and simply took in the short drive to work. She thought back to her son's pouty face and her heart warmed.

And then she quickly thought about the length and thickness of Dwayne's penis.

The swanky place where Miki was employed was an urban inner sanctuary with panoramic views located in the center of glamor, in the foothills of Beverly Hills. It was the luxurious W Hotel in Westwood, decorated in brown, dark red, and blue. The designs and ambiance were vibrant and sophisticated. The mood was contemporary and mod.

Just before one in the afternoon, Miki sat at her chrome-and-glass desk in her office while on the Internet, surrounded by the best of the best décor and furnishings. An imported, violet Victorian droplight shone brightly over her flat screen computer. She'd logged on to a top-rated Blog Talk Radio program to listen to a show called *Chicks on Lit.* She was trying to keep her laughter at bay as she listened to the three female hosts discuss the topic of sex addiction; one of them advised women that in order to keep from being dick dumb, they should just get themselves a BOB—battery-operated boyfriend. Miki chuckled and said aloud, "I heard that. If only. Sure would cut down on all this crazy-ass shit."

Miki lowered the volume on her computer and picked up her office phone as it rang, keeping an eye on her computer screen.

"Are you free for lunch?" her sugar daddy, Robert, asked.

"No. Not today." She grinned, thinking, *Speaking of Bob.*

He gave a long, low sigh. "How about in the next day or two?"

"I'll check with you then." Her words were fast as she read an e-mail.

"What's going on?" he asked.

"Nothing."

"You seem distant, Miki."

"No. Just busy." She clicked her wireless mouse to send her reply. "Just trying to stay on top of things around here."

"I got it. Well, I've got the rest of your money."

"You do?" she asked, turning from the computer for a moment. She glanced out of the oversized window behind her, crossing her legs.

"Yes. And I really would like to see you. I mean in private."

The outside view of towering palm trees and powder-blue skies met her sight. The morning had crept away and it was already early afternoon. She turned back around to check the time on her screen and logged off. "How about if I call you tomorrow and we can talk about getting together?"

"Okay. I can even come by there and get a room like we used to do."

"Maybe. But I'll call you." She swung her chair to the side and stood up in her tailored, burnt-orange skirt and blazer.

"Okay. Don't work too hard. Bye."

"Later."

She hung up her desk phone and grabbed her iPhone, stepped her pointy bronze fuck-me pumps upon the polished concrete flooring, and sat back against the butter-yellow leather sofa that was angled next to her desk. She leaned against a large brown-and-orange-striped pillow and prepared to send a text, when her phone rang.

She answered it quickly. "Hey Dwayne." Her face was nonexpressive.

"Hey there. I was thinking about you and wondered how you were."

"I'm good. How are you?"

"Cool. All is well. Just getting things going with our promotion for a celebrity event at the club coming up. You know I own Club Sunset. You should try to make it out one night."

"I'll do that." Miki crossed her legs.

"Good. Listen, I mean, I've been wanting to ask. What's up with you? I mean you got a man or what?"

She spoke matter-of-factly: "I won't ask you that and I won't tell."

"Oh, so it's like that?"

"Dwayne, we both know what we've got going on as far as what we're trying to work through. It's the same stuff for both of us. It might be smart to not go there. Let's just take it for what it is."

"So, those other evenings. What were they to you?"

"It was a reaction to temptation. I have those all the time."

"You do?"

"Dwayne, please. First of all, don't act like you don't know about me. And second of all, don't act like temptation isn't one of your major issues as well. I mean, I have fun and all, but I think it's best to leave our conversations in the bedroom—where we've had them twice already." Her face stayed bland.

"Okay. That's cool. I mean I guess it's gotta be cool, right? I was just asking if you had a man or not, that's all." His television could be heard in the background.

She uncrossed her legs, looked up at the clock again, and said, actually managing a grin, "So basically, Dwayne. Here's my question for you. Do you wanna fuck again or what?"

"I do."

"I do, too. Are you going to the next meeting?"

"I am."

"I am, too," she said, scooting to the edge of the sofa. "Cool."

"So I'll see you then. Bye, Dwayne." She hung up and focused on her phone again when the manager's assistant entered her office.

"Excuse me, Ms. Summers. I'm sorry to bother you, but Valencia's waiting outside for you. I just saw her when

I came back from lunch." The woman looked barely twenty.

"Okay, thanks. I was just about to text her when I saw I had a missed call from her."

"And Ms. Summer, I picked up your desk phone in the lobby. You've got a call on hold. They said it's urgent."

"At my desk? Who is it?"

"They wouldn't tell me."

"Wouldn't tell you? Okay. Wow. Thanks a lot." Miki stood, grabbed her handcrafted purse from atop her desk, and rushed to exit her office, walking behind the assistant. They both headed in different directions. Miki stood over her concierge lobby desk and picked up the phone. "Hello."

"Bitch." The voice was flat and angry.

"Hello?" Miki said with a question mark.

"Since you like to fuck, I'm going to fuck you up. Bitch."

Her eyebrows dipped. "What? Who is this?"

*Click.*

Miki looked at the receiver and then checked the display on the phone but it no longer read the caller information. She pushed the receiver to its cradle, stood still for two seconds, looked around, and then headed straight out of the front lobby doors.

"Good afternoon, Ms. Summers," the doorman said to her, as she put on her gray Gucci shades and moved fast in her high-heel pumps.

Her head spun in a daze while the tacky and dirty threatening words swirled in her mind, but she put on a temporary happy face as the sun's rays grabbed her. "Hi. Good to see you." She saw Valencia's truck, stepped to it like a model in her heels, and opened the door. "People are losing their damn minds."

"What's wrong with you?" Valencia asked.

Miki hopped in and closed the door, jerking herself back upon the leather seat while the air-conditioning cooled her frustrated-looking face. She pulled on the hem of her tight shirt and crossed her legs.

"Just got some dumb-ass bitch who called my office. Some female talking about fucking me up." Even though frowning, Miki leaned over and gave Valencia a hug.

"Fucking you up? For what?" Valencia looked puzzled as she hugged back.

"Hell if I know."

"And you don't know who it was?"

"If you ask me, it sounded like Anthony's dumb-ass wife."

Valencia put the car in drive and pulled off. "Well, then, you need to call and tell him to check her young butt."

"Done that before." Miki cut her eyes outside of the window as the fancy city went by. "With her paranoid ass."

"Paranoid? You two are fucking around now, come on."

"You reminded me of that before already. And we're not fucking," Miki corrected her.

"Please. He's eating your pussy like it's a ripe-ass grape, girl. The word *oral* before the word *sex* does not excuse it qualifying as fucking."

"Well, it's not called oral fucking. Besides, she's still paranoid."

Valencia put her right hand up. "Anyway, I say you need to have that call traced and report it."

Miki looked at her and crinkled her mouth. "Not at my job. I can't even begin to make a big deal about this. Besides, that's all they need so they can start fucking with me again. Knowing corporate, they'll turn it into a reason to yank my ass right on outta there and into the unemployment line. No thank you."

Valencia used her turn indicator and made a left. "Whether it's them fucking with you or some bitch saying she's gonna fuck you up, just make sure you watch your back. That's not the kind of fucking we need or want."

"Just shit talking."

"Are we going to the SA meeting tomorrow night?" Valencia asked.

"We are." Miki looked as though her mind was ten minutes behind their conversation.

Valencia looked at her. "Come on now. Don't be a Debbie Downer. Cheer up. Let's go eat. Purple? Lemon pepper chicken?" She made it sound like a threesome with Denzel. "You know you love that kick-ass lemon pepper chicken."

Miki acquiesced, uncrossing her legs and adjusting her pumps along the floorboard. "Purple it is." Her face was only slightly enthused.

# 15

# "*Rehab*"

## Sexaholics

It was the next evening, on a Tuesday. The gentle breeze, casually delivered by the Pacific Ocean, was Santa Monica's usual summer blessing. Teela strolled into the outpatient treatment facility looking glad to see her new friend, Brandi. She energetically pointed her finger Brandi's way. "Hey, what's up with you, girl? And what is your problem?"

Brandi's face jumped. She opened her eyes wide and her mouth wider and gave a girlie giggle. "What do you mean? What happened?"

"How come you never answer your damn phone, woman?"

They walked together, step for step, while Teela kept her stare on, waiting for a reply.

Brandi popped herself on the forehead with the palm of her hand. "Oh I know, Teela, girl. I'm sorry. I'm just so silly. I always forget that I have the ringer on my phone on silent once I get off work. We can't have our cell phones on in the actual classroom. And what do you think I always end up doing, like a ninny? I forget to turn the ringer back on and then this happens. I mean, my own mother can't reach me sometimes. But it's not like I do anything when I get home anyway. I'm such a homebody."

"Yeah, well, homebody or not, you need to answer your damn phone, shit. And anyway, this Friday night, it's you and me. Period."

"Okay, that sounds so great. I mean really, it does."

Teela looked at her sideways. "Well that sounds oddly fake for some reason. What's up with you? But either way, here's what we'll do. You meet me at the bar of the W Hotel in Westwood after work on Friday and we'll have a few drinks. I'll be in the Whiskey Blue bar. I'm not gonna take the chance that you don't pick up that damn phone, so let's agree on this now. I'm not about to hunt you down, woman." Teela wrinkled her forehead. "And you'd better be there. Last time we talked about getting together for a drink, I tried. You, Miss Lady, didn't." Teela aimed her finger at Brandi's nose. "So be there."

Brandi smiled as they stood at the door of the meeting room and leaned toward Teela, extending her arms to give her a hug. "Wow, of course I'll be there. Again, I'm sorry. It won't happen again."

"Good girl. Now let's sit our asses down and learn some shit." Teela hugged her back, then entered the small meeting room first and approached the circle of seats.

"I'm right behind you."

Brandi took a seat next to Teela on one end, and Valencia sat next to Miki on the other end. All four were dressed in their work clothes: Teela in her tan sweatsuit, Brandi in dress slacks with a silk blouse, Valencia in jeans and a monogrammed tank top with the Cravings Restaurant logo, and Miki wearing a bright red Escada pantsuit.

Dwayne sat two seats away from Miki wearing his own designer suit. He and Miki played eye games with each other. He smiled; she grinned. He winked, and she blushed, both simultaneously realizing that Rachel Cummings had already begun speaking.

The other members of the group said in unison, "God, grant me the serenity to accept the things I cannot change, the courage to change the things I can, and the wisdom to know the difference."

Miki scooted back in her seat and sat up straight, loosening her shoulders, and giving a look as though she didn't miss a thing. She smiled at Rachel Cummings, who was looking right at her.

"Hello," she said directly to Miki.

"Hi," Miki said, nodding.

Rachel continued, "Okay, family, listen up, all of my dear, sweet anonymous friends. We say 'anonymous' at SA because, as I'm sure you've noticed, we don't ask for your last name. We don't need to know your full name. It doesn't matter. As you are all aware, we charge nothing. There's no contract, no dues, no membership process. Each of you has already acknowledged that you're a self-admitted sexaholic, so this is the place to be. We just ask that you show up. And let me thank you one and all for coming back. So here's the deal. Tonight we'll focus on a few of the recovery steps.

"Basically, as I told you before, SA is a spiritual program of recovery based on twelve steps. We'll go over the first three in a minute, even though we touched on the first one last time. I hope you've all been sexually sober for the past two weeks. No need to raise your hands. You know your own sobriety date, and we'll share our length of sobriety at an unannounced point in time. Maybe tonight, maybe not. When we do that, I don't want anyone to have any outward reactions whatsoever. The individual already knows what it means once they start over. And the most important thing is that the individual who is stating his or her own length of sobriety is completely honest. Not honest with us, but with himself or herself. Honesty and admittance got you in here seeking help. Honesty and admittance will get you through this. You'll be constantly surprised at how 'not alone' in your wagon falls-offs you are. That's the beauty of the group dynamic. People who come together in fellowship are important. One sexaholic sharing with another, telling what worked or hasn't worked, is healing for everyone. There's strength in numbers and safety in knowing you're not unique. I believe that your innermost feelings can be understood this way. We're a group of people suffering from a similar issue who strive to find our way out, all the while respecting each person's privacy. That's the SA dynamic.

"The thing we have is common is the fact that the sex part of our lives is a problem. But it's only a side effect of the true problem. There's something within me, and within you, that if we don't address and continue to address, then staying sober won't work. Sexaholism is an illness.

"This is a program which is spiritual, as in 'we believe in a Power greater than ourselves that can and will restore us.' No matter what your God is defined as, you must believe.

"First off, the first step it seems you all have already taken, and that's admittance. You've admitted that you are powerless over lust. That your lives have become unmanageable.

"Second is believing that you can and will be restored to, as we'll call it, sanity. Illness can be cured. But like I said, you must believe.

"And third, you have to make a decision to turn your will and love over to God as we understand Him. If this is a problem for anyone, or if anyone has a concern regarding Power or faith in general, please let's discuss this now. In our opening prayer we asked God to grant us serenity, courage, and wisdom. Did anyone have a problem with that prayer?"

"No," everyone said, except Miki, who seemed distracted by her own head.

Rachel Cummings noticed the look of thought on Miki's face and asked, "Did you, Miki?"

Miki shook her head strongly. "Oh no. Not me."

"Good. So, how have the last two weeks been for you?"

"Fine. Things are fine." Miki scooted from left to right.

"Are you still feeling that the *nympho* label owns you?"

"Owns me? No, not owns. I wouldn't say own. I'd say rent. It rents me." Miki grinned and looked around at people's faces as they grinned back.

"Oh, rents you. Okay. So it stays for a while and leaves, or do you say rents because you intend for it to only reside temporarily?"

"I hope it's temporary."

"Good. So how did the last two weeks go?"

"Well. Life as usual."

"Okay. And what about your sobriety? How long have you been sober?"

"One day." Miki put up one finger and smiled. "Okay, five hours. Lunchtime today." She gave Valencia a warning stare.

Valencia said nothing.

"Okay. I see. And what's been your biggest challenge?"

"Just trying to resist. I mean I can put an opportunity off but I usually make sure it happens. Even when my brain tells me the timing is bad or it's wrong to do it, I guess you could say my vagina just won't stop nagging me until I do."

"Really? What was your biggest challenge?"

"Just ignoring the turn-ons. The opportunity for getting laid and foolin around. Honestly, it's kickin my ass. It's like I have zero power."

"Don't feel alone, Miki, because you're not. I chose you tonight because I think your situation applies to step one, which is being powerless over lust, which you just mentioned. And also the fact that you need to believe that there's a power greater than you that can restore you. There is a certain sanity that we lack as sexaholics, and we need to restore ourselves to that sanity. It means resisting and it means thinking before we act. It means telling ourselves no, and telling the other person or people no. It means having faith that God's got you."

Miki looked conflicted. "I know, but I've thought I needed to do more than just pray about it. I've always understood that to mean I need to do something about it myself."

"But how do any of us do anything without Him? We're powerless without Him. This brings me to the third step, which is deciding to turn your will over to the care of

God. You need to have faith and believe that you will be delivered through this. But you, just like all of us, must take the first step toward believing."

"That's why I'm here."

"Good. Very good. Lastly, I must ask: in your opinion, what is a nymphomaniac? I mean, how would you define it?" Rachel Cummings asked Miki.

"I guess it's abnormal sexual cravings by a female. Like wanting repeated sex all the time."

"Do you want it or need it?"

"I need it. I crave it. It's all I think about. Before I finish an orgasm I'm honestly thinking about the next one."

"Then perhaps you are indeed addicted. But you may or may not be a nymphomaniac. They're not necessarily one and the same. Sometimes nymphomaniacs just have high sex drives. Some really need attention and gratification. It goes beyond the bedroom or the backseat. It's really a need that even if met four times a day, still wouldn't be enough. The root of the matter is attention, needing to be desired. Needing attention from more than just one person. The majority of nymphos can't be monogamous."

"Well, I'm telling you now, that sounds like me."

"Do you want to be monogamous?"

"I don't know."

"Okay. See, you claim this is temporary. You say it's renting you. So evict it. If you keep letting it live within you, chances are you'll constantly cheat on your mate and have failed relationships. The truth is, we do tend to attract who we are."

Miki nodded and twisted her mouth in thought.

Rachel Cummings said, looking around the room, "All

of you who can relate to what Miki is feeling right now, this goes for you, too. What you need to do first is find out why. Why do you need it? Does it fill a need? Why do you need the attention? What gratifies you about sex? Those are your big questions.

"You weren't born this way. None of us were. Marianne Williamson said our deepest fear is that we are powerful beyond measure. What are we afraid of, and who taught us to be fearful of ourselves? And what road would we need to take to fully love ourselves? Once you get that lesson learned, then you can begin to feel the power of healing. Then you can step through these doors knowing you're on the road to healthy sex, one week sober, one month sober, one year sober, whatever. We all deserve it. This is serious. It's life-saving serious." She again looked at Miki. "You fell off the wagon, Miki, but it's okay. We're all family here. We're you. Just get up and start over again. This is your life. It's time to hug a new day."

She looked at everyone. "Repeat after me. Stop lusting and become sober."

"Stop lusting and become sober," the members said back.

Valencia offered assurance to Miki by touching her fist to her heart.

Miki touched her fist to her heart back.

"Anyone else?" Rachel Cummings asked, looking over at a tiny woman with a red face, who had been sitting with her head down during most of the meeting.

The woman raised her hand and began to tell the story of what the last two weeks had been like for her. Sleeping with her boss on his desk in the middle of the day at work and getting caught. Losing her job. Leaving her toddler at home all night long while she snuck out to sleep with the man she met in the grocery store earlier that evening.

Miki sat still and listened. Her mind shifted to trying to recall all the exact words of her sponsor. *How did I get this way?* she asked herself. *That's a damn good question.* She thought of her relationship with Tariq for a moment, and then thought back to her mysterious phone call.

After the meeting, as Miki waited in the hallway for Valencia to use the bathroom, Rachel Cummings approached.

"Hey Miki." She gave Miki a hug. "I hope you don't think I delved too deep there."

Miki patted her back, smiling. "No. Not at all. That was helpful, actually."

"Good. Listen. I know that I bring up faith as part of this program, and I wanted to invite you and the other new ladies to come by my church next Sunday if you can. It's in Westchester. They're cool there, you know, supportive and open. It's more positive thinking than anything. Just thought you might want to come by. Not sure if you have a church home or not."

Miki said, "I do, but I haven't been in a while. I go to West Angeles but it gets pretty crowded there."

"Yeah, I know. I've been there before. This is a much smaller congregation. I've already spoken to Brandi and Teela. They said they'd try to make it."

"Okay. Sure. I don't see why not."

"I'll ask Valencia, too."

"Oh, I'll tell her about it. She's in the ladies' room." Miki pointed toward the bathroom door.

"Good. I'll send all of you an e-mail with the address. It starts at eleven in the morning. I hope to see you there."

"Great. Thanks."

"Have a good evening." Rachel Cummings turned to step away as Dwayne approached. "Hi Dwayne. Excuse me," she said, as she passed.

"Sure. No problem." Dwayne took a second to watch her walk away, right around the area of her rear end. He stepped to Miki and spoke in a low voice. "Hey. Are you coming by for a minute?" he asked, touching her arm. He gave her a suave look of irresistibility.

"I am."

"Good. So I'll see you in a few."

"Okay." Miki heard Dwayne's "Atomic Dog" ring tone as he walked toward the exit door.

He answered, and said in an even lower tone, "Nothing. I'm going home and going to bed. Talk to you tomorrow. . . . Love you, too."

Miki's world was mightily rocked from the rooter to the tooter and all areas in between. Dwayne had serviced every inch of her. Tonight, even more so than the first time when he'd put her in wild-ass hood mode and had her talking shit, hanging off the bed. This time, he even found an erogenous zone she didn't even know she had. That was one reason why she broke her rule and laid up with him upon his disheveled king bed, talking. Neither had on a strip of clothing. The soft lights graced the outlines of their long frames.

He lay on his left side, facing her. "Funny. You've never asked about my SA deal."

She lay on her right, facing him, and said, "I told you it doesn't matter." Her hair was mussed.

"What do you mean?"

"I mean, it's not gonna change anything."

"But don't you even care?"

"I do. I figure you'll tell it when you're ready."

"I'm ready. It's not all that uncommon. The regular members know all about me." He rubbed the smooth, brown softness of her upper arm with his massive right hand while looking in her eyes. "Rachel Cummings labeled me a womanizer. And I agree. And just so you know, I have a woman."

Miki did not blink. "I figured that much."

"She knows about the first night we got together. She and I argued. But we got back together. But believe me, you're not the only one."

"Okay. But, does she know that?"

"No." His eyes darted to the ceiling. "Well, yes. She thinks she knows it. I tell her she's imagining it all. She believes it after a while. But such is life."

"And why do you do that to her?"

He gave Miki a serious stare. "Same reason you do it. With so much opportunity and so many women all around, it's all so easy. It's just about finding the right woman who'll deal with it. And she's the one for now."

"Why even have a woman, then?"

"Why do you have a man?"

She placed her arm over her head as she spoke. "Someone who I let myself care about, a little. Someone to share my day with."

"And what if he wants something permanent?"

"I won't let that happen."

"But what about what he's doing? Your man, I mean."

"I can't worry about that. I guess I'd deserve it. I've screwed around on men so much, life needs to give me a taste of my own medicine, I guess."

"I guess." He removed his hand from her arm and rubbed his eyebrow. "You don't want more?"

"Like I said, I don't let that happen. I don't use the word *permanent*."

"Some things are beyond our control." Dwayne readjusted the pillow beneath his head.

"True."

He asked, "So doesn't it bother you that I belong to someone else?"

Miki explained, "Sounds like your body doesn't mind. That's on her." She gave him a *comme ci, comme ça* look and massaged her hairline.

"Do you ever think about whether the men you get with are married or taken? Do you ever think about what could be going on in the minds of the women who're being fooled around on?"

Miki said flatly, "I think most men are taken anyway. It just happens that way. And that's on them. I mean, a woman can't really even ask a man nowadays if he's single. We have to be specific because a man will lie to the hilt to get in our pants. We have to ask: Are you married? Are you living with someone? Are you in a relationship? Or better yet, is there someone who'd think she has the right to kick my black ass for getting with you?"

He chuckled yet looked serious. "I guess you and I could both say yes to that, huh?"

She nodded. "I guess so. But you still haven't told me your deal."

He rolled onto his back but turned his head to look at her. "I can never have enough sex. Enough women. Enough orgasms. I guess I'm the male version of you."

She propped up her elbow and rested her head upon her hand. "Or I'm the female version of you."

He explained, "Maybe we're both right. I grew up with my father. My mom died during childbirth. And Dad was your typical rolling stone. I'm a chip off the old block. Only I'm thirty-six and don't have any children."

"How'd you manage that?" she asked, looking amazed.

"Condoms. I use them even when I'm fucking someone I'm seeing all the time. But yeah, my dad has nine kids, all by different women. He never told me to chase women but he showed me how to do it. He showed me every trick in the book without even knowing he was showing me. I opened the nightclub just so I could meet women. I've always had public jobs just so I could meet women. I can't be in a grocery store or Target or Lowe's without looking at, lusting over, hitting on, flirting with, or trying to get at a woman. And everywhere I go, I see women who I'd fuck. It's just that there are so many different physical traits that turn me on. They can be short, tall, fat, skinny, light, dark, big ass, no ass, huge tits, no tits, blonde, brunette, black, or white. I have fucked every nationality, I have fucked four women at the same time on the beach, I had sex on a plane with a stewardess, sex in the movie theater, and in the back of the fire truck when I was a firefighter. I got more numbers back then. And I get ten times as many now. I have all the chick-magnet factors. A big house, a little money, nice car, I dress nice, and I'm fairly decent looking, so I've been told."

"Fairly." She grinned. "They didn't lie."

He smiled for a quick second. "And still, I'm not satisfied. I need all the pussy I can fuck. I always wonder what it feels like inside the pussy of the one I see wherever. It's simply my mission to find out."

"I don't know if I'd use the word *simply*, but you know. They say it doesn't feel much different from the previous one most times. It's all about the conquer. Sounds like it's not much of a challenge to you. Sounds like chasing the pussy comes pretty easy to you."

"It does."

"So why me? Why me more than once? Why'd you call me? Why me instead of the other ladies in the group?"

"Oh, I did get with one before you got there, but she's been cured and moved on. And yes, I did hit on Rachel Cummings's fine, luscious ass, but I got nowhere."

"Really. Rachel?"

"Yeah. She's not feeling the dick anymore, anyway. But listen. I've been in group for eight months now." He turned back to his left side to face her and, this time, rubbed his hand along the curve that joined her waist to her hip, up and back. "I guess you just seem different. It doesn't feel like a fling with you. It's like if I were right. If I was healthy. If I was fixed. If I was sober, we'd be cool. You fit the image of who I think I could be with."

She blinked fast. "You don't even know me."

"I know." He looked at her chest and then down at her belly button. "I mean your look, your class, your energy, your sexual appetite. It's hard to explain."

"And why isn't your woman the one?"

"She could be. She's conservative and square. She thinks everyone online is gonna get AIDS. Even if they have a MySpace page. God forbid they'd be on a dating site. She's very reserved. Almost passive. I've just been trying to get her to loosen up. I think with you, we'd match better. But, it's just a thought."

"So that's it? You're a womanizer who's never satisfied. Kinda like a pussy packrat, huh? That doesn't sound too uncommon to me. Sounds like a whole hell of a lot of other men out there."

"Miki, the truth is that I got arrested for assaulting my best friend's wife when I was staying with them for a few days in Chicago. He went to work and she left the door to their bedroom open while she was getting dressed. I peeked in. She saw me looking and gave me a look back. I guess I misread that look because I opened the door and came on in and she said I forced myself on her. I thought she wanted me to. But I did jail time for that."

Miki raised her eyebrows and formed her mouth to say slowly, "Wow."

"I got arrested another time when I came to a traffic light and made eye contact with the girl in the car next to me. She smiled. I followed her home and she called the police. Another time, and this wasn't that long ago, it happened after I had too much to drink. I was at my club, and a couple of dudes I know and I went home with this girl. She wanted us to run a train on her. Her man came home and pulled out a knife on us. We jumped him and we were all accused of assault. She claimed we tried to rape her. As part of my probation I agreed to counseling. They suggested I check into a sexual rehab program, and so here I am. And it really doesn't feel like it's changed much. I'm still thinking and feeling the same way. I think every woman wants me, Miki."

Miki smiled and reached down to find his hand and

their fingers interlocked. He held her hand back and they looked each other square in the eyes. "I had no idea. Not every smile means 'fuck me,' Dwayne. Lord knows I know about variety, though. I believe I'm wired to cheat. But damn, that is some serious shit."

In the next second, they heard a banging at his bedroom door. Miki released his hand and jumped out of her skin. Her smile vanished.

Someone tried to turn the knob over and over fast but it was locked. A piercing, high-pitched voice dug into their ears. "Bitch, get the fuck up outta there and get at me face to face. Fucking with my man again. I'll bust the windows out your ugly-ass car if you're not out of this room in three seconds. Or make it your Corvette, Dwayne." She began to bang the hell out of the bedroom door. The door frame shook with each thud.

His hazel eyes leaped. "What the fuck?" He sprung from the bed, scrambled for his boxers, and jumped into them. He made a mad dash for the bedroom door, exited the room and quickly pulled the door closed behind him.

The livid woman continued to rant. "You dog. You need to get a fucking hotel room with your stupid ass. Why the fuck would you bring a bitch back to your house anyway? And as far as that skank-ass bitch is concerned, I'm not done with her." She bellowed toward the door again as he snatched a baseball bat from her hands. "He told me you like to fuck. He told me you're a damn addict. I will kill you, bitch. Come back over here again, okay? Try me. I ain't no punk bitch. Bitch."

Dwayne yelled at his woman, "Get your ass out of here, now."

Miki held the black silk sheets to her neck. As much as she'd tried to look, the door had only been open long enough for Dwayne to exit fast, and she didn't get to see the deranged woman's face.

The woman still berated him with a shrieking mix of panic and rage and hurt. "Dwayne. You lied to me. You told me that night was the one and only time, and now you have the nerve to have her back over here. Have you lost your mind? You told me tonight you were going home and going to bed, but you didn't say who the fuck you were going to bed with. I put up with so much shit from you. I'm sick of this. And you, bitch, in my man's bedroom. You'd better get the fuck up outta there, bitch."

Miki hurriedly hopped up and scrounged around to grab her stuff while the two argued outside of his bedroom door. She looked around, trying to find a closet to hide in, when she noticed a window near the television. She yanked on the wooden shutter's drawstring and slid the window lock tabs, lifting the sash as she kicked out the screen.

Miki climbed out with her shoes and purse in hand, and took off as fast as her bare feet could carry her. She reached her truck, pressed the car alarm, jumped in, started the engine, and took off down the street doing eighty.

Now, just like in the past, there was one more man in Miki's sex life who had a woman she didn't give a fuck about. Just another silly, jealous woman who needed to get a grip and learn that all men will shuffle the infamous fucking-around cards and deal them one by one. It was just that Miki had learned you have to come up with your own deck of cards and slickly deal them just as well.

Miki spoke loud while looking through her rearview mirror after making sure she wasn't being followed. "That's what the fuck I get for staying too long and laying up after the fuck. My bad. Damn, I guess I didn't hug a new day very well today."

Miki then thought to herself, *Damn. Did he say she was reserved and passive? Not. And wait. Was it her voice that called my office that day?* Miki tried her best to recollect the tone and the pitch. Especially of the specific word that was used to refer to Miki more than a few times . . . *bitch.*

# 16

"*Single Ladies*"

## Teela

It was a happy hour Friday, and time for Teela and Brandi, newfound friends, to bond one-on-one. They found the last two available seats at the bar of the sleek and chic Whiskey Blue, where all of L.A.'s hipsters hung out. It was a trendy oasis-style restaurant, with ginger-colored bar stools and liquid-lava bar tops, cinnamon swirl walls, and laminate floors.

There were no more open bar stools, and every single dinner table was taken. The myriad of voices was gleeful and thick. The smell of crab-stuffed mushrooms and garlic-steamed clams soaked the air.

Teela was extremely upfront and inquisitive from the moment they sat down. "So, how'd you get all fucked up into all this addiction shit anyway?"

The bartender lady stood before them. "What'll you have? We're known for our martinis."

Teela replied, "I've heard about those. You know, I'll have a redheaded slut." She wore black leggings, black sandals, and a baggy black top.

Brandi's eyes bugged. "Oh my goodness. What is that?"

She still wore her work outfit, a conservative, navy blue knee-length skirt and matching blazer.

"I think it's Jägermeister and cranberry juice, and . . ." Teela gave a look as though trying to recall.

"Peach schnapps," the bartender said.

Teela snapped her fingers. "Peach schnapps. That's it."

Brandi said, "Wow. That's a big-girl drink, there."

"You should try it. It's strong but good," Teela told her.

"Sounds tempting. I'll just have Patrón, please."

Teela said, "Cool. We can do shots."

"So, a shot of Patrón?" the bartender asked Brandi.

Brandi told the bartender, "No. A glass, please."

"A glass? That's gonna cost a lot more, you know?" she asked.

"Okay. That's cool."

The bartender placed two napkins along the bar top before the ladies. "Okay. We always say have it your way. I'll be right back."

Teela said, "Damn, Brandi. Talk about big-girl. Look at you. Ordering a glass of that hell water."

"My love of booze was passed down from my parents. I mean it's not like you're drinking Kool-Aid yourself."

"True." Teela nodded and crossed one leg over the other. "So. Go ahead. Tell me. What's got you so addicted?"

"Well, nosy, if you must know, I've always had cravings for whatever it is that'll take my mind off of my life. I've been that way for as long as I can remember. To be honest with you, I was on antidepressants when I was only twelve." Brandi leaned her elbows onto the bar.

"Twelve? Why so damn young?"

"Who knows? I think it was around the time when

kids my age started teasing the crap out of me and ripping me down every day. Even in the seventh grade."

"I'll give you that. That damn puberty stage can be the roughest."

"I was unremarkable. That's the only way I can explain it. Teela, this may sound stupid but when I was young, it took me a minute to grow into my ears, lips, feet, and nose. My nose was so big they said I had a snot locker. I was a geek like you've never seen before. I wear contacts now, but in school I wore eyeglasses, and I had braces, too."

Teela said, "Yeah, but you sure got some pretty-ass teeth now, girl."

"Ha, ha. Thanks. In school they called me Miss Urkel. They even joked and called me B.C., meaning I was like birth control cause I'd never get pregnant. Nobody wanted me." Her shoulders started to slump and she gave a nervous laugh while Teela only semismiled. "I mean it was bad. I even loathed myself. So much so that I tried to kill myself after this quack doctor put me on these pills. And my teachers and parents thought I was healed only one week into the meds, like it was some wonder drug. I was always like an actress. You know, like the song "Tears of a Clown" when there's no one around. That song could have been written for me. I mean I was restless. Couldn't concentrate. Couldn't sleep or eat. I was just sad inside. I mean really sad like gloom and doom, stuck in the mud, quicksand sad." The bartender placed their drinks on the napkins as Brandi sat straight up. "Thanks."

"Looks good. Thanks," said Teela, using a black straw to stir her drink. She said to Brandi, "I mean what were you sad about? I can see you must have felt bad and kids can be cruel, I know. But other than that, what was going on? Please don't tell me it was a hardheaded boy."

Brandi took a big swallow of tequila. "Yep. Pressured me to have sex at age eleven and all of his attention just stopped. I worshiped that little skinny fool. That shit felt good too, and that's all he wanted. I wanted more. I wanted him something bad. In the worst way."

"Damn, that must have been some killer-ass puberty dick. I guess young or old, they're all the same."

"Well, something flipped in my head and I started stalking him and sitting across from his house at night. One day I peeked in his window and listened to him talk on the phone to other girls. I even put sugar in his gas tank and then threw horse shit on his dad's car. I was off."

"Damn, Brandi." Teela sipped again. She shook her head at Brandi. "What kind of meds did they have you on?"

"Back then it was Citalopram. That and whatever alcohol I could sneak from my parents' bar. They drank for breakfast, lunch, and dinner."

"Wow. And how'd you try to do it? Kill yourself, I mean."

"I slit my wrist." Brandi held up her left arm and showed the inside of her wrist. The cut was halfway around and had keloid scarring over her skin. "My mom came in the room before I even passed out, yelling at me to wash the dishes, as usual."

Teela touched Brandi's back and gave her a soft rub. "Holy shit, girl. All of that mess over some boy."

"Him, and all the other mess that life dishes out. Life is a bitch."

"Life's a bitch and then you die. That's why they say live like there's no tomorrow. You need to count your blessings."

"You're right. And I do." Brandi took a double swig. She looked at her watch.

"You have somewhere to go?"

"No. Just checking the time. That's all. I don't stay out late."

"Why not? It's Friday."

"Oh, you're right. I forgot."

"But really though, this sex-sobriety shit is gonna take some real miracle work."

"You ain't never lied."

"So where's your man nowadays?" Teela asked

"Don't have one," Brandi replied matter-of-factly.

"By choice?"

"Don't want one."

"But, when was your last relationship?"

"Never had one."

"All your life you never had a relationship with a man?" Teela asked, poking her head toward Brandi.

"Don't want one." Again Brandi spoke plainly.

Teela shook her head. "I don't believe you."

"Go ahead and believe me. Cause it's the truth. Nobody's going to suffocate me."

"So you go around fucking men on the street but never had a man of your own?"

"It's easier."

"Wow, well aside from never having a man, you need to cut that street shit out. There are some crazy MFs out there. You could get killed."

"And?"

"And? Don't you sit here and act like you don't care. Like you're out there just so you can put yourself in a position to be attacked or some shit. Or even get arrested again."

"I'll just jack off the D.A. again and get out. They don't care. I don't either."

"Yeah, well, I don't believe you wanna die. I believe you're bigger and better than what's happened to you. I believe you're more powerful than you know."

"Teela, the good side of me is the weaker side. Believe me."

"You've bought into that. I don't have to."

"No you don't." Brandi looked down at her drink and took a gulp. She swallowed and then said, "But I hear you. I guess I am trying to fix this. That's why I'm in the group."

"You can do it. We both can."

"Heck, what about you? You think you can stop watching folks get down?" Brandi tilted her head at Teela, tossing the subject her way.

"I know I can."

"And what about your man. Where's he?"

"At home. We live together. Austin is as freaky as a man can get. I let him be a dog right in front of me because if I don't, he'll do it behind my back anyway. He's a mess. But I love him."

"See, I think being alone is a lot easier than that. But as long as you're happy. That's all that matters."

"Hold up now, I didn't say all that now."

"I hear you. For now I'll stick to my wham-bam-thank-you-sir, hit-it-and-quit-it style. I'm cool with never going back twice."

"I say one day, God's gonna cure you of that. One way or another."

"Maybe that's what's up for us both."

"Maybe."

"In the meantime, here's to you." Brandi held up her glass, which contained one more swallow.

Teela held up hers. "And to you."

And they clanged glasses.

A voice said from behind them, "What are you ladies drinking?"

Teela turned around, looking surprised. "Hey, Miki. What's up?"

Miki stood behind them as they turned their heads. She said, "You two do know I work here, right?"

Brandi said with an extrasmiling face, "You do? Girl, this is a nice place. You're Hollywood style here, huh?"

Miki gave a tug on the hem of her tailored black blazer. "What can I say?"

Teela asked, "Why don't you join us?"

"Can't. I'm meeting my man for a few drinks in a minute."

"Hey, Miki," Tariq said, as he stepped up to the bar. He looked half black and half white. His hair was fresh in a 360 wave. His urban style of dress was youthful, and he was about five inches taller than his woman.

"Hey, baby." He and Miki kissed and he hugged her around the waist. "Tariq, this is Teela. And this is Brandi." She pointed to each.

"Hello," Tariq said, greeting Teela.

"Hi. Nice to meet you." She smiled and nodded.

He looked at Brandi. "Hello."

"Hi."

He looked around and asked Miki, pointing to a private VIP area with awaiting leather chairs toward the back of the room, "You wanna go over there now?"

"Okay, yeah. They're holding that for us. I'll see you ladies later." Miki spoke to the bartender, who had walked up to take Brandi's empty glass. "Garcelle. The next round is on me."

Garcelle asked the two ladies, "You'll both have the same?"

"Yes," they said together.

Brandi said, "Awww, thanks. That's nice of you."

"No problem. You guys gonna try to make it to Rachel Cummings's church next Sunday?"

Teela nodded. "I am."

"I'll be there, too," replied Brandi.

Miki nodded, looking pleased. "Good. Well, I'll see you both later."

"Okay. And thanks for the drinks," said Teela.

"Sure."

"Good-bye," Tariq said without looking back at them, as he and Miki stepped away, hand in hand.

"My goodness. That's her man?" Brandi squinted at them.

Watching Tariq from behind as he stepped with a smooth swagger, Teela said, "He's fine as hell. A big fine-ass box of chocolates."

"Yes he is. From head to toe and in between. But you know what they say about chocolates. You never know what you're gonna get," Brandi joked, placing her elbows along the top of the bar.

Teela looked confused. "What's that mean? You know him?"

"Nothing."

"Oh, I see. That's just you being allergic to boyfriends. Hating, actually. Don't trip. That's a fine brotha."

"Okay."

Teela turned back and said, "What, Brandi?" just as the bartender set their drinks down.

"Thanks," said Brandi, then she told Teela again, "Nothing." Brandi rubbed the hairs on her forearm. She picked up her second glass and took a long sip and swallowed. "Better left alone." Her head spun.

Before Teela headed home a couple of hours later, she pulled up to the tiny park area in Marina del Rey. It was full of old, overgrown, broadleaf oak trees and weeping willows. The bright green grass was healthy and fresh. The sun had set long ago. The swings were abandoned and the slides were quiet. Kids were fast asleep in the now-quiet beach neighborhood. Only the adults occupied the night.

Teela made sure to park her Z in one of the spaces that allowed for the best visual access to areas from left to right. If she were to sit and chill long enough, chances were she'd see something worth waiting for. Something kinky. Someone who was exhibitionist enough to hope that someone like Teela lurked nearby. Lurked in a window or on a bench or on a balcony or in a car. Just hoping that someone, somewhere, wanted to watch them get wild and raunchy in public. Sooner or later, the exhibitionist giver and the voyeuristic receiver of the exchange desired to be sated.

Teela turned off her ignition and turned off her headlights. She sank down into her soft palomino driver's seat and leaned it back a bit. She left on the cool sounds of the FM radio station that played twenty-four-hour jazz. A smooth Dave Koz saxophone melody called "Honey-Dipped" softly met her ears.

Her eyes waited for a meeting like a lion seeking its prey.

She waited and waited.

She heard the sound of a text message.

Peeking at her screen without picking it up she saw that it read 1 message. She did not read it.

Teela watched each and every car that passed by.

Every person who walked a dog.

Every movement in the dark.

And she sat, and sat some more.

Her cell went off again. It read 2 messages.

Ignored.

A car pulled up beside hers. It was a tiny yellow sports car. Hardly one that would blend into the notion of not being noticed. And a man got out. He went around and opened the passenger door for a woman. They hugged and she giggled, and she ran ahead of him into the park, kicking up her heels, wearing a flowing flowered dress. He closed her door, set the alarm, and looked around as he approached her.

Teela ducked down.

The woman grabbed his hand and they hugged as she turned to him. They began tongue-kissing like they were receiving the very life-sustaining air they needed to breathe.

They kissed, and kissed, with everything they had inside their mouths. They began bumping each other with grinding moves, like they were dirty dancing, and she made sure to place her leg between his legs. He reached down to hug her tightly. And then they turned to take a few steps closer to a huge sycamore tree.

He looked around and up toward the many windows of the apartment buildings that faced him on the left. And then on the right.

He looked back and placed his hand along her waist, moving her to stand in front of him. She giggled some more and leaned over, with her blond hair hanging down. He stood behind her and lifted up her dress. It looked as though he moved her G-string to the side.

Teela sat up a bit, peeking over her dashboard just as he looked around to his left again and unzipped his jeans.

He bent his knees to release his size from his underwear and took hold of his dick while the woman took a step back from him, bending all the way down. She bent so low that her hand touched the ground. Then she braced herself with both hands, shaking her hips back at him. Then she looked around, still giving silly laughs and still bending over.

He pressed forward and pushed himself into her from behind. He began pumping like a dog in heat, first slowly and then faster.

Teela lifted her blouse and stuck her hand under her bra, fingering her nipple. She scooted back just enough to allow her hand to slip down her panties and rubbed her clitoris back and forth. She felt a heated rush watching them that made her own hand job even more sensational.

The man pumped and pumped, and the woman's hair jerked each time he pushed himself back the farthest. She stayed bent over with her legs straight and kept her hand along the ground, allowing him full access to every inch of what she had inside.

Teela stuck her middle finger inside and smoothed her wetness around. "Damn, I'm wet," she whispered.

She massaged herself and began panting, still keeping an eye on the couple. She wondered what they'd do if she walked up and bent down to lick his balls from behind while he fucked his woman. She wondered what they'd do if they knew she was masturbating to their uninhibited sex play. In fact, she knew just what they'd do. They'd cum even faster. Even harder. And just as if they did know, or at least hoped they knew, the man banged against her more urgently, and his head raised up to the sky, no longer looking around, and she pumped backward like she was working for her next meal.

He yanked himself out of her and she stood up, stepping away a few steps and he jerked his sperm all over the grass, cumming onto the ground in spurts, yanking and squeezing himself to drain every last drop onto the earth.

The woman rubbed her pussy, laughing while he put away his dick and zipped up his pants.

She lowered her dress and stepped to him to stick her fingers in his mouth. He sucked them fully and they hugged, once again looking around as they turned back toward their car and to Teela, who had just finished cumming on her seat. She ducked down as they reached their car.

He let his woman in, but not before she tongue-kissed him again. He closed her door and came around next to Teela. He got in the car, leaned over again for a wet kiss, started his engine, and backed out. They simply left.

Teela sat up, readjusted herself, and started her car.

She backed away.

Mission accomplished.

Well, sort of.

She always knew just what to do to get herself off as a preliminary.

And it worked like a charm every time.

She drove away dripping like a faucet, headed home to Austin, her own private maintenance man, who had texted her twice.

She knew he'd be more than happy to fix her plumbing.

Or let's say he would have been happy if he'd been home by the time she got there.

"Hey baby, where were you?" Teela asked cautiously, giving him an astonished look as he walked in the back door two minutes after her. He wore jeans, a white tee, and a white NY cap.

"I should be asking you the same thing. You didn't reply to my text when I tried to see when you'd be coming home."

"And so what? You just decided to leave?"

"I had a maintenance call."

"To do what?"

"There was a leak."

"A leak?"

"Yes."

"This late?"

"That's usually when it happens. People usually make the emergency calls after the office is closed. Always after tenants get home from work or after going out. You know that."

"Who was it?"

"A lady in building ten."

"Oh, really?"

"Really. Anyway, where've you been, since the third degree is being dished out tonight?"

"Just riding around. Nowhere special."

"Okay, nowhere special."

She stepped close to him, paused and then walked to the sink. "You smell like perfume."

"I do not."

She turned to walk away. "Good night."

"I'll be right in. I'm gonna take a quick shower."

"Okay. I'll be asleep by the time you get out. I'm really tired."

"You tired? Yeah, okay."

Thirty minutes later, in spite of their aphrodisiac called tension, Teela and Austin were fucking, fantasizing, and freaking as always.

And one time, on the down-stroke, Teela could have sworn Austin called her Payshun.

But she came hard, with multiple visuals from the park in her mind and multiple eruptions rumbling through her vagina.

Within five minutes, she was in a deep sleep.

So deep that she'd missed the sound of the repeated text alerts on her man's BlackBerry.

# 17

⸺ ❧ ⸺

# "I Want Your Sex"

## Valencia

That evening, after Miki and Tariq conversed and shared a few rounds of pomegranate martinis at Whiskey Blue, they headed up the hotel elevator to the huge, sexy penthouse for a little fun. The elegant suite, newly decorated in wheat and merlot, was like a three-bedroom apartment, complete with floor-to-ceiling glass mirrors, a full kitchen, Beaverwood handcrafted floors, hand-painted light fixtures, and four plasma televisions.

But the most impressive thing awaiting their arrival in the room was Valencia, wearing her reddish-brown birthday suit. She'd put on a Biggie CD and the current song was "Fuck You Tonight." The room was dim with a red-light special glow from the red-shaded European floor lamps. She'd dabbed a bit of Eat Me Raw essential oil behind both ears and on her navel. She said aloud while posing before them at the foot of the bed, "No lovemaking, simply backbreaking," and giggled as she slid onto the cherry fitted sheets.

Fifteen minutes later, Valencia cheered on the twosome sexcapade Miki and Tariq had started. "Ay, baby. Hit that ass real good, okay? And I'll take care of that sweet *chocha*," she told Tariq, looking serious as a heart attack. He lay on his back in the lap of sexual elegance upon the oversized platform bed while Miki squatted, riding him like she was making an exercise video.

"How the hell are you gonna do that?" Tariq asked Valencia, while she was lying next to him, placing new batteries into her toy.

"This shit right here is my little *papi chulo*, baby." She showed him her ebony, curved, harness-type, G-spot dildo. It was a monster strap-on.

"Little?" His eyes popped at the sight of it.

"Okay, plus size. Just like you, Big Poppa."

Miki said, "Don't worry, baby. She knows what she's doing." She stopped grinding.

He said, looking scared, "You gonna stretch my baby's pussy outta shape."

"Please. Like I said, ain't like you little down there, *mijo*."

"I'm just saying."

"Why are you two arguing? Damn, you'd think you two were an old married couple or something." Miki ceased her squatting and raised up from Tariq's dick.

Watching her climb off of him, he said, "I'm just saying." His glazed dick still stood at full attention.

"No, I'm just saying," Valencia said, mocking his words. "What you need to do is scoot down to the end of the bed so she can lay on top of you, on her back. Scoot down, baby," she told Miki, while standing up and putting on her black swirl corset harness.

"Okay." Miki moved to where Tariq scooted, admiring the full design of Valencia's body as she wore her equipment. She looked at Tariq and rubbed the side of his wavy head and smiled, noticing the excitement on his face, and then got on her back, on top of him. Valencia grabbed a bottle of apple-scented lube and placed it along Miki's butt hole and squeezed a big glob onto Tariq's awaiting shaft.

And Valencia positioned herself between both Tariq's legs and Miki's legs. She told Tariq, "Take that dick and press it inside her ass. *Pero suavecito.* That means 'gently,' baby," she explained.

"Done that before," he told Valencia, looking at her like he wanted to remind her that he owned Miki.

Valencia said, rolling her neck, "I can't tell." She asked Miki as he inserted himself eagerly, "Are you okay, *mami?*"

"Yes, baby," Miki said after taking a deep breath.

Valencia held on to her dildo and pressed forward, bending her knees slightly while she found Miki's pussy with her tip. Tariq was working himself deeper, slowly but surely. Miki's body shook as the sensations grew.

"Oh hell yeah," Valencia told him, as he got his groove going.

He grinned from behind Miki. "Glad you approve."

Valencia slowly slid her fake organ inside of Miki's awaiting pussy walls, pressing past her well-lubricated lips. She inserted herself halfway, and Miki reacted with a grunt and a sigh. Tariq's dick was on the other side of the layer of skin that separated the rectum from the pussy. "Let's do this," Valencia told him, as if they were a tag team.

He did. He followed her smooth lead and pressed when she pressed. Retreated when she retreated. Miki froze as they pumped. She tightened her eyes and made oval and sidewinder shapes with her lips, sucking her tongue and twisting her face.

Valencia fucked her friend along with her friend's man as though one.

He groaned, "This is the shit, here."

"You like that, Tariq?" Valencia asked. Her voice was softer.

"Hell yeah." His was harder.

Valencia sounded like a seductress. "Can you feel me right above you on the other side of her wall? Your dick moving with mine? Your thighs pushing like mine, and my left thigh up against your balls? You like that, right?"

"Yeah."

"*Papi*, let's cum together?"

"I say hell yeah."

"Miki, you wait cause I'm gonna make you cum with my mouth and let Tariq watch that shit, since that's what he wanted so bad. But right now, my pussy is throbbing and I feel like I'm gonna pee on myself. Oh damn, yo, I think I'm gonna cum all over her, Tariq." Her purring voice was loud.

"Do that. Let it go," he said. "Aww, this is the shit for real."

Miki yelled while tightening her grind, "This is some good-ass fucking here. Uhhmmh. I'm getting double-fucked like crazy."

Valencia sounded like she was ready to blow. Her long, dark, curly hair swung according to her energetic pumping. "Ahhhh, *coño*, cum with me, Tariq. Cum now." She rolled the *r* in his name.

The visual of his woman getting fucked by a woman, and his dick deep inside of her ass, had Tariq one step ahead of Valencia. "Nnnng. Uhhg, I'm cumming, Valencia. I'm cumming Miki. I'm cumming. Every fucking body. Shit, I'm cumming. Arrrggghh, fuck. Dammit."

"Ahhh, I'm shooting dat, awww." Valencia froze. Tariq froze. And Miki started grinding like her body was begging for more from both ends. Valencia shot her orgasm and growled. She paused, then let go of another slow rumble that ripped through her like she'd been stabbed. She gave a deep breath, whined like she was wounded, and panted. Her multiple was exquisite. She then said to Tariq, "Good boy." She pulled out her black shaft. "It's your turn," she told Miki.

"Damn. I wanna see this." Tariq pulled out and Miki rolled off of him. His eyes and his nose were wide open.

Valencia said to Miki while unstrapping her penile apparatus, "Lay back down on the bed. Right there, *mami*. Let me taste you so you can cum, too." Miki scooted back and Valencia said to Tariq, "*Mira*. Watch how I do this. Take notes."

He did not argue. "Oh, I'm watching all right."

And Valencia gave Miki what she knew she liked best. It was called the pleasure plank. Miki loved the sensation of having her pussy eaten with her legs together, stretched out in front so that her legs remained straight and she could flex out the length of her orgasm.

Valencia held Miki just above her hips with her hands, and straddled her closed legs, taking her clitoris head on from the top of her vagina.

She gave feathery strokes and then flicked her tongue quickly like it had fluttering wings, slurping her lips as though Miki's clit was the last bit of hard candy on a stick before hitting the sweet Tootsie Roll that was inside. She placed Miki's tender clitoris between her top and bottom lip and moved her tongue down the center first, then to the tip. She used the soft underside of her tongue and then the rough topside.

Tariq's cock twitched as Valencia's lips feasted upon his lady.

Miki ground into Valencia's face as though they were fucking.

Valencia kept her hands firm upon Miki's, gripping her hips to control her speed and tempo.

She pressed Miki's clit with her tongue steadily and made a humming sound while waving her tongue. The vibration sent Miki into revving mode, which signaled to Valencia that it was time to add more stimulation, now using the soft side of her inner lip to caress her tender pearl. She extended her suck more aggressively and Miki started to moan more and more.

Tariq did not miss one split second of Valencia's skills. "What the fuck are you doing?"

Valencia kept her cunnilingus focused, only looking up at Miki's face to keep track of her level of pleasure. And there it was, written all over Miki's face.

"Ahh, ahh, ahh, ahh. Oh, Val, I love the way you eat me. Like you need to eat to survive. Shit. I love it." The oral aerobics had her head swimming.

He said loudly, "Damn, I love it too. Suck that clit."

Miki began to throb and buck and pant and groan as she neared the edge of her euphoria. She pressed her pussy so far against Valencia's face that you couldn't see Valencia's eyes, nose, or mouth.

"Eat all that cum," Tariq said, cheering them on. He held on to his again-hard dick, stroking his shaft and using his thumb to travel up and down from his head to his veiny middle.

Valencia licked all the nectar she was given and came up for air, saying, "Naw, baby. You needed to be taking notes, like I said. Her legs don't always need to be wide open." She stuck her own finger in her own pussy to do a wetness test. "Damn, she turns me on." The giver in Valencia was replete.

Tariq's eyes were as wide as his mouth. He picked up his chin while taking in the look on Miki's orgasmic face. "Mental notes taken."

Miki began to come down from her tremble, working hard to catch her breath. "Go wash your dick so you can fuck Valencia, honey." Miki turned to Valencia with considerate eyes. "Is that okay?"

"Ay, sí."

"Ay, sí, me too. I was wondering when I was gonna get some," he said, almost running to the restroom.

Tariq was back in two point two. Valencia was on all fours, and she and Miki had just kissed. He positioned himself behind Valencia and stuck his dick inside. His erection appeared and then disappeared within her. Her creaminess could be seen and heard. Her breasts moved along with his sway. She bounced her ass back at him, bucking as he rode her. The booty clap was loud.

Valencia said softly, "Oui, daddy."

He gave about six good pumps and stopped.

Miki looked at him. "Wait baby. Don't cum in her."

"I'm not," Tariq said with a tight jaw.

"Here. Fuck me." Miki moved over to the same position as Valencia.

He pulled out and readjusted to enter Miki.

"Are you soft?" Miki asked immediately.

His eyes were adamant. "No." His dick disagreed.

"What happened?" Miki looked back at his hanging, smiling dick.

"Nothing. I'm just excited."

Miki told Valencia, "He's normally a one-round man."

"I'm fine with that," Valencia said, moving over to lie on her back. She fingered herself and tasted it.

Miki told her, "I can use the dildo on you."

"No. I came, remember. I'm good. Very good, actually." She continued to play with her pussy.

"That you are," Miki said, also moving over to lie down.

"Fuck. I've gotta get used to this shit," Tariq said, fiddling with his dick.

Valencia grinned. "Yes you do."

"Val, whatta ya say we all move in together?" Miki asked, sounding serious.

Tariq added, "All you have to do is say the word and both of you can move in with me, hell."

"Don't tempt me. *Pero*, what would I do with Greg? After all, he *is* my fiancé, you know," Valencia reminded them.

"Small interferences," Tariq said with a sarcastic edge. He gave a minilaugh.

"Cut that out." Miki gave him a motherly face.

"Yeah, watch your mouth, softie," Valencia said with a minilaugh of her own.

Tariq said, "You? The bossiest woman on earth telling me to watch my mouth. Directing the fucking like you're directing traffic."

Valencia batted her mascara-laced eyelashes. "I know. *Mami es muy malo*. Very bad. And you love it."

He nodded. "Yes. I admit I do."

Miki said, "All I know is, if that Greg shit ends up not working out, you know where we are."

"Fa sho."

Tariq added, "And just for the record, I, for one, am fine with you two fucking. Perfectly fine, unlike some brothas." He lifted his brows and gave an eye roll.

"That's obvious," Miki said.

"Selfish is what it is," Valencia said. "Hell, I see three sexaholics in this room. Not two. You know what I'm saying." She held up three fingers.

Suddenly Miki adjusted herself to the middle of the bed and scooted down and met Valencia's pussy with her mouth.

Tariq sat back against the headboard and watched. Again, he was headed for a blood-filled dick, all because of Valencia receiving his lady's mouth.

Valencia looked over at him and blew a kiss.

Miki was deep into her zone.

He smiled.

"That's my girl, you know? I love that girl," Valencia told him, pointing to Miki and then moaning while her eyes were closed, "Oh, yeah."

"Good, then. Then maybe we really can be one big happy family."

Miki was all ears, and then she asked Tariq with inquisitive frustration, "Did you cum inside of her?"

# 18

## "Anytime, Anyplace"

### Brandi

He moaned and groaned.

She didn't.

It was nearly two in the morning after a quiet Saturday night on a random street in West Hollywood. It was the front seat of his car.

"Oral sex is my thing. I love giving head," Brandi told the man, while she sat upon him in the driver seat. She faced him braless, with her blouse unbuttoned, chest skin to chest skin, and pressed her breasts to him. She felt the quickened beat of his heart having a panicky fit inside of his chest. His dick was deep inside of a condom deep inside of her throbbing pussy. He had a hold on her supple ass as he bounced her up and down from his base to his tip. His dick stood at full attention all through her. It was like his dick had a heartbeat of its own.

"Then shit. Do your thing. For real," he told her. His breath smelled of rum.

Her breath smelled of tequila. "Lean back," she instructed while climbing off of him, scooting to her right to sit her bare butt into the passenger seat. He removed his condom while she leaned over to his lap as he reclined and she put his wideness into her mouth, spitting on his dick and massaging her spit with her lips. The blade of her tongue slid up and down and she used her hands to fit him in her mouth, coming back up while keeping her hands in sync with her mouth tricks. She gained a rhythm by sucking on his head and matching the cadence with her hands on his shaft toward the base of his penis.

Brandi quickly brought him to the cusp of his climax, being that the ambiance and anonymity factors were exquisite for freakiness.

He clenched his fist with manly strength. His sperm began to travel up through his bulging dick, and she could feel its path pulsate with her right hand. He took off like a rocket and reached his arm around the back of the leather seat to choke the headrest while he let it rip. She swallowed all of him as though she knew him.

She licked his dick skin and leaned up, scooting all the way over into the passenger seat.

He took long blinks while his mind came out of the orgasm fog and carefully brought his seat back upright, giving fast breaths. "Damn, you suck dick like you made that shit up."

"This I know," she said, slipping on her red hot pants. She then readjusted her ruby-red curly wig and checked to make sure her fake eyelashes were still glued on. They were.

"I'm not mad at you. I can tell you do love it. Hell, I love it, too." He reached over in front of her and opened his glove compartment, pulling out his wallet and reaching in to grab five twenties.

Inside, just before he closed it, Brandi noticed a small

leather holder and a police officer badge, but said noth-ing.

He held out the cash. "Here's a hundred."

She shook her head while buttoning her blouse. "No. It's cool."

"No, it's not."

She bent down to slip on her red platforms. "I'm not a hooker."

"I know that. I want you to have it." He held the money closer to her, still sitting with his pants to his knees.

Brandi grabbed on to the passenger doorknob. "I met you at the bar. We got together. It's that simple. I never do anything I don't want to do. You got yours. I got mine. I'm good." She opened the door, grabbed her tiny purse from the floorboard, and stepped out. "Good night."

"What's your name?" he yelled quickly.

She replied by shutting the door and walking away.

And in one quick minute, he simply pulled off.

Another night of Brandi chasing lust.

She just couldn't stop.

Not for the life of her.

# 19

## "Addicted"

### Miki

Miki stood over the double stainless steel sink in her rectangular kitchen after a few days of T.J. being home. She washed the few ebony dishes by hand from the evening's dinner, when her home phone rang.

T.J. was in the great room on the laptop, logged on to Nickjr.com. It was his favorite thing to do, and the main thing that could occupy his time and keep him quiet.

Miki took the kitchen towel and wiped her hands, and grabbed the cordless from the kitchen counter. She saw the caller ID and pressed talk just before the fifth ring. "Hey Mom. Haven't talked to you in a while."

"You haven't called. How are you?" Her mother's voice was soft yet slightly curt.

"Good and you?" Miki began to dry and put away the dishes.

"I'm okay. Didn't think you were going to answer. But yeah, I'm just a little tired. You know this menopause thing Oprah told all of us women to embrace is no joke. It's a nightmare. I take more naps than your little niece, L'Oreal." Her own chuckle was weak.

"I'll bet."

"Speaking of your niece—have you talked to Adore lately?"

"No, Mom."

"And why not?"

"I've been busy." Miki rubbed her chin along her shoulder.

"Miki, I just don't understand. You two never would've gone a day without talking to each other. She said it's been a month now."

"Something like that."

"Then why not give your sister a call? You know she's going through a separation from Tommy. She's ready to file for divorce, but he's begged her not to. He wants to work things out. Working out forgiveness when it comes to infidelity is a given, if you ask me. I think it's negotiable. Anyone who's been married for a long time knows that. They haven't even been married that long."

"I know." Miki put the pot of leftover Tuna Helper in the refrigerator. "That's why you and Dad are still together."

"Adore needs to keep her family together. Little L'Oreal deserves it. The grass is not always greener on the other side."

"Tommy did creep on her, and you know how she feels about that."

"Creeping, or whatever it's called, temptation is real. Sometimes it's not worth walking away from a marriage because of infidelity. That's the problem today. People don't live up to their wedding vows."

"I wouldn't know, being that I've never been married. But think about it. For all you know, maybe Adore can't forgive him. Some things are more complicated than what we see from the outside. It just depends on the situation. That's her life."

"Well, we're not on the outside. We're family. And like I said, that little baby deserves to have her parents together. And when are you going to go by and see your brand-new niece anyway? You still haven't even met her?"

"No, Mom. How is she?" Miki's face shifted to a frown.

"You need to find that out for yourself."

She fought the urge to react. "I will. Soon enough. I'm working on it."

"How hard can it be?"

"It'll happen." Miki's cell rang from inside her purse on the counter and she immediately said, "Listen, tell Dad I said hey. That's my other line. I'll call you back tomorrow." She folded the kitchen towel through the chrome ring.

"All this call-waiting nonsense is just rude if you ask me."

"Mom, it's not call waiting. It's my cell phone."

"Whatever it is. Cell phone. Call waiting. Anyway, give little T.J. a kiss from his grandma. Tell him I love him."

Miki's short sentences were rushed. "I will. Gotta go. Bye." She hung up and hurried to her purse, took her cell, and said, "Hello."

"Hey there," he said.

"What?" Her eyes hit the ceiling.

"When can I see you?" he asked with a deep voice.

Her shoulders shrugged. "You can't. Bye."

Her thumb hovered over the end icon when she heard, "Meet me at The W in an hour."

"Tommy. I can't."

"You can't?" His voice got deeper.

"No. Not in an hour." She fought herself. "Give me two." She was surprised by her own words.

"See you there."

Miki yelled to T.J. as she hung up, "Your grandma called. She said to tell you hi and that she loves you."

He spoke quickly, trying to talk loud. "Okay. Love her, too."

"Your dad will be here in half an hour. Go into your room and make sure you've got everything ready for the week."

"Oh, Mom. Can I stay until tomorrow? Please?" His voice carried even louder.

"No." She turned off the kitchen light and headed into the den, talking along the way. "I've gotta go into work tonight and get some things done. Now come on. Get going. Get off that computer, now." She shooed him with a rushed hand movement.

T.J. reluctantly scooted off of the desk chair. "Aww, Mom. You and me never have any fun."

Her voice was firm. "Yeah, well. Life is rough."

Miki glanced at Anthony and turned away immediately. "You're late."

"I know. Where's T.J.?" Anthony walked up the driveway to the single-car garage, which was open.

"He fell asleep waiting on you." Miki was in the garage, sifting through the back seat of her Montero.

"I'm only late by twenty minutes."

"Look, I have somewhere I need to be."

"Where're you going?"

"None of your business."

He ignored her attitude, instead noticing her long legs. "You're looking mighty nice. I remember when you'd dress up for me like that. Must be a date."

"None-yum." She looked at him like he was excused, then walked back to the trunk and opened the hatch, reaching inside.

He stared at her hips from behind. "Hold up. I thought you had a man. Could it possibly be a new man? You foolin around on him already with a new dude, or are you dressing up for him? Cause usually after a few months you stop trying to look like that. Whitcha fine ass."

She spoke with her ass aimed his way. "Excuse you, Anthony. No, I only fooled around on you because you're a worthless ass. Besides, stop trying to figure me out. You don't know a damn thing about me."

"Oh, but I do."

"Well, maybe you're right. Knowing you, you ask that poor kid a million questions."

"Please. I would not use him like that." He watched her pull out an empty box and an old newspaper, and step to the trashcan to throw them away. "To be honest, as long as it doesn't affect him in a negative way, it's all good to me."

"And vice versa. By the way, I just know your little jealous-ass woman didn't call me the other day threatening me, did she?"

"My woman? Why would Kiki do that?"

"Cause Kiki's ass is crazy. Unplugging the phone when we talk, and shit like that. That bitch is insecure and deranged."

"Well she's not anymore."

"Oh, so she's not busting the windows out your car anymore, huh?"

"No."

"Glad you worked that out. But don't put anything past her. I sure don't."

"Hold up. So someone called you and got on your ass, huh? Some woman whose man you're fucking with?"

She sucked her tongue, pressed her lips together and turned. "Whatever, Anthony. T.J. is on the sofa in the den knocked out. Go ahead and get him and leave. I've gotta get going as soon as I'm done."

"Okay. Calm down." He walked toward the door that led from the garage to the kitchen, and flicked off the garage light.

"Hold up. What are you doing?"

"Nothing."

She reached inside the trunk again and bent over, trying to gather up old stray crayons T.J. had strewn in her car over time.

He walked toward her as she leaned inside.

"Anthony, I can't see. Turn the light on. Quit playing."

He stepped up behind her and placed his hand on her back.

She scooted back out and stood up. "I said quit playing. Not tonight."

"Why not? You know it won't take long," he said, as though bragging.

"Just go and get T.J. before he comes out here."

"You said he's sleeping. I just wanna talk to you."

"Anthony, stop now. Come on."

"No, you come on. You know how I feel every time I

see you. You know what you do to me. Looking all good in that sexy black dress, showing all those curves I miss so much. Just let me taste you. Bend over and let me lick it right quick. Come on."

"Anthony."

"Here. Right here. Climb inside. On your knees. I've got this."

"Anthony. Please."

"Please nothing. Come on."

She sighed, then slowly climbed inside on her knees, keeping an eye on the door that led to the kitchen.

"Good girl." Anthony reached under her dress and found her to be pantiless. "That's my girl." He bent down to kiss the back of her thighs and up to her ass from behind, separated her cheeks with his hands and found her honey-laced pussy, then parted her lips. He stuck his extra-long tongue inside and gave long licks, then pointed his tongue as far inside as he could.

"Anthony. Wait."

He didn't. He scooped her meat with his bottom lip to meet her clit and rolled his tongue, found more pussy with his upper lip, then closed down on all that he could get in his mouth, and sucked her.

She whimpered. "Ohh, damn. Anthony. Damn."

He gradually devoured her entrance and tunneled her canal with his stiff tongue, slyly slipped his tongue and bottom lip back to meet her clitoris again. Miki felt herself swell and felt her wetness accumulate. She braced herself upon all fours for what she was given, pressing her pussy toward him harder and harder, the more she felt the sensation of his warm mouth pleasing her.

"Awww, damn. Umh, umh." She took a second to

think about what would happen if T.J. woke up and saw his daddy kissing his mommy between the legs. She thought about what would happen if her neighbor, Constance, who shared a twin garage on the other side of the wall next door, came home and shined her headlights on the X-rated, freaky sight of Miki getting eaten alive from behind in the back of her own SUV.

And all those thoughts added to her thrill. She could feel her dizziness approach as his lips extended over her outer lips, bringing her sex organ to a sneaky eruption.

"Yes. Oh my God. Oh, dammit. Yes." She bit her lip as his jaw and mouth continued to work. He shook his head and hummed. Then he found her asshole with his middle finger and inserted it slowly through the puckered opening, and slightly inside. Her ass gripped his finger, and he pressed inside even more, all the while sucking relentlessly upon her pussy.

"I'm cumming. Oh no. I'm . . . ," and Miki came in Anthony's mouth at the same time she heard a female voice say, "It's me, baby. Pick up the phone."

It was Anthony's woman, Kiki, ringing in to the sound of her own personal ring tone voice on his cell as Miki shot her orgasm into Anthony's mouth. The phone rang and rang and she came and came from the back of the truck, with him leaning in to take what she couldn't help but give him: her pussy juices.

He backed away and wiped his mouth with the back of his hand, and actually took the call, looking right at Miki's ass. "No, I'm just leaving. Yes, he's fine. Uh-huh, we'll be there in a minute. Bye."

"Daddy, where's Mommy?" asked T.J., whose voice moved slowly.

Miki immediately shook her fog and pulled down her dress, scooting over to sit down in the back of the truck.

"She's in the car. We're talking. Go back inside and get your things so we can go."

"Okay," he said, rubbing his eyelids and turning back inside.

Anthony stepped over to turn on the light as Miki climbed out. She said, "First of all you need to wash your hands. And you need to leave as soon as you can before your girl comes over here and shoots us both."

"She's fine."

"Yeah, well, she shouldn't be," Miki said, standing behind the truck, preparing to close the back hatch.

T.J. came through the door and into the garage. He handed his dad a small bag and hung his backpack over his shoulder.

"Let's go, son. I missed you."

"Missed you, too. Bye, Mom," T.J. said without looking at his mom.

"Bye, honey." She watched them walk away.

"Daddy. Where's Kiki?" Miki heard T.J. ask.

"She's at home."

"I miss her."

Miki fought to stop her mouth from falling open. She continued to watch her son head off to be part of his father's complete family.

Anthony put T.J. in the car and looked back at Miki. He waved. "We'll see you later." He ran his tongue over his upper lip and said, "Bye sugar."

She spoke up quickly and loudly and sarcastically. "Yeah, yeah, whatever. And tell Kiki she's got absolutely nothing whatsoever to worry about."

Her thoughts were busy. *How strong could that marriage be when he's eating my pussy nearly every week? I'm gonna let that shit go on and on. I've got nothing to lose. But little wifey, stepmother Kiki surely does.*

"Why am I here?" Later, Miki stood in the hotel room at the W. Her brother-in-law sat on the unmade queen bed. The room smelled of the leftover supreme sausage pizza from the cardboard box on the floor.

"I don't know. I guess if you have to ask, I have to ask, too. Why are you here?" He looked like he needed a haircut and a shave, bad. He wore only basketball shorts, two sizes too small. His boobs were almost as big as hers. He stood up.

She eyed his body. "I have no flippin idea."

"You talk to Adore lately?" he asked casually.

Miki stood near the wall by the door. "Let's not talk about that."

"Fine with me." He stood and took a cautioned step toward her. "I've been thinking about you for a while now. I'm basically separated and I was wondering if, maybe."

She put her hand up. "Oh please. You thought maybe we could try to what?"

"Well, you know."

"No, I don't."

He turned back to the bed. "So, you'll fuck me but nothing more."

"Exactly. And I'm not even sure if I can do that again." She looked at the random sprouts of hair on his back and felt like she could gag.

"So why are you here?"

"A part of me can't tell you. That's part of the problem."

He turned to her. "Is it that bad? To think about being with me again, I mean. Damn."

"You're my brother-in-law. Hello!" she shouted like somebody needed to wake up. She scowled at him.

"So? That didn't stop us before."

"I hoped it would be enough to stop us now."

"Is it?" He gave her a lustful, hungry, wanting look that she caught.

She swallowed and sighed. "No. Do you have a condom?"

"I do."

Miki began to remove her clothes, placing her dress on the red guest chair. Tommy was all eyes. He stood and started to pull down his shorts. The bulge that contained his penis looked like he had a squirrel inside. Miki turned away and stepped toward the bathroom.

"Damn, you look good," he said, looking at her ass as she walked away.

She heard a sound like a cat meowing. "What was that?"

"What?"

She exited the bathroom and pointed. "I heard something in the bedroom. What is that?"

"Oh. That's just L'Oreal."

Miki's voice jumped. "L'Oreal. My niece?"

"Yes." He tossed his basketball shorts onto the floor.

"You brought her here to the hotel with you?"

"I had no choice. I have her for the night and—"

"And what?"

"And I wanted to see you."

Miki headed back to the guest chair and got dressed, fast. "You had to see me now. Tonight. You couldn't wait to see me later when you didn't have her. Is that what kind of father you're going to be to her? Bringing her on fuck dates with you?"

"No. Just tonight."

She aimed her finger at him. "Tommy. I don't believe you. I hope Adore never takes you back." She opened the door.

He yelled, "Miki! Hold on!"

"Good-bye, Tommy. What in the hell was I thinking?" She stepped out.

He stood in his way-too-tight orange underwear. "But Miki. Your niece is in there. Don't you even want to see her? I heard you've never even taken the time to meet her."

She fought not to yell. "When and if I do see her, it definitely won't be like this. I've gotta go. Bye. And lose my fucking number."

She closed the door softer than she wanted to and left her brother-in-law and her new, unseen niece inside.

# 20

# *"Toxic"*

## Teela

In the middle of the next week, Teela arrived home from a long day at work after a staff meeting with some corporate executives at the health club. The meeting started at five in the afternoon and lasted past the dinner hour.

There was no need for her to worry about cooking any meals tonight. She peeked into the side-by-side refrigerator and saw a foil-covered dinner plate Austin had prepared for her earlier and put away. It was her favorite meal of pork chops and cabbage with turkey necks.

She said aloud as she grabbed the plate, "That boy is trying his best to fatten me up." She inhaled the smell.

"Hey, sweetie," Austin said, placing his Nokia phone into his pants pocket as he stepped into the kitchen. He smelled of a freshly dabbed splash of his masculine, sandalwood signature cologne. "I see your meeting lasted longer than you thought."

"It did. But I'm home now. And I am starving." She peeled back the foil. "This looks really good, thanks."

"No problem. Things were pretty quiet around here today. Just a few work orders. Mainly an air conditioner and a couple of water heaters." His cell rang from his pocket. "Excuse me a minute," he told Teela, turning his body. "Hello." He began to walk out of the room.

She said out loud, standing next to the oak-and-limestone island. "Since when do you leave the room to talk on your cell?"

He replied from the hallway, "Huh? No." He reentered and opened the fridge while still on the phone.

"Who's that?" Teela asked.

He replied while bending down to grab some grapes from the crisper. "Oh, it's Payshun. You know, our neighbor. Payshun."

"Oh, as long as it's not Falon. She's not getting her fake ass back over here. She's one of those "fuck you till you're asleep and lie to your bitch" hos. Anyway, tell Payshun I said hi, and ask her when we're all gonna get together again." Teela stood at the counter in front of the microwave and transferred the food to a microwave safe dish.

"Oh, okay. Yeah, Teela wants to know when we're all getting together. . . . I know. . . . Yeah. . . . Uh-huh. . . . I will. Okay. . . . So everything's cool with your closet then. . . . Okay. . . . Okay. . . . Yeah. Bye." He closed his phone and the fridge and popped two grapes in his mouth, chomping down and chewing with his mouth open.

"What's wrong with her closet?" Teela asked, placing the container inside and pressing the Start button.

"The sliding door was off the track."

"It's those cheap doors. So she's calling you instead of the office?" she asked while the microwave did its thing.

"Well, considering we know her pretty well, I guess she feels she can call directly."

Teela asked, "We know her? No. I don't know her at

all. But the original intention was to get to know her. Is that something you still wanna do? What did she say when you asked her?" She opened the silverware drawer and took out a knife and fork.

"I did. She said she can't. She's studying for a real-estate exam. She's been really busy."

"I see. I didn't mean tonight. Anyway, did you eat?"

"I did." His cell rang again. "Hello. Which unit? I'll be right over." He popped two more grapes in his mouth and stepped to the side door. "That was the answering service. Unit 203 has a problem with their air conditioner. I'll be right back."

"Okay. I'll be right here, tearing this food up."

He left as Teela opened the microwave and checked her plate, which was still not hot enough so she reset it. She leaned against the counter and turned around to look out the window over the sink. She glanced around at the building next door, and on the first level, she saw a man standing in the window. The vertical blinds were open, and he was butt naked, standing in front of someone. Teela stood on her tiptoes to see exactly what was going on when suddenly one of the lights was turned off and only a faint shadow remained.

Immediately, without thinking, Teela darted out the side door and ran down the stairs to the bottom level. She tiptoed over near the window and climbed onto the small balcony, quickly pressing her back to the wall and then leaning her head over to take a peek. The room was still dark, but she could see a man getting head service, and the person giving it to him on his knees was also a man. Teela's jaw dropped and she held her breath. She kept looking. The bald-headed male receiver had big butt cheeks that flexed tighter and tighter as he pressed his dick in and out of the man's mouth. Teela's heart took off in an instant and she felt a rush of heat consume her, but just that quick the sound of a yapping dog got louder and louder.

The receiver quickly turned around and Teela darted her head back against the wall. She counted to three, then started to lean her head into the window again when she heard, "Who's that?"

Teela sprang from her place and jumped over the rail like it was a hurdle, dashed around the corner to the other side of the wall, and crouched low near a bush. The dog still yelped, even more panicky. Now Teela's heart raced so hard you could see her chest rise and fall. Suddenly a door opened, and a couple hugged as the male gave a cheek kiss. He walked away, dropping the hand he'd held. The sexy girl said, "I'll see you in the morning." The floral bouquet scent of Perry Ellis for Women tickled the air.

"Yes, you will," he said. Then he turned and his eyes met Teela's shock-filled face. "What are you doing?" he asked, at the same time the girl's door could be heard closing.

Teela sprung to a stance. "The question is, what the hell are you doing? I thought you had a call for an AC."

"I did. Did you follow me?"

"Hell, maybe I should have. That's not building two. You said 203. That's building ten." She pointed toward the door. "How long has that shit been going on? Is that where you were when I came home late the other night? With her?"

"What? Who?"

"You and Payshun, dummy?"

"I told you she called about her closet before. I was just checking to make sure it was still okay. I was only there for a second."

"Well, that was a warm departure hug to thank someone for fixing a closet door." Her words were piercing. Her face was red. "What the fuck is up with you two, Austin?"

He took a step toward their place as though she would follow. "Nothing. Let's go inside. Come on."

"No." She yanked on his arm but her one word was loud enough to stop him. "What's up? Fucking tell me now." She stomped her foot.

He jerked himself toward her. His dreads flung to his right. "Nothing."

"Boy, I will fucking knock on that bitch's door and kick her black ass."

"Teela," he said, as though begging for her cool side.

"I'm not playing."

"Okay, wait." He looked as though he was regrouping his thoughts. "This is my place of business here. Don't start any shit, now."

"You already started it. And this is *my* residence. You moved in with me, remember? Now talk." She started counting. "One. Two."

He spewed his words fast, speaking up though his eyes said he shouldn't. "She and I got together a few times."

Finally, the dog's wails ceased.

"You what?" Teela got even louder. "Why would you do that when we all agreed to see each other? I don't fucking understand."

"She didn't want to keep seeing both of us. She only wanted to see me."

"And your ass was okay with her only seeing you?"

"No. I just came by a few times. That's all. Nothing more."

"I'd call that seeing her. If it was nothing more, you wouldn't have hidden it from me."

"Teela, she doesn't want to be with a woman. She's not into women."

"Well that's news to me but, hell, I'm not, either. But you fucking lied to me. As open and honest as I've been about setting you up with women, and you up and do this behind my back. There was no reason to do this, Austin. Especially with our own neighbor. Damn." Teela's eyes began to fill with tears.

In spite of her tears, he now flailed his hands about. "Hold up. Falon told me you two fucked some dude named Reggie. You did that behind my back. Did I make a big deal? I gave you the benefit of the doubt and said nothing."

She stepped right up to him. "I'm not a bit surprised she told you. She was so deep into your ass that night she was willing to eat your shit if you asked her to. You know what, Austin, yes we did. You're right. We did. But I didn't fuck him. That's surely not what you can say about Payshun's ass."

He looked around toward Payshun's door. "Yeah, right. Like I believe that."

She pressed her finger to his chest with each word. "I didn't. You weren't supposed to fuck other women without me." She then pointed her finger in a circle and gave a major head roll. "You asked for that. And still, that wasn't enough for your greedy ass."

"You hook me up and then get all jealous and shit." He

looked at her like he hated the very sight of her. "Hell, maybe you do need some counseling from the group because you are out of control. You don't know what the hell you want. A man. A man and a woman. A strange man and woman. Or a fucking puppet to figure it all out and do as you say. Well, I am no puppet."

"No, you're a dog just like all the rest of em. So you know what? Go ahead and move in with Payshun, Austin. Because there's no way in hell you're getting back in my fucking place."

"Fine. I guess I'll just call the police."

"Go right ahead."

He took a deep breath. "Quit playin, Teela." He gave her a stern look, but her return look was sterner. "You know what? Fuck you. I can call the office in the morning and they'll put me in a place no questions asked."

Suddenly, Payshun's voice sounded: "Fuck her, Austin. Come on in."

Teela turned and took two steps. Austin took three and turned to stand between them. She yelled over his shoulder, "Screw you, you ghetto-ass bitch. You can have his sorry ass. You ain't nothing but a jump-off anyway. And he can come get what little bit of shit he moved in after I leave it at my door in the morning." She pushed his shoulder and he stood firm. "And you, asshole, if you even think about trying to get in tonight, I will shoot your horny ass. Now take that to the police."

"Horny? Look who's talking," he yelled as he headed toward Payshun's open door.

Teela stormed away and ran up the stairs crying. She slammed, locked, and bolted her condo door. "And I'm having the fucking locks changed," she yelled into the air.

She heard another door slam hard. Payshun had shut the door with Austin inside.

Even though her heart burned like a cigarette, instantly Teela wiped her tears and sniffled, ran upstairs, and started packing his shit.

She didn't say a word but her mind was loud. *Freak-ass muthafucka. This is it. No more. This crazy-ass shit will fucking kill me.*

Her phone rang and she peeked at the caller, which read *Austin*. She picked it up and pitched it against the off-white bedroom wall. The back of her cell broke off. The dent in the wall was deep and scuffed a shade of black, like the phone.

There was a knock at the door. She rushed over to open the nightstand drawer, took out her chrome .22, and flicked the switch from Safety to Fire. She headed downstairs to the front door and said loudly, "Who is it?" She cracked open the door.

"Ma'am, excuse me, but, were you peeking in our balcony window?" asked a frowning man. He held a miniature pinscher who looked her dead in the eyes, like he could serve as an eyewitness for the prosecution.

*Oh fuck*, she said loudly in her mind.

It wasn't the first time she'd peeked at her neighbors. But it was the first time she got caught.

This time, her own curiosity had not only snagged Austin red-handed but snagged her red-handed, too.

# 21

# "Crazy, Sexy, Cool"

## Miki, Teela, Valencia, and Brandi

It was late morning that following Sunday. All four ladies stepped through the church doors at the same time, turning heads, looking like Carrie, Miranda, Samantha, and Charlotte from *Sex and the City*. All had on higher-than-high heels and short skirts, and all wore bright colors. They looked like they had it all together. Like your average Jane but with a sexy diva flair. Though all that lived within them was in need of some true, down-home healing.

The all-white, cathedral-style church with the old-fashioned steeple was packed. With traditional pews and a pulpit, and a small choir to the side, it was quaint and had a holy feel. And it was fully occupied.

"Over here," Rachel Cummings said softly, gesturing with her hands for the four of them to come over to where she was sitting in the second row. She and her black, younger, Afro-wearing wife scooted over and made room. Her wife waved and smiled as they filed into the row and sat down one by one. Each held a church program in hand.

The choir stepped up and began to sing "You Changed

My Life." Miki, who sat on the end, leaned in to Valencia's ear and whispered, "Yolanda Adams wore that song out, girl." She touched her hand and Valencia smiled, tapping her foot to the beat and clapping her hands along with Teela and Brandi, who sat closer to Rachel Cummings.

They stood as the song wound down and applauded. A few *amens* and *hallelujahs* resounded with serious, soulful rumblings.

Gray-haired and handsome, Reverend Honeycutt stood tall. His pint-sized wife had led the choir, and everyone showed their appreciation for the hard work. She smiled a big, contagious smile, looking proud.

The reverend approached the podium in his hunter-green, perfectly knotted power tie with matching silk pocket scarf and two-button wheat suit.

"Praise the Lord. Now that is what I call letting God know you praise Him. Amen. Remember that your destiny is better than your history."

Rachel Cummings let out her own "Amen," holding her woman's hand as they all took their seats.

Reverend said, "Some say don't sweat the small stuff. I say don't sweat the big stuff, either. Forgive and forget, literally. God's got you. God's truly got you. And besides, we're all a work-in-progress anyway. Each and every one of us. And yes, we fall down, but we get up, too. Get on up, as James Brown said. Get up!" he yelled.

He did a quick rendition of James Brown doing the mashed potato, snapping his fingers while the band did their short version of the song.

The church members clapped along with him and laughed as he wound up his energetic sermon.

He laughed, too, and wiped his forehead. "I feel good," he shouted, ending with, "Hallelujah."

The crowd replied the same way, and some spoke in rhythmic tongues.

Reverend Honeycutt walked from behind the podium to the right side of the room. "You know, today we'll talk about finishing the course. We all tend to get bruised and worn and torn down. It's pretty much a guarantee in life. From the moment we're born, we get another day closer to our last day. And our experiences show who we are at every turn. Sometimes things happen that we asked for, and most times, things happen to us that we didn't. Some of us have been used and abused, but you must choose to walk as a whole human being. You'd better believe it's all for the good because it's all God. It's all divine and meant to shape you up before you ship out. Isn't it funny how we tend to remember the times that left the biggest scars? The scars are there to remind us of the lesson. Through the lessons, we find that we have an opportunity to be better. It's not what happens to you. It's what happens through you. It's how you respond that matters. You can play the victim role, or you can play the victor. No matter what's happened to you, it's your call. But the bottom line is, sight unseen, you need faith. Believe and know and claim and accept and let go. Let God. Do the work. Show up." He walked from the right side of the room to the left side. Miki looked down the row and smiled at Rachel Cummings, who had leaned forward to smile back.

"Every test is a testimony. Count yourself fortunate to have gone through some stuff. Okay, so you were abused. Okay, so you were left. Okay, so you were beaten. Okay, so you were let down. Okay, so you were molested. Now what? You don't get a pass for that. Make something of it. Don't let your mess go to waste. You've got to turn your mess into your message.

"Winners are losers who refuse to quit, so remember that. You have to fall before you can get up. And for now, I want you to turn your bibles to 2 Samuel 21, verse 1." He paused a few moments while everyone flipped to the correct section. Brandi didn't have a bible, so Teela leaned in close and shared. Valencia had a frayed and beat-up tiny black King James version. And Miki had a study Bible, all highlighted in yellow, with *Can I Get an Amen* written in silver glitter on the front.

"Then there was famine in the days . . ." The reverend continued to read from four verses, then spoke to his congregation for the next forty-five minutes before he said his final words.

The reverend pulled a handkerchief from his coat pocket and wiped his brow as he headed back to the pulpit. "You must be determined to release your mess and move on. Have a funeral for it and let it die. A setback is a setup for a comeback, folks. Victory is on the other side of inconvenience. God will not let you out of your trouble until you get what you need from it. God never flunks you. If you don't get it right, he just gives you a retest. And believe you me, you'll go through it again and again until you pass."

He began to preach louder and louder. "It's a new season. It's time for a new level of consciousness. Time to find someone who's gone on to where you want to be, someone who will be tough on you. That's how you get your greatest development, under someone who doesn't cater to your every whim. You need to get a hookup to look up. What you commit to build, you empower to grow. We are imperfect people, and loving yourself is number one, and that means making an unconditional commitment to that imperfect person within. And you can enhance that commitment by trusting in God. Don't be afraid to cry sometimes. Tears are a language that God understands. I want you to remember this: nothing is more powerful than a made-up mind. Endure hardness as a good soldier. Stay the course. Don't give up. Can I get an amen?"

"Amen," the churchgoers replied, most looking around at one another. Teela nodded to herself and said it twice.

The service drew to a close after the final song and prayer. The ladies exited the sanctuary and walked into the lobby, standing near the front door.

Rachel Cummings was dressed in khaki pants and a loose blazer. She said, "Thank you all for coming. I hope you got something out of it. I don't like to preach at our bi-weekly meetings, though I do think our faith is what's most important. Like I said, we can't do it alone."

"I agree. I appreciate the invite. He is good. Very inspiring," said Teela.

"And by the way, this is my wife, Trish. Trish, this is Miki, Teela, Valencia, and Brandi."

"Hello. It's very nice to meet you all," Trish said.

Valencia said, "Nice to meet you, too. You've got quite a woman here."

"I know that. We've been together for a long time. She's my rock."

"That's a beautiful thing." Teela gave them a look of admiration.

"Yes. It is," said Brandi.

Miki suggested, "How about if we all go and grab some breakfast? There's a great diner near here, and the food is pretty good."

"I'm game," said Valencia.

"Me, too."

"Sounds good to me. What about you two?" Teela asked Rachel Cummings and Trish.

Trish replied, holding on to her wife's arm, "We've got a meeting that we facilitate that starts in a few minutes and goes most of the afternoon. But you ladies enjoy yourselves."

"Oh, okay. Well, thanks for telling us about the church. I know I'll make a point to come back," said Miki.

Rachel Cummings told them, "Good. See you all on Tuesday."

"Have a good one. Adios," said Valencia.

About thirty minutes later, all four ladies were seated at Dinah's restaurant near Fox Hills. The high-school-aged water girl served them coffee, juice, and water. They placed their breakfast orders and reminisced about the sermon.

Teela spoke calmly yet sounded moved. "That whole thing about going through it again until you get it right brought me goose bumps. I mean, I've thought that so many times. That every time I say I'm going to do something differently, it gets the same results. And then it happens again. It's like, okay, God, enough."

Valencia said, "I'm telling you, it's been awhile since I've been to church. Hearing what he had to say does get you to thinking. It's like a pattern we fall into that's sometimes like a comfort zone. Even when it's a bad pattern, it ends up feeling comfortable because we get so used to it. I don't wanna stay in my comfort zone anymore."

Teela added, "Well, if it's true that God hears tears, then he should hear me loud and clear. Austin and I broke up. Austin's my boyfriend who lived with me, but I caught him with a girl we both got with who lives in our complex."

Brandi looked caught off guard. "Oh, I'm sorry," she said, sitting next to Teela.

Teela shrugged her shoulder. "No, it's cool. I spoiled him rotten anyway, and with me trying to detox when he stayed so freaky, we just didn't work well together. I found myself always trying to find strange women for him to get with. I mean, it fed my fetish, but it wasn't gonna help me get past it any sooner."

Miki asked, holding on to her coffee mug with both hands, "So he's just as lustful as you are?"

"More so. He just doesn't see a problem with it." Teela sipped her ice water.

"Well if he's seeing someone who lives in the same place behind your back, that sounds like he's a little out of control to me," Valencia said, looking at Miki.

"Don't look at me. I am no judge on control," Miki said, shaking her head.

"Me neither," said Brandi. She glanced at the clock on the wall, then tapped her fingers along the table.

Miki asked Teela, "You don't think you two will get back together? I mean, where's he gonna live?"

"He lives with her. I kicked him out that night."

Brandi looked sad for her. "Wow. Have you heard from him?"

"I have. He calls and I don't pick up. He sent me a

text, apologizing, saying she can't compare to me. And he said he'll always have love for me. Whatever the hell that means."

Valencia explained, "That means let's be friends for now while I see what else is out there, since I'm free, but don't move on with anyone else until you take me back when I'm done. Funny how they never learn until it's too late."

Miki shook her head. "See. That's how men are. Valencia will tell you, I've learned to dish it right back out. I mean, what's good for the goose is good for the gander. Girl, please. If you were busy doing your thing on the side like he was, then he would've been hit right back with a taste of his own medicine and you all would've been even-steven."

Teela replied, "Well even or not, I'm sorry, but I don't wanna share my man any longer unless I'm there."

"What's the difference? There or not, if you're not the only one he's fucking, then you're not the only one, period." Miki took a cautious sip of her brew.

Teela leaned forward with her elbows on the table. "True. But fucking behind my back is cheating. Fucking with me is not."

Miki placed her coffee mug down on the table. "I don't get it. I watch Tariq with someone else and I'm cool if I'm there. But I also know if he was with someone and I didn't know, as long as I'm doing the same, no problem."

Brandi asked, "So you'd have no problem with him if he had a life aside from you where he did things you never knew about?"

"No. I really wouldn't have a problem."

Brandi looked at Teela, who gave her a *don't tell* look,

then back at Miki. "Wow. See, that's why I just don't have anybody. That keeps things a whole lot cleaner."

Valencia took a small sip of juice and told the ladies, "Well, I wanna get married. I want kids soon. That's all I know. I want my fiancé Greg to be my husband because I want the life, the dog, the picket fence, and all that goes along with a good life. I want all of it."

"And he wants you to stop fucking, right?" asked Teela.

"He does."

Miki admitted, "See, I think I'm safe in telling you this." Miki looked at Valencia, who nodded. "I mean, it's no big deal to us. See, Val and I have been lovers for a while now. Her fiancé knew it before and he was cool, but now he's not. My man is very cool with it. I mean very, very cool."

Brandi asked, "Really? So you guys are gay?"

"We're not gay," said Miki quickly.

Valencia corrected her. "We are."

Miki leaned back and crossed her legs under the table. "I'm not. Speak for your damn self."

Teela said, "Funny, if a man slept with a man we'd call him gay. But when we do it, we just say we're what, curious?"

Miki replied, "No. Not curious. I sure as hell know my way around a pussy by now to be way past curious. Call it what you want. I just want a woman every now and then. I know what I do and do it very well, thank you."

"Oh yes, she surely does," said Valencia, making a move like she was squirming in her seat.

Brandi said, "Well, that's not me. I mean, I just don't

wanna work that hard. And that looks like a whole lotta work. Eating pussy. I'll stick to sucking the dick."

"Like anything else, you've gotta like it. Put on your knee pads and stay a while, hell." Miki looked around for the waitress.

"You ever thought about trying it, Brandi?" asked Valencia.

She turned up her nose like she smelled sour cheeks and smooched her mouth to the side. "Oh hell no. I just like the way a man reacts to me. That's it. I could care less about a woman."

Teela exhaled loudly and readjusted her hips. "Well, I see we got all that out on the table. How about we eat?" she asked, winking at Miki.

Miki winked back at her as the waitress approached with plates piled high. "There she is," she said smiling from ear to ear. She inhaled the smell of the sweet pancakes and licked her lips. While the waitress stood there passing out the orders, Miki asked, "Who out of all of us is the freakiest?"

Teela pointed to Brandi. "She is."

Valencia pointed to Miki. "She is."

The waitress grinned and blushed and shook her head and walked away.

They all laughed while grabbing their forks to begin eating their meals. But not before Miki and Teela and Valencia closed their eyes and looked down for a silent prayer. Brandi watched them and then did the same.

The four ladies enjoyed their meals and shared stories of life, love, and what it would be like to one day live normal sex lives.

After about an hour and a half, as they all pulled off in their rides, Miki sent Valencia a text.

R u still comin by 2nite?

U know it. Can't stay long. But hell yeah I'm there.

Good. We'll c u then. U looked hot 2day.

Thanx. U 2. ☺

# 22

## "You Sure Love to Ball"

### Valencia

Intensely, Gregory's voice rang from Valencia's wireless earpiece while she hurried from Inglewood to Brentwood as fast as she could.

"Where the hell were you this time?"

It was that same Sunday, almost midnight. Valencia had spent another late, freak-filled evening with Tariq and Miki. It was one hour past the time she'd agreed to come to Gregory's house and spend the night.

"I'm just running late. I'm on my way."

"From where? Okay, of course. Don't tell me. You were with the love of your life, Miki, right?"

Valencia tried to hide the sound of an exhaustive sigh. "Yes, I was at Miki's. She was helping me with wedding plans. Time just slipped away."

"She was helping you with wedding plans? With our wedding plans or yours and hers?" His cynicism was thick.

"Greg, please don't start that. I'll be there in thirty minutes. Bye." She sped up the 405, way past the speed limit, racing to get her fast ass to her future home.

By the time she arrived, Gregory was sitting at his desk

as usual. "Are you always on that computer?" she asked, as she put her purse beside the bed.

He kept his back to her. "Are you always with Miki?"

Valencia took her overnight bag and unzipped it, taking out her black silk PJ's. "Do you want to talk or can we go to sleep?"

"You look pretty tired. Maybe you'd prefer sleep."

"Tired? You haven't even looked at me. But, yes. I guess I should."

He spun around and spoke with an edge. "Well, I'd prefer talking."

"Greg." She shook her head and took her toothbrush and pajamas in hand, heading to the bathroom where she closed the door.

Twenty minutes later, she exited showered and dressed for bed.

He asked, still sitting in the same position, "Tell me, cause I wanna make sure I get this right. You and Miki went over what, exactly?"

She stood at the bathroom door, looking over at him. "We just went over different options for reception locations. And we looked at some dresses online."

"And what else?"

"That's it." She walked to the bed and pulled back the checkered satin covers.

"And it took all that time?"

"Yeah. It did. Any more questions?" she asked, fluffing up the foam pillow.

"Yes. So, what's this about you and Miki being together with her man?"

She paused. "What do you mean?"

He blurted, "What I mean is this exactly. Quote, unquote. 'Val, baby, Tariq and I had a sexy-ass time again. Let's not let it be the last time. And just so you know, we went at it again after you left. All in your name.'"

Silence swelled. Valencia's eyes rose and her mouth dropped and she swallowed a gasp. She looked over at her purse, which was wide open. He held up her BlackBerry. "You went through my phone?"

"Tariq went through my pussy?"

She stepped to him fast. "Greg, you have no right." She snatched her phone from his hand. "Jerk." She dismissed him with her angry eyes.

"No, you are not gonna turn this one around on me. My fiancé's cell vibrated and I picked it up and read it. I'll gladly trade that with you as far as who has to deal with what."

Valencia scrolled through her phone and began yelling, "You know what? We did. We fucked. All three of us fucked and it was damn good."

"Why?"

"Because." She stared at him with a look like she could beat his ass like he stole something.

"Oh, I see. Just because." Now he yelled. He also stood. "Why the fuck did you have a threesome with your best friend and her man when you have a man? A fiancé. We agreed that if anything, it would only be women. Damn, Valencia. I agreed to you getting with Miki at times, but not fucking her and her man while I sit here waiting on you as usual. What the hell is that? I thought you could show me you were ready for marriage. But I guess I was wrong. I guess you can't turn a ho into a housewife after all." He flashed a scowl.

She did not even blink. "Maybe not."

"Just tell me fucking why."

"It's complicated." She sat on the bed, still looking at her phone.

He walked to her. "I guess it is. So complicated that you can't even explain cheating on me when we're supposed to be married early next year."

She put one hand up. Her eyes were flat. "Greg. Please."

"Please what? Are we gonna have to go back to bringing people into our bed like we'd been doing since college, just so I can have you in my life? Will it ever be you and me? I was even willing to do the 'you, me, and she' sometimes. Damn, Valencia. What the fuck?"

Her voice lowered a notch and grew soft. She spoke without looking at him. "I don't sleep with men alone. You know that." She played with the long, curly ringlet that hung over the right side of her face.

He got louder. "And you have the nerve to think that matters? Like that makes a difference. Like I should be happy you don't let dick inside of you unless there's another person in the room. Valencia, you're not supposed to sleep with men period, other than me. I don't give a fuck how it was before."

She looked up at him and cut her eyes. "Greg, don't you go and get all saintly on me. Your ass was so fucking into men I thought you were a damn fag. You sucked dick with me in the room and I didn't go flippin the fuck out. We were freaking. That's what we did."

He stepped even closer. "Right, that's what we did. Past tense. And as far as the man, it was one time and it lasted three seconds and you were the one who begged me to put my mouth on it. But that's not what we do now. I stuck to my end of the deal to stop the sex-crazed, swinging, risky lifestyle we had together for years. I wanted us to get on the straight and narrow and be husband and wife and raise a family. You broke your end of the deal. You will never be straight or narrow."

She stood up, six inches from him, towering over him. A sneer darkened her oval face. "And you can just pass judgment on me when your ass sits here logging on to porn websites, chatting with folks while you jerk off your dick like it's a damn squeeze toy, up all night 'cause you can't get enough of a cheap thrill." She pointed to the computer and then to his dick. "You choke your little shit so damn much you barely even have skin tough enough to fuck me. Shit, who'd wanna fuck when they've cum six times already in one day? You stopped fucking me cold turkey and you expect me, a woman who's trying so hard to fight her cravings for sex that I just joined a sex rehab group, to go cold turkey just like that?" She headed to her bag and began taking off her pajamas. "You've been so busy masturbating and getting on me for being with Miki, that you won't even try to deal with your own sex addiction. You cut back in your own way and I don't sweat you, and so now, I'm trying to do it in my own way."

"Your way won't work. It is not acceptable. Besides, when I wanted to be with you, you didn't make time. Like the other night. But I let that slide. Not anymore."

"Then just fuck it." She went into the bathroom and her voice screamed from the other side of the door. "You are not my damn father. Take this damn ring and stick it up your faggot ass." She threw it into the bedroom where he stood. "But, I'm sure you'd like that. And I hope you're not logging on to Down-Low Blowjobs while you're molesting that poor keyboard. Fucking freak." She exited the bathroom fully dressed, took her bag and purse, and stormed out of the bedroom door.

He yelled behind her. "Fuck you. Go run to your woman, Miki. You're fucking in love with that bitch and can't even admit it. I can't compete with that shit. I won't compete with that shit. Maybe I can compete with her man, but not with a pussy."

"You will never compete with him. Your beat-up dick is just as short as you are. You haven't grown an inch since I've known you."

Her loud footsteps headed toward the front door and he ran the many square feet to catch up with her. "Get the fuck out. But gimme my damn key back first."

Her hand was on the quartz doorknob that led to the garage. "With pleasure." She made a quarter turn in his direction. Her face was pissed off. "And I'm the reason you have that good-paying job of yours. I got you that job by fucking that recruiter years ago because you wanted me to, after your dreams of an NFL career crumbled. You've been with UPS since you graduated from college because of me. You owe me some money, Gregory. This is not the last of me. And you know what? Maybe I just wasn't good enough for you anymore. Maybe you need a square girl who probably wouldn't want your weird ass anyway, money or not. But you're far from square and neither is your family. So don't go calling this kettle black when your pot is black, too." She jammed her hand into the purse and ripped the single gold key out of her wallet, pitching it at his chest. She exited abruptly and slammed the door so hard the house shook like an L.A. earthquake had hit the scene. "Fuck you, shawty," she yelled while inside the garage.

Valencia jumped into her truck and pressed the remote that rested on the visor, rolled down the window, and tossed the tiny clicker out along the lawn as she yanked the car into reverse. The song on the radio that blasted extra loud was "How You Gonna Act Like That" by Tyrese.

She twisted the dial to Off, heaved the car into Drive, and sped down his street and away from the man she'd labeled as her now ex, wealthy, no-pussy-eating, judgmental, jack-off of a fiancé.

Once again without a family, Valencia was abandoned.

Once again she was not good enough to keep.

Once again, because of her past, she was unable to have all that goes along with the good life.

And to top it all off, she was still addicted.

# 23

———— ✺ ————

# "You're Making Me High"

## Brandi

**W**hy in the hell is it so cloudy out tonight? What's going on? And wow, when are they gonna fix this damn bumpy-ass road? Seems it got worse just since last week. And it even seems like the road got narrower. I mean, was this a single-lane highway before? What's with all these cars? And what in the world is that loud-ass noise? That ringing in my ears that keeps shouting louder than the hip-hop station that's on full blast. Who is that talking bout, "I'm da biggest boss dat ya seen thus far?" I hate rap music. And who in the hell is singing along with the lyrics like they're on BET Jams? But I suppose a better question would be, what in the heck is up with that siren? That glaring-ass, loud-ass siren.

Brandi quickly pressed the Down Volume arrow on the steering wheel with her left thumb, while looking straight ahead.

"Miss Williams. Miss Williams."

"Who the hell are you?" she asked out loud, while still looking at the road ahead, which was playing dirty little tricks on her mind.

"Miss Williams. Stop. Don't you see the police cars behind us? They're flashing their lights with their sirens blaring. I've been telling you to stop and pull over." The voice was male, yet with an almost-grown pitch.

"Who are you?" she asked again, looking over to her right. His face was familiar.

It was a face that was puberty-ridden and acne-filled, coated with fright. The male turned back and then forward, over and over and over again in a deep panic. "Stop and pull this mug over," he said again, as he pulled her right hand away from his now-deflated dick and buckled his pants, pulling down his blue and red *Iron Man* T-shirt.

She shook her head to make room for the eruption of emotions, and kept shaking out her brain as the fast-moving roadside scenery began to blur. Slamming on the brakes, she hit what seemed like a curb, and the *Iron Man* T-shirt-wearing male grabbed the wheel and yanked her fiery red Camaro into an oak tree as their heads jerked backward and then forward.

*Swoosh.* Their faces slammed into the ballooning air bags. Their skin was engulfed by the force. The car skidded and came to an abrupt stop.

A megaphone voice sounded from outside. "Get out of the car with your hands up where we can see them. Now."

The Camaro would be no more.

Brandi did as she was told.

And thirteen-year-old Keyshaun, laced with Brandi's X-rated fingerprints, did as he was told, as well.

When she arrived at the sheriff's station that handled the East Compton area where she was arrested, Brandi was locked in a large, bright holding cell alone, awaiting arraignment the next morning on five felony counts, two of sexual assault on a minor, one of endangering the welfare of a minor, and two counts of statutory rape. That had been the first time she was with someone twice. Ever.

She sat on a wooden bench. Agony filled her face. Her weighted shoulders hung low.

"You're allowed to make one phone call."

She replied as though in a daze, massaging her sweaty palm with her thumb. "I'll call my mother."

"What's her number?"

"I don't know. It's in my cell phone."

"I'll be right back," the female deputy said, looking like she wanted to bitch-slap Brandi personally.

Late in the afternoon, two days after pleading not guilty during an initial hearing, where she was represented by an attorney who was a friend of her mother, Brandi sat in a plain-looking room at the Lynwood Regional Justice Center. It was an all female, midlevel county facility. And she was in the library.

She read through a few books on a shelf. Some of the books were by Ray Bradbury, Walter Dean Myers, and Walter Mosley, her favorites. Brandi took a seat on a steel chair and sat back, wearing her official orange jumpsuit.

"Gimme that," demanded a woman wearing unkempt cornrows and built like Queen Latifah.

"What?" Brandi asked, looking shocked and worried. She stood up immediately.

"That book. That belongs to me."

"No. That was on the shelf here." Brandi shifted the book from one hand to another. It was a copy of *Fallen Angel*.

"Oh but you're wrong, oh tender fresh meat. I own that shelf. It's got my name on it. See. My name is Library. And this is my friend, Cafeteria." She pointed to her buddy on the left. "My Latino lovely here is named Shower." She pointed to her buddy on the right. "And anywhere you go, one of my other friends will be there to greet you."

Brandi simply extended her unsteady hand, offering the book as she was told.

The grim-faced, oversized black woman threw it against the wall. "Hey, we hear you raped a child. Is that true?"

"No." Brandi's one word sounded like a question.

"Oh, don't tell me. You pled not guilty, right?"

"I did."

"Yeah, we all did. The thing is, we don't believe you. And just in case you don't get what the fucked-up justice system should have coming to you, I have an idea. This game right now is judge and jury. And you are about to do your time for fucking a little boy, bitch."

"I didn't."

The woman skidded her head toward Brandi. "You did. We know you did. We know you're a pervert. We know who you are. We heard all about you. You got off on this child. He's a child. He may have acted like he liked you, but he's a child."

"I didn't. I'm telling you. I gave him a ride home and I was drunk." Brandi leaned away, bracing herself for the tongue-lashing.

The woman leaned forward. "Then how did you end up with his sperm inside of you? How did you two end up at a motel together the day before? See, they try to change the paperwork around here with codes so that we don't know the real deal with certain inmates' charges. But we have our ways. I think another question is, how did a thirteen-year-old end up drunk in your car with the tequila you bought him? Let me guess. Patrón, was it?"

Brandi's face was red. "It wasn't like that. I'm telling you."

"Well, I'm telling you. It's like this." She stared at the area near Brandi's pussy. "Pull your pantsuit down. Now."

Brandi took one step back. "No."

The woman grabbed her upper arm with her right hand. "Bitch. Say no again and I will shank your ass." Random sprays of spit shot from her mouth. The woman opened her left hand and flashed a piece of metal with a pointy tip. "Pull em down."

Brandi pulled her arms of out the sleeves and pulled her jumpsuit down to her ankles. Her eyes began to water.

"And your panties."

Brandi's thumbs eased her panties downward. She stood for a moment, fully exposed from tit to twat, and stepped out of both.

"Now bend over," the woman said, pointing to the chair.

Brandi's eyes seemed to beg. She acted as if she'd heard wrong. "What?"

"Bend the fuck over. And shut the fuck up. Do as you're told." And the lady with a deep voice and oversized body had a ripe, yellow banana in hand. She stepped in front of Brandi, facing her full on, and held the banana between her own legs. "Now suck this."

Brandi whimpered but placed her knees on the seat and bent over the back of it.

The woman ordered her buddy, Cafeteria, who held on to a white hand towel, "Put that fucking towel around her neck."

Cafeteria began to place the towel around the circumference of Brandi's throat and she tightened it, giving it a firm jerk. And the third woman, Shower, covered her mouth as Brandi squirmed for a second and then froze.

"Now, Shower is gonna move her hand and you are going to suck my fake dick or all three of us will pull on this towel and choke the fuck out of you. Now do it."

As Brandi shut her eyes, she felt the tip of the banana at her mouth.

"Open."

She parted her lips and took it in toward her tongue and swallowed hard. The woman pushed and pulled it. Brandi gagged.

"Suck it. Suck the fuck out of it."

As Brandi was bent over, doing her best to suck as little as she could, she felt an object pressing near her asshole and she jerked, tightening up.

"Close your mouth and take it to your tonsils. Don't let up."

Shower, who stood behind her, inserted the handle of a cylindrical brush fast and deep.

"Uggghhhhh. Uhhhhh." Brandi's grunts were joined by heavy tears rolling from her eyes to her cheeks to her chin.

The woman taunted her. "Why you crying? Oh, you can't take it big and forceful, huh. You like the little puberty dicks, I guess. Cut out that whining and take that up your ass, bitch. Whether you get out of here or not, whether they transfer you or not, I bet your fast ass won't be fucking no more kids. Ya see, I'm a mother. See, you basically fucked my kid and every kid of every other woman in this place. Suck it, dammit."

Another woman rammed her fist, knuckles and all, inside of Brandi's pussy, pumping her whole hand in and out, deep and furious.

Brandi began to pee on herself.

"Good girl. That means you feel that shit. I would pull this banana out of your mouth and make you lick my pussy but if you bit me I'd have to stick your ass."

She continued like she was preaching. "Yeah. You're gonna be worth something up in here. I'll make sure you never see another dick for at least a year if they say you can stay with us. I'm gonna do my best to make sure your sweet ass ends up right here at Lynwood Regional. You ain't gonna get no Paris Hilton treatment up in here. Me and the ladies right here, we have very close ranks with those who matter, so don't even think about making a big deal of this little cherry-busting moment, otherwise the next time we'll lock your ass in a broom closet and bring Dildo Devine in here. Or have Judy the Ripper fuck you in the boiler room or the laundry room. But you need to know, no matter who finds out in the ranks, they don't fuck with us when it means we're getting in the ass of child molesters. They'll tolerate murderers and rapists before you. They prefer we teach you an early lesson just to welcome you to the family. See, statutory rape gets you fucked every night. And even if you do tell, there's still a nice, horny female officer who'll show up at your cell after the nine-o'clock count and make you lick her ass with grape jelly. Fuck with us, okay?"

Brandi moaned and her body quaked with fear. She fought not to cry but was losing the battle. She wept and sucked and received and wept some more.

"What's wrong? Oh, I see you don't like women very much. Go ahead, Shower, pull that shit out of her ass." Her partner in crime did as she was told, drawing the long, wide handle from Brandi's asshole. "I think it's time to focus only on that coochie." The woman stepped back and released the now-dented banana from Brandi's mouth. Brandi gave a long, gagging cough and started breathing unsteadily. "I wanna watch this up close and personal." She stepped back around Brandi, standing to her side. "Fuck my friend's fist back. You got that nice big fist up your tight pussy. Fuck her like her hand is the very dick your sick ass was used to. Since you like to fuck so much."

Brandi pushed her hips back. With every insertion she pressed forward. With every withdrawal she retreated. For a dozen times more she got plummeted with the woman's fist until the fist was yanked out abruptly. A little more urine escaped from Brandi's urethra.

The woman bent down to speak in her ear. Her breath was hot and stale. Brandi closed her eyes. "Now get the fuck up and pull your pants up and get the fuck out of here. And baby, this little incident ain't nothing new. You're a statistic, part of a very high percentage, so get used to it. And now that you've been branded, your ass is mine. Pleased to meet you, with your pretty pussy. Oh, and by the way, my real name is Coffee. I have five more months here so we'll have lots of fun." She stood up straight and continued. "Yeah, you're my new bitch, bitch. Oh excuse me, your new name is Brandi bitch." She took the bristle part of the brush that served as her dildo and popped Brandi on her backside. "Nice ass." The three walked away.

Brandi trembled from the coldness of being scared and kept her eyes closed as she heard the six footsteps fading away, then she heard a door open slowly and creak to a close.

She held her breath and turned around to sit in the chair she'd gotten raped on. She exhaled madly. Her mind sat with her in shock. Her whole body and the air around her smelled of pee. She sniffled and wiped her eyes, and rubbed the dripping snot from her nose with the back if her hand. She saw her wet jumpsuit that had been sitting in the spill of her own piss, slipped her feet into it, still wearing her rubber-soled shoes, also wet, and balled up her panties, gripping them tight in her hand.

The sobriety game was over.

And a whole new game had begun.

The next afternoon, Teela sat at the light gray counter of the visiting area on the other side of the thick glass, which separated her from her friend, Brandi Renee Williams, also known by booking number 3743330, who was in deep trouble. She was still in the large, sterile-looking, cold jail facility.

"What in the heck happened?" Teela asked in obvious amazement, holding on to the chipped, black receiver. "Brandi, what were you thinking?"

Brandi didn't move her body. Only her lips. She barely blinked her bloodshot eyes. "It's so easy for people to throw stones when they live in glass houses." She sounded like she was dying of thirst.

"But Brandi, a minor?"

"I was drunk."

"Girl, you know alcohol is no excuse."

Brandi held tight to the receiver and licked her chapped lips, swallowing hard before she spoke in a monotone voice. "I've heard that from everyone, from my mother to my new ex-boss, Mrs. Ross, to my attorney. But you know what, Teela? If what I've been through in just the short amount of time in this hellhole is called paying for what happened, then as bad as it's been, I'm accepting the fact that I'll stay right here and finish out what I have coming to me until God says I'm done. Like Reverend Honeycutt said in church that day, we need to endure hardness as good soldiers. And no doubt, I have to be one. I have to be. But I can't help but think that no matter if they put me in isolation or not, the truth is that even when I get out, I'll have no job, no family, and no life. So as of right now, if the best you can do is intensify my guilt level, go right ahead. I can take that easily. That thirteen-year-old boy didn't have the luxury of isolation. So as of today, I'm guilty as charged."

Teela nodded and looked down, and then glanced to her left, eyeing the many visitors who sat in a row. She looked down again and spoke. "By the way, I was accused of peeping in the window of a neighbor."

"Teela, did you?"

"I was looking for Austin, that's all. That was the night we broke up. That's how I found him."

"So you peeked in every condo?"

"He was in the one right across from it. It was by accident."

"Accident. Okay. Damn."

"Damn is right." Teela sighed and rubbed her upper arm. "So, what's your bail?"

"Too high."

"What is it?"

"Five hundred thousand. I need fifty thousand to get out."

"Damn again."

Brandi began to hold on to the receiver tighter, talking straight up. "Teela, do you know that I went to a sex shop to see what was up with the glory hole you talked about the first night I met you? I've continued pretending to be a streetwalker, fucked strange men, giving them head more times than I can remember. I have no control over what I do any more than I would have control in here. Honestly, I hope I stay in here and get treated like shit. Because I *am* shit. If I couldn't start this whole 'stop lusting and become sober' shit before, I guess I have no choice now. It might just take my freedom to change me. I'm willing to do whatever." Her face looked like she was ready to cry, but no tears fell.

"I understand. But Brandi, for right now, you have to stay focused on your case. You'll be fine. I just know it."

"I guess have to. I won't be having a drink or a good fuck up in here."

Teela carefully examined every line and feature on Brandi's face. She looked ten years older than she did only days ago. "Are you okay? What's going on in there? I know this is hell, but you just look like you're zoned out."

"This is probably just the real me. No tequila. No need to be charming. Just me."

"Okay," Teela said, as she looked around. "Girl, I'm gonna have to run. I've got a guy coming in with his employees to get a tour soon. But I'll be back to see you. Okay?"

"Okay."

"Stay up."

"I'll try. Teela. By the way, I liked him." Brandi's eyes were glassy and far away. She looked down at the scar from her slit wrist, and back at Teela.

"You what?" Teela looked like her ears were deceiving her.

"The thirteen-year-old. My student. Keyshaun. I liked him." Her face was swaddled in guilt.

"Oh, Brandi." Teela gave Brandi a warning look and then leaned back and reached into her pants pocket. "Girl, I'm gonna see if I can send you this coin." She held up the silver SA chip. "I got it at the last group meeting. On the front it says, 'To thine own self be true.' It celebrates twenty-four hours of recovery. No sex."

Brandi said, "Congratulations." Her voice was still unvaried.

"Thanks." Teela pushed her chair back a bit. "And by the way, it has the Serenity Prayer on the back. Remember to ask this, 'God grant me the serenity to accept the things I cannot change; courage to change the things I can; and wisdom to know the difference.' I mean, it couldn't hurt."

"Thanks, Teela." Brandi still looked stone-faced. She then said out of the blue, "I'm not usually one to tell, but I think I should let Miki know something."

"What?"

"The night we met Tariq and I told you I knew him. Well, he's a cross-dresser. I did him one night when I was on the streets, and he was dressed like a straight-up bitch, getting off on schoolgirl role playing."

Teela's eyes expanded. She poked her head forward. "Are you kidding me?"

"Not even. Will you tell her?"

"Oh no, I don't think so. It shouldn't come from me, if it should be said at all. I don't know."

"Well. I just had to say that."

"Good-bye." Teela hung up, then ran her fingers through the back of her hair and stood, taking departing steps, seeming confused as she looked back.

"Bye," Brandi mouthed while hanging up.

And as the guard approached, Brandi still watched Teela and gave a single wave as she walked away. Free.

The guard took Brandi by her arm. Still locked up.

She walked slowly, thinking about how her Camaro alter ego had heard the voice saying she was unlovable.

It was the voice that tapped against her childhood.

And Brandi realized her heart heard it, too.

That voice was why her heart had been broken.

She walked back to her solo cell and said in response to the Serenity Prayer that was still in her head, "I accept. I surrender. Amen."

And she prayed for an unbroken heart.

# 24

---

# "Insatiable Woman"

## Sexaholics

It was Tuesday, and another Sexaholics meeting had arrived. Seven members showed up—all except Brandi, of course, and Dwayne and Miki. Not that their reasons were in any way related. It was Dwayne's birthday, and Miki had a date with Robert.

With a half hour left to go, after discussing whether or not sex with spouses was allowed throughout detox, and after two members shared their experiences over the past two weeks, Rachel Cummings decided to ask Valencia, "So, how's it going with your willpower? I mean as far as abstaining from pushing the limits." Teela sat right next to her, looking glum.

"I've failed." Valencia's face was empty.

"I wouldn't use that word. Nothing is ever over. Failure is not an option or a word to consider. There's always another way and another day."

"Well, today I'm no longer engaged. My ex-fiancé found out some things and he couldn't deal with it any longer."

"Like what? Would you mind sharing?"

"Like, he found out I was having sex with a woman I had feelings for."

"So was it just that you were having sex with her, or was it that you crossed the line into feelings?"

"Both. He tried to pretend he could deal with the girl-on-girl every now and then, but he was threatened by our connection."

"Some men are like that, especially when you're engaged to them. They'll play with two girls, but when they prepare to marry you, if they're the type to wed a woman due to virtue issues, to them another woman is cheating. It's adultery."

"But we had a deal. He changed his mind."

"I can tell this really hurts you. What you must do is really try to stop beating yourself up. People have opinions and experiences, and the way we look at things is our individual viewpoint. His viewpoint and your viewpoint differed. That doesn't make him bad or you bad."

"Bad is exactly how I feel. I feel like I'm worthless. Like I have no morals. Like I never will be worth marrying. I'll never settle down and have a family."

"Valencia. Was it just about your girl? Or something else?"

"We used to have sex with other people all the time. He'd watch me fuck other men right in front of him. But this time, he found out I had sex with my girl and her man. He broke it off with me and I haven't heard from him." Valencia's eyes were cloudy.

"So, it's about infidelity in his eyes."

"This man has a masturbation fetish that I could call infidelity, too. I mean he lusts after anything and everyone. But we met under these circumstances. We're both freaky. I know who he is. I know what he craves. I loved that freak in him. And I thought he loved the freak in me. I guess I didn't meet his standards of virtue. Not enough to be his wife, anyway."

"And so I guess whatever deal you two had must have changed for him. In his eyes you probably violated the terms."

Valencia shook her head and gave an exasperated sigh.

"Valencia, the fourth, fifth, and sixth steps apply. Number four is to make fearless personal inventory of ourselves. We all must do that without blame of anyone else, including ourselves, but we must be fearless in what we might find about ourselves. You must take inventory of Valencia. And fifth, admit to God, to yourself, and to another human being the exact nature of your wrongs. Whoever that another human being is, is up to you. But you must verbalize it out loud because you can't heal what you don't acknowledge. And sixth, be entirely ready to have God remove all your defects of character. All of them. Be ready and ask. Seek and ye shall find. You're here. You have sought. And so, you shall find. But not overnight. These rules will be flushed out and broken down and repeated and broken and recommitted to and spoken of again, and again, and again. Know this. And not only know better, but be better so you can do better. Really look over your twelve steps, not only here but when you're at home, at the doctor's office, at work. Reinforce and know it. It can and will save your life."

Valencia leaned forward. "Can I start with the fifth one tonight, please?"

"You can start wherever you want. There's no real order. Only that you focus on getting all twelve."

"Okay." She leaned her elbows along her thighs. "I

guess I really do think I'm this adult who tries to distract herself from what's normal with what's abnormal, like I did when I was a little girl. What's abnormal is comfortable to me. I tell myself I want normalcy, but sometimes I think I don't deserve it, so I screw it up. I guess I just can't say no to my weird thinking. When I have sex, I don't think or care about anyone who would not approve. I don't even really think about sex itself. I just do it. It's like it's all body and no mind. I was a lonely child. And now, even when I'm with people, I still feel lonely. When I'm having sex, it's the only thing that means something. I guess at some point I learned if no one wanted me, I was nothing. My parents, who were murdered when I was twenty-one, didn't want me. And it's not like they gave me up to anyone else, but maybe they should've. And most Puerto Ricans are very family-oriented with strong ties. Unlike her strong-willed mamma, my mamma was passive and followed my poppa's lead, no matter what. She had very few maternal instincts. I took a backseat to their place of business. I was latchkey without a key. They didn't even lock the doors. From the age of nine, I cooked, bathed, cleaned, let myself in, walked to school, put myself to bed, and did most things I wasn't supposed to do, too. I felt empty and alone. I say some things are not better left alone. And I was one of them.

"I would always watch my parent's dirty movies when I was a child, and believe me, they had a ton of them. The X-rated feelings distracted me and eased my loneliness. I couldn't wait for my mamma and poppa to leave so I could be alone with my pornos and masturbate. The people in the dirty movies were wild and loose and free, and they didn't judge my ordinary life. I can kind of understand anyone who gets off by masturbating. But today, I crave more of the turn-on. It turns me on, turning someone else on, especially if it's kinky. I got addicted to that shit. I'm always thinking of it. Turning someone else on by doing what I can to get them off is intoxicating. I guess you could say if I had to take inventory, all of that spells out the exact nature of my wrongs. I guess right now I'm too broken to be devoted to one man. I did fuck up. But maybe someday I can be. I mean I'd like to be." She leaned back. "And yes, I'm confessing this out loud to all of you, other people. Other addicts. That where I come from." Valencia pressed her breath through her lips and looked at Teela.

Teela gave a warm look of approval.

Rachel Cummings took a moment to make sure Valencia was totally finished. She nodded and prompted Valencia's eyes to meet hers, and she smiled. "Thanks, Valencia. Let's all say thanks to Valencia."

"Thanks, Valencia," everyone said in unison, offering face hugs.

"We say thanks because not only are you helping yourself, you are helping everyone here in one way or another to see themselves through your openness, honesty, and admittance. See, no one is born a sex addict. I've said this before. We must face our childhoods as you just faced yours. Sex gives us emotional power and control. So how do we get hold of our own emotional power without sex? Valencia, I'm sure you feel judged by a fiancé who didn't approve of your choices. But you must approve of your own. You must make the choices that make you proud. And you must be honest about what you're feeling. For yourself. And for others. You can escape your past by finding strength to forgive your parents so you can be a fully functioning human being. The goal for now is to get healthy sexually. You need to nurture, connect, and love. You have to have a sense of worth and make emotional attachments that are mutually compatible. The one with your ex-fiancé was not. It's time to change that. I know it's true that we learn what we live, but the time to heal is now. You are here. That's the biggest step. Your sharing is appreciated.

"By the way, we have a member who is going through an example of what can happen when we continue to lose control over our lust and our lives. Eventually, we can lose it all. Let us all pray for Brandi. Please hold hands and bow your heads.

"Dear Lord, Please bless Brandi's soul and deliver her. Keep her strong and let your will be done. Amen."

"Amen," the members said together.

"Now, in Brandi's honor, we should mention the next few steps which include taking personal inventory when we're wrong. Admitting it right away. Next, praying and meditating to improve our conscious contact with God. We'll talk more about how to do that later. And the last one is to have a spiritual awakening as a result of all of the steps that we learn. In that, we carry this message to others, and constantly practice what we preach. Good night. See you all in two weeks. Stop lusting and become sober."

The members all said, "Stop lusting and become sober."

Rachel Cummings had Teela's attention especially.

# 25

## "Take You Down"

### Miki

Later that evening, Miki wore the timeless gold diamond tennis bracelet Robert had just clasped upon her left wrist. It jingled, as did his gold neck chain and charm, as they ground upon each other. His grind was out of a longing lust for a young lover to remind him of his youth; hers was out of an appreciative receivership, knowing exactly what she'd been telling herself, it was what it was.

And as usual, Robert wore a rubber and a brass cock ring on his rock-hard penis to slow the flow of blood and make his sometimes dysfunctional erection last longer. Unlike the rumor that all white men go down, this man did not go to the pussy promised land. Again, Miki had accepted it.

Robert said with a deep voice, "If I could just fuck you morning, noon, and night, you'd never have to work another day in your life." The vociferous sentence spoken out of sheer ecstasy sounded like a pornographic offer and a sugar-daddy promise.

The room was chic and dark and modern, with gray and red and white artwork. A small golden fluorescent light shone over their bare bodies from the corner of the huge room near the hardwood Asian platform bed.

"Is that so?" Miki spoke softer than he did. She was all ears while riding Robert, bouncing upon his thin but firm frame while he watched her ex-stripper fuck skills through the wall-to-wall beveled mirror in suite 4118 at The W Hotel. Robert had strategically adjusted the cream-colored, padded settee so that he could get a down-home view of himself being fucked by his hot tenderoni, Miki Summers.

"I'm telling you. Just say the word and I will move you into my Newport Beach house, and you and T.J. will never have to want for anything. I'm serious, Miki. I want you." He spoke to her back, then caught another glimpse of her round-the-way girl moves through the mirror.

Miki watched herself in the mirror, too, pumping him all the way back to his brass ring. "You don't want me. You just want this sweet pussy, that's all."

"This pussy is good, but it's all about you. You've been available to me for years, and it's time to go to another level. I'm not getting any younger. My money can be your money."

"And what would I have to do?" she asked, getting her serious grind on.

He spoke a notch lower. "Just understand about my wife. You know the deal. She's sick. A man has needs. Just be available to me by living with me. I wouldn't be able to be there all the time. But when I am, you'd get all my attention."

"So I'd be your hideaway mistress, then?"

"I wouldn't call it that."

"What would you call it? And why are we having this conversation while you're fucking me, Bob?" She bounced upon him aggressively to accentuate her question and his eyes shut tight. He grunted and looked like he was holding his breath.

Even as Robert obviously focused upon fighting the timing of his normally premature orgasm, hoping the ring worked, Miki straddled the settee, one leg on each side while he lay on his back in vagina heaven. Her French-manicured toes flexed and pointed along the russet shag carpet. She was facing the other way, and she bent over to grab the wrought-iron side of the bench to brace herself. Still on top, she faced his feet while he stroked her back and grabbed handfuls of her loose booty. Her ass flopping sounded like thunderous, pornographic clapping along his stomach.

Miki placed her right hand between her legs and along her own pink love muscle, stimulating herself manually while his narrow penis stabbed her vagina. She thrust her hips and masturbated. The more she teased her swollen clit, the more she felt a rush begin to travel through her soul. The rush that could bring her to her own peak.

"Damn, you're so wet today. My balls are dripping wet from this juicy vagina. No dry pussy here." He sounded as though dry pussy was his norm. He pumped her harder, to the left. "You like this angle, don't you?"

"Yes." She watched him watch her.

"Look at you. This is how it should be always. I've never met a woman in all my life who can get me off like you. No inhibitions. No hang-ups. Just so damn sexy, Miki. So, so sexy. Heck, I'd have to go to Rio to find a woman like you."

Miki leaned back a bit and rocked him back and forth with her hips, sliding his white dick in and out of her black pussy with a more side-to-side motion. She rubbed her ass along his pubic area and ground his dick all the way inside.

He slapped her ass and it wiggled in response. "Never seen ass like this before in all my life." He was in love with it.

"You love that big black ass. You can't get enough of it, can you?"

"No. Never." He switched his sights from her ass, to the mirror, to the ceiling, to her ass, and then back to the mirror. "Grab my balls. Grab em."

She leaned forward again and did as he asked, grabbing him by the testicles, fondling them between her long fingers.

He watched her work. "Grab em. Harder. Squeeze em."

Miki maneuvered his tawny-colored balls, getting rough like he liked it.

"Ohhhh, that's it. That's it. That's my Miki. Grab them. Grab my balls."

His voice told her he was deep into his approaching cum-factor. The cock ring was no match for her. Miki squeezed even harder.

"Oooooowwww, yes. Ooooohh, uhhhm, yes." He jerked his body and let out a high-pitched scream. "Ahhhhhhhhhhhhhhhhhhhhhhh. That's my bitch."

Miki ceased her bucking motion and her hand job against his balls. He would always call her the B word when he came. It was the way it was. She'd gotten used to the routine. He'd either jack off by looking at her ass while she stood in front of him, or they'd take a position where she could grope his balls and get him off the way he needed to. Either way, the name he always called her was *bitch*. This time, for some reason, she climbed off of him and said nothing.

He didn't move but said, "There's some money for you on the dresser. That was amazing." His breathing worked overtime.

He lay back to calm himself and closed his eyes.

His cell rang six times while Miki got dressed, putting back on her black skirt suit and red heels. He simply lay back, and then he began snoring, resting upon his back with a loose condom half off his limp dick, still breathing hard with a nasally sound.

Miki looked at him again and shook her head. She headed toward the door and his phone rang again. And again. He didn't move an inch, but he did break out into a loud, foghorn snore as he always did. And that always did drive her nutty.

She left. This time, without taking the money.

He didn't even notice.

As she exited the elevator and entered the hotel lobby, she was greeted. "Oh, hi, Miki. Wow, you're here late. I thought you were off already. I was going to call you," the hotel VP's executive assistant said. The woman wore cognac eyeglasses and had upswept hair.

"I just had to check on something. Call me about what?" Miki fluffed up the hair on the back of her head with her fingers and then rubbed her under eyes, checking for remnants of stray mascara.

"Miki, Mr. Walton asked me to set up a meeting with you for tomorrow morning. What's a good time?"

"Maybe late morning."

"Oh, I know for a fact he's booked. How about first thing, like nine o'clock?"

"Okay. I guess I have no choice."

"Good. I'll let him know. See you in the morning." The woman walked away.

"Okay." Miki exited the front door, stepped out into the early nighttime, and answered her phone. "Hello."

"Since you like to fuck so much, consider yourself fucked. Bitch."

Miki stopped in her tracks. She tried to keep her reaction down. "Look, bitch."

*Click.*

Miki noticed the doorman looking past her and then looking the other way quickly. She gave an exasperated exhale, tossed her phone into her bag, and headed toward her SUV, which was parked near the front in the end stall. Miki removed her keys from her purse at the same time she heard her phone ring again. She snatched it and read the display.

"Val. Hey, girl."

"Hey, Miki. I was wondering. Are you free to hang out tonight? I really would like to talk to you. Some shit happened with Greg and I wanted to tell you at the meeting but you didn't come. Greg found out about me and you and Tariq." Before Miki could reply, Valencia said, "Wait. Hold on for one second, baby." Miki was a few cars away from her own when she heard a *click* and then a voice. "Yeah. Hey, can I hit you back? I'm on the phone with Miki right now."

A familiar male voice said, "Okay. Can you meet for a minute? Just maybe a half hour. At our regular spot?"

Valencia answered him saying, "I was gonna ask her to meet me but yes, I guess I can. I'll call you right back."

"Okay, sexy."

"Bye." And then Valencia spoke to Miki. "Hello."

Miki's eyes bugged. Almost in automatic mode, she aimed her keys toward her car and it beeped. She said as though begging, "Val?"

"Yeah. Oh, wait. Hold on. Let me check and make sure it hung up."

Miki heard silence.

Valencia said, sounding like she was moving around while she spoke. "Yeah, okay. Sorry."

From behind Miki, headlights suddenly blazed, and an immediate, horrendous sound of screeching rubber against pavement shrilled into the nighttime air. A *thud*, an insurmountable shove, and a crushing weight struck Miki's frame. She was pushed up against her truck. Her fancy bag and iPhone were catapulted into the air as a monstrous force squashed her flesh, bones, and organs, crumbling her hips and legs into a flat mass. Her head jerked back, and she fought to keep her mind alive.

The three-thousand-pound vehicle rapidly shifted into reverse, allowing Miki to crumble to the ground. Her head met the concrete. Only the sound of skidding tires and the smell of hot fiery rubber lingered.

Suddenly standing over her and peering down into the recesses of her eyes, an older man with fear oozing from his face asked, "Ma'am, are you alive?"

Miki's blood wet lids barely separated. The look on his face told her he expected her not to answer.

She was completely still, laying in the darkness.

Physically and mentally.

The only thing moving was a heavy tear that gravity sent traveling down the side of her shocked and frightened face.

The concerned and boisterous male voice said, "I saw the license plate. It read 14KGOLD. If you can hear me, help is on the way. Please don't even begin to try to move."

She didn't.

She couldn't.

She felt absolutely nothing.

# 26

## "Sugar Walls"

### Teela

Teela visited Brandi right after work the next day. Brandi had changed her plea to guilty, her bail was doubled, and she was waiting to have her trial date set. She was not leaving anytime soon.

It was a one-sided visit, and Brandi said very little to her new friend. The conversation from the other side of the glass was taken in by Brandi, who looked deep into Teela's eyes and only listened. This time it was Teela who spoke like a robot. And this time, Brandi was indeed crying.

"I remember the sound. It was right next door to my room. I was nine.

"Daddy would wait outside of their own master bedroom upstairs, standing guard, most of the time with his arms crossed over his wide belly. He'd have a stern look on his face. And the louder the sounds got, the sooner it would be over. When it became quiet, he'd open the door and go inside, and the visitor would leave. But not before handing my dad some money in the hallway or at the front door.

"One time, while the loud fucking noise went on, Dad

opened the door and watched. And he reached in his pants and pulled out his thing and yanked it.

"One night Dad went ahead downstairs and slept on the couch while the man was with my mother all night. I heard them go on for a while. And this time, I was the one who just had to see. The door was left half open, and by the dim light of the tiny bedside lamp I watched him mount my mother. They were under the covers and his butt thrust was like he was on fire. She moaned and turned her head up toward the ceiling with squinted eyes. I saw them do it and I kept watching. My mother was in a pained pleasure state. It was like she wished it would stop or wished it wouldn't. But the look on her face was a glow of passion that made my heart ache. They kept going and going, in the same position. And it took a long time before he finished his business. But I guess I still kept watching, a long time or not. I had told the members of SA before that I'd watch my parents have sex. But the truth is that I watched a strange man fuck my mother while my father slept downstairs.

"About four long years later, around the time puberty had just about beat me up, my bedroom door opened and a man in the dark walked in my room. My door then shut and the man came closer. I screamed and my dad jerked the door open, walked up to me fast, stood over me with his evil, scruffy face and his overweight body, and removed his belt. 'You will keep your mouth shut. I'll be right back. You do as you're told.' And so I did. I can still hear the sound of that belt buckle jiggling as he walked out. That man he left in my teenage room was my own uncle.

"I remember one night, my mom made noises from her

room, and I made noises from my room at the same time. We moaned this particular night, together, with only a wall separating us. At one point, the louder I got the quieter she got, and I could have sworn her moans turned to whines, like she was crying for my pain. But then her groans stopped. And I heard her bedroom door open and close. I never heard her working in her room again after that. For the next five years, I guess I was the sexual breadwinner of the family.

"I can't explain it but in an odd way, I learned to like the feeling. It felt good to have a man's dick inside of me. It felt good to have my neck kissed. It felt good to have someone's mouth on my vagina and their fingers inside of me. I'd have an orgasm while I cried, but I couldn't stop it from rushing. I'd hear my door open and my heart would stop, yet I'd begin pulling down my panties by the time the stranger got into my bed. It wasn't like I learned to hate those men so much. I just hated my dad for allowing it to happen.

"My mother sent me far away to go to school, and he died while I was in college. I missed the funeral on purpose. But still, she didn't leave him on her own. Kinda why I could never understand her telling me to leave Austin. I went to see her the other day for the first time in years and probably won't go back. She's still grieving over him. See, God took my dad, otherwise they'd still be together today. By the way, he died after having a massive heart attack while he was fucking a hooker less than a mile away from our home. Some things never change.

"I suppose all of this is what taught me to be fearful. I was sold by my father. Through sex, I took back the power I didn't have as a child. And only God can grant me the power of the healing I need so badly now."

Brandi's eyes were red from shedding stinging tears for her friend. She lowered the receiver for a minute and wiped her face. The tears clouded her vision, and she fought to focus her eyes and mind upon Teela. She put the receiver to her ear and simply said, "I'm so proud of you." She sniffled like a five-year-old. "And since I'm sure he never apologized, I want to apologize for what he did to you. I'm sorry, Teela."

Teela's nose was flushed. Her eyes were dry. She winked. "Thank you. And I'm sorry for what you're going through." Her voice was nasal.

Brandi nodded as a simple acceptance of Teela's words. "Sometimes, we have to get lost to find ourselves. In time, I'll be good as new."

"Me too, Brandi. Me too."

# 27

"Naughty Girl"

## Miki

*More than one year later*

It was early September, the very beginning of fall, though the stubborn summer temperatures still held on tight as the late day's heat clung in the motionless air. At The Addiction Center, the Sexaholics meeting for the evening was a special one, with a guest speaker that Rachel Cummings had invited personally.

The meeting was held in the theatre-style auditorium in the main complex of the rehab center. The comfortable, cushioned seats were jet black. The new room with a stage was added to the complex less than two months earlier.

There was standing room only. Miki sat in her shiny new wheelchair on that stage, ready to address the group. And everyone was all ears. The theme for the evening's meeting was *Make Your Mess Your Message*. Not a member was stirring. You could hear a pin drop.

"I was just a shy kid, and very, very skinny," Miki told the dozens and dozens of people. She wore all white, with silver jewelry and silver flats. Her hair was freshly straightened, and her sheer makeup was flawless. Her eyes were wide, and her face gave off a humble glow. Her expression almost seemed pure. "But I grew out of both, as most who knew me a year ago can attest to. My younger sister, Adore, has always been thin. Built like a twelve-year-old. Her slender little self is right there standing near the wall." People followed Miki's gesture at her sister, who stood in the back of the room with a soft smile. Also standing in the back was Miki's mother, with a face identical to Miki's. "My sister got that body from my mother, who's back there also." She nodded to her mom. "She helps take care of my seven-year-old son, and my niece, who's my sister's fourteen-month-old. Yeah, my mom is just hitting sixty, and is still one hundred eighteen pounds, just like she was when she was in her twenties. But for some reason, especially when I was younger, I was handed the body of the women on my father's side. Hippy and rumpalicious. They say I was built like a cross between JLo and Janet. I'll admit that I used my body to my advantage. In my case, the boys never noticed me before I started to fill out. But I quickly saw their attention as my fuel. It drove me. It gave me what I didn't have. I got noticed.

"I worked as a topless dancer, once I got some serious breasts after high school, and then I stripped for a while. That got me paid. I never went to college. I wasn't very smart like my baby sister, but I got by. In my mind it was dumb to spend another four years in school when I didn't end up graduating from high school until I was nineteen. I was held back twice.

"I was the fast one, not my sister, Adore. Right around the time I started developing and my attention-getting booty made its long-awaited appearance, I would sometimes sneak out of the house. I'd go to the homes of boys in my neighborhood and give them blow jobs. I'd have phone sex with girls from school while they masturbated. Girls whose voices I knew, though I couldn't even tell you what they looked like. I just took their calls and got them off. I even had threesomes the summer before ninth grade. Needless to say, I became very popular. By the age of thirteen I lost my virginity and lost my mind. I loved sex. It was heaven on earth. I immediately craved it after the very first time. My first-time sex partner was a virgin, too, but we took each other to fuckdumcum. It was all I could think about afterwards. I came four times. He came five.

"What I knew for sure was that sex was the one thing I was really, really good at. I used it to my advantage. Call me a ho or a slut, but I admit that I got what I could from men because I believed they'd surely try to get what they wanted from me. I saw my vagina as valuable. Not my mind. But my vagina.

"No one could have ever really given me what sex did for me. And no, no one raped me when I was little. No one assaulted me. My father or uncles never tried to do freaky things with me. I will say that my father was a little distant. A little constipated as far as communicating his emotions. More so with me than with my baby sister. Or so I thought. Some will say that is the root of it all. But I say, the bottom line is, he was there. My mother made up for his inability to connect emotionally. I don't think I ever blamed myself, like something was wrong with me. Yes, my sister and I battled for attention and wanted what the other had. Maybe I thought she had Daddy and I didn't, but nothing earth-shattering happened until I crossed the line and pushed the limits with the ultimate sister betrayal. I slept with her now ex-husband. As I said, I just didn't care. Some say I was a nympho. I mean like Samantha from *Sex and the City*, I had to have it. But, I say I was just hypersexual with one hell of a nerve. Plain and simple.

"Years ago I left my son's father after being with him for four years, but I kept on seeing the few men I had on the side the whole time I was with him. He moved on and got married. I didn't care. I continued to let him give me what I needed physically. He desired and pleased me. That was all that mattered.

"Over a year ago I was sleeping with—no, I was *fucking*, a fellow SA member. The sex was really good. He was my cohort in crime as far as falling off the wagon. The benefit in being with him was, again, that he was someone to please me and temporarily fill my feelings of worthlessness with being unlovable. It was just another means to cope, I suppose. The thing is, I never took the time to stop and ask him if he was available. I just didn't care that I was fucking someone else's man.

"I was even fucking a woman. My best friend, who I never noticed had fallen in love with me. In a roundabout way, I pushed her right into the arms of my boyfriend. I didn't notice that, either. But what the hell, I mean I did bring her into our bed.

"I also had an older sugar daddy. He handed over the cash when I needed it and I'd break him off some pussy, so we were good. He was way old enough to be my father and threw down well enough to keep my attention. He could have been on Viagra, I don't know. Like I said, I usually didn't take the time to ask questions. I didn't assume his wife knew about it. After all, she was suffering from dementia, and from what he told me, their marriage was sexless. He got what he needed. What I needed was new clothes, jewelry, and the latest shoes. I was his mistress and I used him for my financial benefit.

"I'd just finished fucking him in a suite at the hotel where I worked, on the night before my boss was going to fire me for having sex in the hotel rooms during business hours. That day, I was wearing a pair of red Manolo Blahnik shoes I'd bought with some cash my sugar daddy had given me not long before, as well as a diamond bracelet he'd just put on my wrist, when his daughter, who definitely did not have dementia, sped what I'm told was the family's black Benz CL5 straight into me at forty miles an hour as I was about to get in my car, and smashed the curves of my lower body right up against the metal of my SUV. She'd spied on her dad when he called me and waited in the parking lot of the hotel where he and I had just screwed. That was the day her mother died, right after her father left their home to be with me.

"To this day she has never been found. And he, my sugar daddy, moved a young black woman into his home about three months later. But thirty days after that, he drove off a cliff in Malibu and committed suicide, probably from the stress of his wife dying, and because he yearned for his missing daughter. He'd changed his will and left everything to his live-in lover. And so, here I am, cured of my addiction, though I'll never walk again. But I still say, even with all the guilt of that, that day I got hit was truly the moment I hugged a new day." She took a deep breath and gave a deep exhale.

"By the way, my girlfriend and my boyfriend are now

a bona fide couple. The night of the accident, she ran to my bedside quicker than he did and even confessed her love for me. But I pushed her away once I remembered the phone call we'd had seconds before I was hit. Her call waiting accidentally became a three-way, just like the three-way in my bed, and I overheard them make plans to meet that evening at their regular spot. Or maybe she meant for me to hear. I'll never know. They'd been seeing each other behind my back for who knows how long. And the funny thing is, as bad as she wanted to be a mother, she got pregnant by my man the very first time we all slept together. I remember the no-condom moment well. They have a three-month-old son named after my ex. The baby is the spitting image of his biracial face.

"But see, all of that has to be okay, because it's the same thing I was dishing out. They were freaks just like me, and when you take risks and push the limits anything can happen. It's part of the pursuit-of-sex game we played day after day. For me, I didn't give a damn about anyone. So turnabout is fair play, right?

"As far as my situation personally, I can never have another genital orgasm because of the extreme nerve degeneration to my body. Though some can experience that, I cannot. I will never again feel a penis inside of my vagina. I can never mount a man and bounce like the stripper I was years ago. I am a paraplegic, the result of a complete spinal cord injury, having no voluntary motor or sensory function below my waist. I have use of my arms, but I have no feeling in my legs whatsoever.

"And yes, I'm here to shock you. I'm here to plead with you. I'm here to beg you. Please don't end up like me. The very thing I craved is the reason why God has me right here in front of you. To be a benefit to those for whom it's not too late.

"Believe it or not, I'm comfortable in my own skin now. I thank God for that. The devil in my head that kept me lusting is gone. So in a strange way, I don't blame the young woman who ran me down. It was a blessing in disguise. I thank God for my life, and never again will I fail to say *I love you,* or to tell someone that I care.

"I pray that you find an easier way to kill the devil in your head than this. I may never take a step again, but you could be one step away from sexual healing. It takes just one step at a time. Don't leave here seeing it as a game. Don't give up. Don't lust.

"As the lovely Rachel Cummings says, you'll always be a sexaholic. But the first day of the rest of your life starts now, with making sure the anniversary date of your sobriety is today.

"By the way—though, as I said, I don't have feelings in my lower body—let me tell you just because I can't control my hip and vaginal muscles, I do, however, have nerve endings above the waist. And baby, the senses in the tongue, lips, hands, and on the skin, mainly face, neck, shoulders, and back . . . watch out." Miki snapped her right-hand fingers, which generated snickers from those who she spoke to. She managed a cute grin. "I give new meaning to the term *oral sex.* The mouth can do glorious things. And touching, kissing, and cuddling never felt so good. And the breasts respond . . . please believe me." Her smile widened and then narrowed. "Sex is what you do. Sexuality is what you are. I'm still sexual. It's a part of our nature to be sexual. But sexuality is about the whole person, not just the genitals.

"I do have feelings in my heart. Those feelings are reserved for my family, my sweet little second-grade son, whose stepmother is now my friend, and for the only man I have sex with now and forever, my husband, who is sitting right there." She pointed her head and touched her heart with her fist to a man with curly hair, about ten years older than her, sitting on the end in the first row. He smiled large, flashing his deep-set dimples as people strained their necks to see him. He touched his heart with his fist back. "He won't stand. He'll tell you it's not about him. I met him at the hospital the day my mother and sister and niece and son came to take me home. He was an orderly who wheeled me out into the parking lot, and we've been together ever since. He loves me, including my atrophied legs and my catheter. He's amazing. And yes, this might be too much information, but even though I told you I'd never feel a penis in my vagina again, that doesn't mean there hasn't been one in there, okay?" She grinned at him and they both blushed. "Plus, he's smiling like that because I'm much more of a giver now. I get my pleasure in many ways. And believe me, he ain't complaining.

"Please know that I wouldn't change a thing." Miki glanced down at her digital wristwatch. "I've been sober for three hundred seventy-nine days, thirteen hours, and fifteen minutes. I've also been a whole woman for that long.

"My name is Miki Summers Bolton. I'm Marcellas Bolton's wife, and I, like you, am a sexaholic. May God grant you the serenity to accept the things you cannot change, courage to change the things you can, and wisdom to know the difference. Thank you for listening to my story. And good night."

The crowd sprang to their feet and began to applaud as Miki nodded. Her face lit up with a smile that led to a laugh. Her husband approached the front of the room and stood next to Rachel Cummings who shook his hand as he waited for his wife to give him the signal to escort her offstage.

Standing in the front row was Dwayne, clapping loudly. Next to him was a new female member, very young, very shapely, and very pretty. He leaned toward her and whispered in her ear. She giggled, looking shy. He laughed, looking proud of himself, took in a quick view of her cleavage, and then continued to look toward Miki, still clapping.

And a few seats over was Teela, with tears streaming down her face as she wiped her green eyes and sniffled. She caught Miki's eye, and they gave each other a wink.

Teela's wink said, *Well done.*

Miki's wink said, *You'll be just fine. Keep showing up.*

Teela decided not to tell Miki about Tariq.

She'd concluded that some things were best handled on their own.

And this time, she was right.

Now Valencia had Tariq.

One who also showed up sitting next to Teela was Austin, a newly admitted sex addict who now had his own place. He kept coming to the meetings just to show Teela, who now owned her own home in Baldwin Hills, he had changed and wanted only her. Though she wasn't quite convinced yet.

All the members in the auditorium had shown up another day to take back their power of choice, step by step, with the goal of obtaining sexual sobriety, though some would take longer than others. The objective was to gain control over their addictions, and to forgive themselves and one another.

And the person crying the most was in the very last row.

Valencia Sanchez.

She caught Miki's eye, too.

"Sorry," Valencia mouthed quietly, touching her heart with her fist, wearing the pain and guilt of her life on her sorrowful face.

Miki nodded and touched her heart with her fist back. She flashed a tiny smile and then it grew a little bigger. Big enough to expose her right dimple and she mouthed, "Love you."

Miki thought, *If Adore could forgive me, surely I can forgive Valencia.*

They had each hugged the possibilities of a new day.

And a new life.

Abstaining.

One way or another.

For information on the 12 Steps and 12 Traditions of Sexaholics Anonymous, or to test yourself by answering twenty questions to assess whether you may have a problem with sexual addiction, you may visit the Sexaholics Anonymous website, at www .sa.org.

*Secrets are a darkness in your heart.*
*Free your mind and the rest will follow.*

*Pynk*

# BEING SEX-SEE

## From the Oversexed to the Undersexed

Thank you for experiencing my second Pynk novel, *Sexaholics*, about the lives of four women who are oversexed addicts. Now, on the other end, there are women who are very opposite from Miki, Valencia, Teela, and Brandi, in that they are sexually repressed, yet they're really quite the same. They're women who are where they are in their lives, regarding families, and jobs, and money, and sex, because of what the world has taught them about each life dynamic. And sex is a dynamic part of life. Sex is a necessity of life.

The title of my next novel is *Sixty Nine*, from which a preview chapter immediately follows. Even though it is erotica, it is not about the literal sexual position 69; it is about three undersexed women, Magnolia, Rebe, and Darla, who were all born in 1969, and who are about to turn the big 4-0. They are dissatisfied with their lives in general; more specifically, when it comes to sex, they yearn for more than their usual missionary positions.

I watched *The Oprah Winfrey Show* awhile back when she had as a guest a sex therapist named Dr. Laura Berman who talked about sexual problems in women. Some women do not have orgasms and they fake it with their men, who are none the wiser because often they get theirs, so that's all he wrote. There are also some women who have little tiny, non-earth-shattering orgasms that don't quite live up to what they see in porno movies or hear about from their sexual-creature-like friends. Some women get so close to having the big O, but then they get stuck and hold back because of a thought that creeps into their heads that tells them they're trashy or slutty for feeling so good.

Orgasms are both physical and mental, and though some women really do have medical reasons that affect their libido and their ability to experience an orgasm— usually involving their pelvic floor, or a side effect of certain medications—a lot of women fall into the one basic sex trap that I feel so strongly about dispelling. The thought that we've bought into from the time we were little: *that sex is dirty*.

As some of you may know from reading my first Pynk book, *Erotic City*, that's the main reason why I decided to write about sex, to hopefully educate through fiction.

I've heard people say that writing about sex is sinful and that if people would only listen to the word of God to guide them, and cease falling off of the "good walk" path, we erotica writers would then and only then be cleansed and pure and righteous. But I am here to tell you I do not buy into that. That is one of the reasons why we women are so repressed today. We are afraid. Well, please know that I am not ashamed or afraid. And I hope you're not, either. By the way, isn't judgment a sin?

While I definitely believe that moderation is key, be- cause we must have boundaries and not run off hog wild, so to speak, it is my desire to contribute in some way to the liberation of women and show all sides of sex, good and bad. But in the long run, I hope my books bring awareness and encourage women to love their bodies and feel good about reading scenes that turn them on so much they can't wait to get home and take care of themselves and/or pounce on their mates. I hope my writing teaches women about what healthy sex should be. Sometimes you learn that by reading about what healthy sex is not. To read erotica is not sinful, and it is my desire that the guilt so many of us women feel will eventually be shattered to pieces.

We must learn to tell the truth about how we feel about sex and about what we think about sex, and figure out where those bad thoughts came from. Also, as Milan Kennedy, the main character in *Erotic City* stated, we must know that women have wet dreams, too, and we cannot be afraid to ask for what we want in and out of bed. We can be sexually equal to men. That's what the feminist movement of the '60s and '70s was all about, a freeing and de-conditioning of gender discrimination and how society views females. It's been about overall equality relating to the right to vote and equal pay, which President Obama protected with a law early in his administration— but also women's rights issues, ranging from reproductive rights, like access to the pill and abortion, to the right to breastfeed in public, and even the need to create specific sexual-harassment policies to define exactly what harassment is, even when it comes to men as the victims.

We women are not second-class citizens. Nor are we sex objects.

All in all, views about sex are sometimes deemed to be issues of morality and issues of sexism.

I'd like women to learn to be what I call, Sex-See . . . seeing sex in a whole new way, mentally, visually, and physically.

After all, good sexual health involves the spiritual and physical body. We are sensual and sexual beings. We are allowed to experience sexual pleasure. We have to let go of negative messages about sex among consenting adults—negative messages that tell us sex is wrong. I believe we can make a conscious decision to dispel those messages that breed guilt.

I'm talking about safe sex. Yes, there are prices to be paid relating to teen pregnancy, HIV, and so forth. As a good friend of mine says, fuck responsibly. And I totally agree. You are responsible for yourself. Make good decisions based upon who you are. And take in the rest as learning tools. When in Rome, don't necessarily do as the Romans do, unless you think it's the best decision for you. Most important, love yourself first.

If you are fearful and keep thinking you shouldn't talk in bed or let go and enjoy your orgasm, ask yourself what it is that you're afraid of. We all had messages about sex when we were growing up. Most times, if sex was brought up, we were told it was vulgar and not acceptable, especially when we were young girls. And we were told we shouldn't talk about it. We got dressed up and went to church and the information we came away with was that sex should be experienced only for purposes of procreation. I know that's how my parents raised me, even though my mother was more liberated than most. Back then, parents who wanted their daughters to remain virgins until marriage surely had good intentions, but the other side of the coin is to encourage safe sex, because most of the time teens are going to do it anyway (I know I did), yet still feel guilty afterward. In my opinion, that's when the confusion starts. When I was in high school it seems a few of the Catholic schoolgirls, the ones who learned about God from the time they were little, were the fastest girls in the neighborhood, simply because the forbidden tempted them so much that they thought they were missing out, which caused them to be even more curious than those who were not as restricted. The more you tell someone they can't do something, the more they want to do it, kind of like Adam and Eve. And from a biblical standpoint, it's all about our own individual interpretations, and that's a whole other conversation.

Now back to the orgasm! ☺ The sex therapist on *Oprah* said when you're about to experience your own orgasm, if you hold yourself back because of the negative voices from your past, you will cheat yourself and disallow the erotic experience of a burst of a beautiful, euphoric, intense pleasure rolling through your body that, from a physiological standpoint, can bond you to your partner just because of the pheromones you produce from the rush itself. That is a proven fact. I know there are some women who still hold back, even though they may not hear the negative voices from the past, because the sensation is so strong that they get scared and freeze up. I'm there with you. I can *surely* understand that! Though a good multiple orgasm might be right behind your fear to cum like the queen you are.

If you're one of the many women who have repressed feelings about sex, and you feel you're too frigid and rigid in bed, maybe you need to think about what you can do to begin to let go of the embarrassing and shameful ties that bind. Refuse to carry those old messages and voices in your head that tell you sex is lewd and immoral and improper. If necessary, think in terms of experiencing romance with your partner, as opposed to quickies, so that you can take the time to really excite yourself and your mate. Take the time to talk about each other's erogenous zones. Make foreplay last longer, starting with a sex text early in the day. Tell yourself you deserve to be pleasured, that it's good and loving, and that you'll still be a nice girl and a respectable lady in the morning. Remember people used to say that women would ask the man, "Will you respect me in the morning?" Why is it that men never ask that?

Anyway, think in terms of nonmissionary, and feel free to masturbate healthily if you so desire. Masturbating in moderation is not slutty either.

Train yourself to replace the outdated messages with new ones. It's called a sexual adjustment. Remember, you are a sensual and sexual woman, and you're allowed to experience a happy and fulfilling sex life. Live up to your full orgasmic potential. Release your inner vixen. Become more comfortable with your sexuality, maybe by taking a pole-dancing class. Try new positions or have sex someplace other than the norm. Go to a Passion Party and try out some of the new products there, like a Triple Tickle Dolphin, with a fluttering tail that stimulates the clit, and tickling tails that can be inserted into both the anus and the vagina. Live out your healthy fantasies.

While you turn the page to check out the characters in *Sixty-Nine* as they struggle to escape from their undersexed worlds, keep in mind that these three coming-of-age women make conscious decisions to explore erotic sides of themselves they never knew existed. I call it sexxxploration.

The bottom line is that *Sixty-Nine* is a liberating story about sisterhood and friendship, and about how our past experiences and beliefs can influence our views about life, and about sex. How shame and dysfunction and abuse can keep us repressed. And how guilt can keep us from truly viewing sex as a pleasurable act. *Sixty-Nine* is a novel about going beyond one's self-inflicted boundaries to fully experience true sensuality. But by taking these risks, we never know what lies on the other side of our comfort zones.

So, my dear readers, enjoy this opening-act chapter preview as Magnolia, Rebe, and Darla find out what it's like to go beyond the missionary, and experience the erotic edge of a real-life sixty-nine.

# PREVIEW CHAPTER

# SIXTY-NINE

⚮

## by Pynk

*November 2010*

# 1

# A Sexier Side of Me

Girl, I started my period on my own damn wedding night. That should've been a definite warning sign that my marriage would not last through the ebb and flow, so to speak, of holy matrimony," Rebe Richardson said with a millisecond smirk on her chocolate face. Her micro-braided head rolled toward the two best friends she'd known since college. She tried to keep her words just above the blaring celebratory music in the background.

Rebe sat upon the contemporary purple leather stool at the huge, fully packed bar with her long, bare legs crossed like a prima ballerina. She even pointed her toes. Her stately gams, formed from her days a dancer, extended far beyond the hem of her little black dress. She sat to the right, with Magnolia Butler in the middle, and Darla Howard on the other end.

The trendy hotspot, called Flavour, was decorated deliciously in pale blues and lavender, with dark wood bar tables, draped private VIP rooms, and two mirrored, elongated bars. Oversized plasma TVs graced every wall, showing last-minute countdowns from most major cities. The nightclub was located in the Coconut Grove area of

South Florida, where two of the gussied-up ladies lived. Magnolia lived in Playland, Florida.

It was New Year's Eve.

The well-promoted, well-attended bash was wall-to-wall packed.

The sounds of Whitney Houston's "Exhale (Shoop Shoop)" serenaded the discolike, neon-lit room. The soft mixture of blue and pink LED flashing-light designs bounced along the walls and from the ceiling. The glass dance floor was a pastel menagerie of light grids that grooved to the beat of the popular R&B music.

And it was 11:46 p.m.

"What? And that stopped you from having sex on your honeymoon night? Because of your monthly visitor?" Darla had made sure to lean toward her friends to speak loudly, with her light brown, precision-cut hair, platinum hoop earrings, and liquid silver minidress. She picked up her fluted champagne glass and took a tiny sip of the yellow label Brut, extending her French manicured pinky as she swallowed.

Rebe squinted her nose and eyes like a foul wind had just blown by. "Ewwww, yes, of course it stopped me," she said, squirming in her seat.

"I know that's right," Magnolia confirmed, taking a big gulp from her blended vodka and peach schnapps. Her scarlet red nails matched her knee-length strapless chiffon dress. Her gold satin slingbacks were high and sexy.

"And you didn't see to it that at least he had fun? I mean, you know," Darla asked.

"I did. Well, a little bit." Rebe paused with a hold-up look for them both. "Hey, why are you guys all up in my stuff anyway? Damn." She sucked her tongue and gave a sassy snarl.

Darla raised her newly threaded brows and darted her head back. "You're the one who took us there."

"Yeah, well I wish I hadn't. I was just trying to share my wedding-night disaster with my girls, that's all." Rebe twisted her glossed lips and raised her glass, tipping a swallow of the ice-cold Pierre Jouët champagne into her mouth.

Magnolia kept both hands on her cocktail glass. "Hell, at least you had a wedding night. It's probably a good guess that I'll never find out what it's like to even say I do. I mean after all, thirty-nine will be gone in, ah," Magnolia peeked at her oval diamond watch, "twelve minutes and counting."

Darla, the dental hygienist, tilted her head toward Magnolia as her full lips smiled, exposing her perfect, bleached teeth. "Me too, girl. I'll be saying good-bye to thirty-nine right along with ya."

Rebe added, "Please. I'm right behind both of you. I remember when we were younger, we thought forty was damn near elderly. I mean all of our parents were the very age we are now. Tell me, where in the heck did the time go? My Lord." She shook her head and gave Magnolia a reflective gaze.

Magnolia's ginger-colored face beamed. "That's true, huh? It was back in 1989 when we were at Miami-Dade, cramming and partying and doing our twenty-year-old thing. Heck, was that two decades ago already?" She had question marks in her huge eyes.

Rebe nodded. "Yes ma'am, it was." Her eyes shifted to

her other friend. "And then Darla, you and Aaron ran off and eloped and left it at only two musketeers. Excuse you."

Darla ran her fingertips along the back of her closely tapered neckline. Her slender face indicated surprise and displeasure. "Oh please. Don't bring him up. Not tonight."

Magnolia's eyes were warm. "Darla, we love you. I know it's been five years since he passed, but you had a solid marriage and a man who loved you. My relationship lasted one damn year before he up and left me, just because I wouldn't act like a stripper in bed, unlike his husband-stealing secretary. Aaron loved you for you, Darla. And for that, you're blessed."

Darla's honey-colored shoulders dipped. She leaned back and then forward. "I know that. But I do miss him. Lord knows I do. But one day, I'm gonna need to move on and get me someone, or should I say, get me some, period."

"But Darla, come on now. Not even one dick in five years? Not one?" Rebe held up a solo index finger.

"No. And?"

"And, how do you do it?" Rebe asked.

"I mind my own damn business, that's what I do. Just like you didn't want us up in your stuff a minute ago." She cut her eyes from Rebe to Magnolia, who gave her a sly grin. "And Magnolia, we know you get more dick than all the ladies up in this club tonight put together."

Magnolia gave a half-gasp and put her hand to her chest. "Oh please, talking about minding someone's business. So now I'm a slut, is that what you're saying? All because Rebe didn't do her man right on her wedding night."

Rebe shook her head and managed a snicker.

Darla put her hand up. "I'm just saying, I mean honestly, you've been in more relationships than we have."

"I have. Yeah. You're right. Don't trip now just because I can catch, you know. That hasn't been the problem. But damn, if I'm so successful in the bedroom, then why did Neal leave my ass for his secretary? Hell, that was the longest relationship I've been in and I got dumped. Shoot, they all leave anyway. No biggie." Magnolia readjusted her long, off-black ponytail, which hung down to the middle of her back. "And Trent left, too. Went back to his baby's mama just because she liked to have threesomes with him. Sorry-ass fool."

Rebe said, "Then that says a lot about him. You two were just different. But I mean, I did hear it's not only about how much sex you have, but also what you're doing in the bedroom that matters. I'd be the first one to say I failed if that's the case."

"Who'd you *hear* that from?" asked Magnolia after she took another swallow.

Rebe looked toward her friends, and then looked past Darla. "I don't remember. Somewhere." Her eyes said she was distracted by nearby testosterone. "Anyway, the point was that we women should get off our backs and get on our knees. It's about opening our minds and our legs. I mean, like definitely having safe sex, but having great sex, too."

Darla stared squarely at Rebe. "Did you hear about that before or after you got stingy on your own wedding night?"

Rebe kept her sights behind Darla's back. "Very funny," she said without even a snicker. "I'm just saying, I mean

I was left by Roderick after he accused me of being too missionary, so like I said, I know how you feel, Magnolia." Rebe smiled demurely, but not at Magnolia, while uncrossing her legs.

Darla added, "Hell, I'm gonna be myself, no matter what. Screw what they want. And I don't care what these women out here are doing in this crazy-ass world nowadays anyway. I'm sorry but I've just gotta be me."

Rebe batted her eyes and inched her sights back to her buddies. "Yeah, but haven't you ever wondered what it would be like to just go buck-ass wild and freak like there's no tomorrow? To fuck a stranger or have an orgy or buy all the sex toys you can and just fuck yourself in every orifice all night long? Haven't you been curious?"

Magnolia said immediately, "No."

"Yes you have."

"Orgy. Hell, no. Masturbate all night, maybe." Magnolia took a drink.

Rebe eyed the view behind Darla again and her cheeks began to blush. "I'll take the first one. Shit, I might just walk right up to him"—she nodded toward a man sitting two bar stools over from Darla, then slyly looked down toward her glass—"and ask him to take me home and fuck me like the new freak I need to be. Like he's mad about slavery and shit. I mean fuck me like it's 1999, instead of 2009. Fuck me like I'm the last fuck of his life and he's about to get hit by a Mack truck in the morning." She shook her torso, like she had shivers running up and down the slit of her vagina.

Darla turned around and saw a big man, very long, like he could be maybe six-seven if he stood, with a low-cut fade and a perfect goatee and light skin, eyeing down

Rebe like she was the last corner of Grandma's secret recipe macaroni and cheese on Thanksgiving Day. "Damn," she said, turning back around to give Rebe a high five with her eyes.

Magnolia glanced over behind Darla, too. "Yeah, right. You do that. And then, and only then, I *will* have an orgy," she said with sarcasm.

"No, you won't," Rebe said as a dare.

Magnolia shrugged her body-glittered shoulders. "I don't have to worry about a damn orgy because you're not about to say one single thing to that man. Not Darling Rebe. And yes, he is fine now. I will say that. Yes I will."

Rebe straightened her back. "Yeah, well, I guess you really don't know me like you think you do."

"Please. You don't know yourself." Magnolia looked assured.

Rebe said, "Maybe none of us knows ourselves the way we should." She turned her body all the way toward them and recrossed her legs. "I'll tell you what. How about if for 2009, we turn up our libidos and make some real resolutions? Some sexual resolutions. Something different. How about if we go into the New Year shattering our beliefs about sex? Living our sexy dreams, out loud." She used her hands to assist her words. "I just think we've set these boundaries for ourselves, and maybe they've limited our ability to really experience the erotic, sexual side of us. I mean, these comfort zones are getting about tired if you ask me. Honestly, I've had enough of this frigid adulthood." She circled the rim of her glass with her fingertip. "I don't know about you two, but I've been thinking about this a lot. I'm perimenopausal, but I'm about to cross over the erotic line and dive off the fucking edge for real. I'm about to say good-bye to my inhibitions. Hell, it's a new year." She leaned closer toward them. "I say we lighten the fuck up like we should have twenty years ago." She swigged her drink.

Darla shook her head. "Rebe, girl, please. After all, we can't go back."

"Who says?"

Magnolia reminded her, "We're forty. Hello." Her eyes said *hello*, too. "Maybe your dynamic hard body forgot your age but my arthritic knees sure as hell remember."

Rebe smirked and glanced up at the time on the television screen over the bar. "Hold up now, we're not forty yet. And for the next five minutes, I'm about to dare even myself and open my mind and my legs in a way I've never done before. I'm about to take back my sexual freedom, and my first step is—get ready for this—I'm gonna start stripping at night."

Darla asked, looking amazed, "Stripping. Oh Lord, that's the bubbly talking now. I know you were a dance instructor years ago and all, but, who's gonna hire a forty-year-old stripper?"

"I already have my pole-dancing class set, if you don't mind."

"What? *You* an exotic dancer?" Magnolia watched Rebe's eyes, which were again focused on the hunk to the left.

The crowd started to get louder.

The buzz was more intense.

Folks' glasses were being filled to the top.

People moved closer together.

"Yes. It's a New Year's class specifically scheduled for brave, sexy, daring women like me who want to break out of the box, or at least that's what the brochure said. So don't hate." Rebe again moved her eyes to Magnolia and Darla. "Anyway ladies, what about you? What is it that you've always wanted to do but never had the nerve to do?"

Magnolia took a long gulp as the bartender walked up. She smiled and pointed toward her and her friends' glasses for fill-ups. The bow-tie-wearing lady nodded and walked away. Magnolia leaned along the shiny, speckled bar and spoke as if she were telling the FBI's most classified secret. "Well, actually, a few months ago I was talking on the phone to this guy, and he told me I sounded like a phone sex operator. I mean he pissed me off a little, but later I actually thought of what it would be like to do that. You know. Turn someone on over the phone while they jack off, and maybe even find a way to get paid for it." She dropped her sexy smirk and sat up straight. "After all, I have been jobless for nearly a month."

Darla wore a look of wonder. "What? I know you got laid off and could use the money, but you, Magnolia? I can't even picture you doing pillow talk, whether it's for money or for free. I mean I know you get yours, but I'm sorry, I just can't picture it." She shook her head. "But I must admit, something's gotten into you lately. Sitting up in here with your little tight red dress on and shit. Usually, we can't even get you out of your velour sweats. You go ahead on."

"Whatever."

Rebe asked, "You mean like have phone sex with people as in on the regular for money?"

"Maybe," Magnolia replied as all three drinks were refreshed. "Thanks," she said to the bartender, who then took another person's drink order.

"Closet freak," said Darla, close to Magnolia.

Magnolia angled her head. "Well, what about you, Miss Stick in the Mud?" she asked Darla.

"You know what?" Darla's eyes got big. "To tell you the truth, I wanted to open a business. I mean, I only have a little life insurance money left. I figure I could try and do something with it before I blow it all."

"Nice. And?" Rebe asked, fighting her eyes to keep them from visually licking the man's face behind Darla.

"And, I was wondering what it would take for me to open an adult toy store."

"An adult toy store? And you call me a closet freak?" Magnolia asked, looking baffled.

Rebe touched her shoulder. "Darla, you should do that. I think that would be sexy and fun and maybe even profitable."

"No, I can't. What would my mom think? And my in-laws. And my brother. Good Lord. Joseph would think I lost my mind."

"Well good, maybe he should. Losing our old minds for new ones might be just what we need. Besides, you don't have to tell them if you don't want to. That's on you." Rebe's eyes flipped between both of her friends. "You know, ever since I can remember, we've been so damn worried about being proper and always so bothered by what people think of us. Well, I'm shaking that off and I'm all for the philosophy of, 'what you think of me is none of my damn business.'" Rebe downed a long gulp and smacked her lips. "So what do you say? Are we all in? All three of us? Me, stripping; Magnolia, you with your phone sex website."

Magnolia jumped in fast. "Oh heck no, I didn't say

anything about a website. I said I'd try it. I don't know how but I hear it can be a legitimate home-based business. Something like that."

"Okay, whatever. Try it." Darla made air quotes with her fingers and again said, "Try it. And you, Rebe, you're opening a sex store. Right?"

"I said I'd look into it. Get it right."

"Good. Let's just do it then. I mean it's not like we're robbing a bank. It's not gonna kill us."

Magnolia tapped her fingernails along the bar and looked left and then right at her friends. "Shit, might as well."

Rebe smiled. "Then the challenge is on."

Darla asked, "Challenge? And what do we win after we do it?"

"Hopefully a hell of a lot of damn good sex and some extra money," Darla said, just as the boisterous countdown began around them. The ladies all arose to their high-heeled feet, standing side by side upon the maple concrete flooring, and raised their glasses high in the air.

"Ten."

"Nine."

"Eight."

"Seven."

"Six."

"Five."

"Four."

"Three."

"Two."

"One."

As everyone began to yell, "Happy New Year," Magnolia said extra-loudly, "Here's to girlfriends never being farther away than the arms of our hearts can reach." It was the threesome's sisterhood mantra.

Rebe and Darla nodded and smiled, and all three said together "Cheers" as they clinked their glasses.

A few of the people along the bar and those who stood behind them offered a touch of their glasses, too, each saying, "Happy New Year," and the ladies saying it in return. Groups of strangers hugged, and loud horns blew and noisemakers cranked, and turquoise and black balloons drifted slowly from the ceiling downward among the many bodies, making a trail down to the floor around them.

"Happy Freaking New Year," Rebe said out loud like she was starting to really get the 2009 feeling, just as she looked over at the big man with the perfect goatee. He stayed seated as people hustled around him. His eyes were only for her. Hers met his and stayed there. She read his thick lips: *Happy New Year.*

Rebe heard him loud and clear and mouthed it back sexily.

She had a new look on her face.

And Magnolia and Darla noticed.

They watched Rebe watch him and then she smiled sweetly toward the big man. She spoke loudly again. "Freaking New Year is right. And I'm about to start right now." She took hold of her little black clutch from along the bar top and pulled on the hem of her short dress. "Listen. I love you both but I gotta go."

Magnolia placed her hand on Rebe's wrist. "No you're not."

"Watch me." She took a tiny sip from her glass and

placed it back down on the bar. "And I might even suck his dick on the way."

Darla's forehead wrinkled. She warned, "Rebe. Be careful. You don't even know him."

"That's the whole damn point."

"Are you drunk?" Magnolia asked over the loud glare of feel-good voices.

"No. Not even a little bit."

Darla spoke close to Rebe's ear, "Look, you text me in ten minutes, and then if you leave, you text me an address. Don't play."

Rebe acted as though she was deaf. Magnolia and Darla watched her sashay away, with her straight, elongated back and long legs strutting like she was on a runway. She gave a girly fling of her skinny braids and stood before the big man, shook his hand, and brought her lips close to his left lobe. Magnolia and Rebe could see Rebe shut her eyes as she spoke. The song "Celebration" by Kool and the Gang played as folks joined in to sing along, some heading to the dance floor.

In thirty seconds flat, after the big man whispered back to her, he stood tall, proving that he was indeed six-seven, towering over her by a foot. He placed some money on the bar and grabbed Rebe's hand, stepping away suavely with an ear-to-ear smile, while she femininely followed, looking back at her buddies, winking, grinning, and giggling like a teenager.

Magnolia said, "Well I'll be damned," almost giving off a smirk of envy. "The nerve."

Darla's mouth was stuck on open. She swallowed hard and blinked three times fast, looking at Magnolia as though prompting her to do something quick, and then she darted her worried eyes back toward Darla's exit. "Oh my God. She did it. She's leaving. Is she leaving, or are they headed to that private room? Where are they going? That child cannot be serious." She turned toward the bar and looked at Magnolia again for a moment. "What happened to the squeamish girl who just used the word *ewwww* a minute ago? She has lost her ever-loving mind at the stroke of midnight." Darla turned back toward Rebe's departure and lost complete sight of the big man and Rebe. She stood on her tiptoes. "Heck, where'd his tall ass take her?"

Magnolia sat down and took her drink in hand. "Rebe's truly taken that forty-year thing to a whole new height. And I guess that means our butts need to get serious too, girlie. Like she said, we just made three sexual resolutions. And I don't know about you, but I'm in." Magnolia again raised her glass for a toast. "Happy fortieth birthday, Darla."

Darla cut her eyes away from the crowd and plopped down on the bar stool next to Magnolia. "Happy fortieth birthday," she said weakly. She and Magnolia leaned toward each other for a hug, and Magnolia patted her on the back. Darla glanced at her tiny barrel purse and opened it, snatching her touch-screen cell and eyeing it with a frown. "That newly freaky girl had better text me. Trying to shake the missionary and get all sixty-nine and shit. She ain't forty yet, dammit."

# PYNK'S SEX DICTIONARY FAVORITES II

## A–Z

**Autofellatio:**
A *Better Sex* Definition: The act of a man performing oral sex, or "going down," on himself.

**Blue Balls:**
A *Better Sex* Definition: *Blue balls* is a slang term referring to testicular aching that may occur when the blood that fills the vessels in the male genital area during sexual arousal is not dissipated by orgasm. When a man becomes sexually excited, the arteries carrying blood to the genital area enlarge, while the veins carrying blood from the genital area are more constricted than in the nonarousal state. This uneven blood flow causes an increase in volume of blood trapped in the genitals and contributes to the penis becoming erect and the testicles becoming engorged with blood. During this process of vasocongestion the testicles increase in size 25–50 percent.

**Cameltoe:**
A *Better Sex* Definition: A vaginal wedgie ("vedgie"), most commonly caused by tight pants that work their way into the crevices of the vagina making a shape that clearly resembles a camel toe.

### Dyspareunia:

A *Better Sex* Definition: Dyspareunia is the clinical name for painful intercourse. This condition can occur at any age, in both sexes, and the pain can appear at the start of intercourse, midway through, at the time of orgasm, or after intercourse is completed. The pain can be felt as burning, sharp, searing, or cramping. It can be external, within the vagina, or deep in the pelvic region or abdomen.

### Eunuch:

A *Better Sex* Definition: A eunuch is a male for whom testicles (and sometimes the penis) have been removed. Pre-puberty removal results in a high-pitched voice and a boyish body. Postpuberty removal results in infertility. Testosterone, produced in the adrenal glands, along with other influences on sexual behavior may provide for sexual desire and erectile ability in the eunuch.

### Frenulum:

A *Better Sex* Definition: The frenulum is the small triangular fold of highly sensitive skin on the underside of the penis, just behind the glans.

### Gonzo:

A *Better Sex* Definition: An extremely low-budget genre of porn in which one person acts as director, actor, and cinematographer. First-person porn.

### Hymen:

A *Better Sex* Definition: A hymen is the thin piece of tissue that partially blocks the entrance to the vagina. It is sometimes called the maidenhead or cherry. It is named after the Greek god of marriage and has no known biological function. Although some women are born without a hymen, most have one, and the hymen varies in size and shape from woman to woman. The hymen usually does not cover the entire vaginal opening, since there must be some way for the menstrual fluid, or period, to leave the body.

## Impotence:

A *Better Sex* Definition: Impotence is the inability to achieve or maintain an erection of sufficient firmness for penetration during intercourse. Health professionals prefer the term *erectile inhibition* or *erectile dysfunction* to the term *impotence* due to the sweeping negative connotation the term *impotence* projects onto men.

## Jill Off:

A *Better Sex* Definition: Female masturbation—a clever play on words that means the female equivalent of "jacking off."

## Karezza:

A *Better Sex* Definition: The physical techniques of karezza, as propounded by Alice Bunker Stockham and others in her circle, are designed to teach control of the orgasm response in both men and women, for the purposes of physical pleasure, partnership bonding, better health, and spiritual benefit. What sets karezza apart from traditional religious teachings such as tantra yoga is that karezza method applies equally to both partners in the relationship, whether they are a man and a woman, two men, or two women.

## Libido:

A *Better Sex* Definition: *Libido* is the term that the noted founder of psychoanalysis, Sigmund Freud, used to label the sexual drive or sexual instinct. He noted that the sexual drive is characterized by a gradual buildup to a peak of intensity, followed by a sudden decrease of excitement. As he studied this process in his patients, Freud concluded that various activities like eating and drinking, as well as urination and defecation share this common pattern. Consequently, he regarded these behaviors as sexual or libidinous as well. Freud also became interested in the development of the libido, which he saw as the basic and most powerful human drive. He believed that the development of the libido involved several distinct and identifiable stages. During infancy, he noted, sexual drive is focused on the mouth, primarily manifested in sucking. He labeled this the oral stage of libidinous development.

### Manscaping:

A *Better Sex* Definition: The act of grooming, shaving, or trimming hair on the male body. Derived from the word landscaping. One of the most recognizable scenes of manscaping is from the 2005 movie *The 40 Year Old Virgin*.

### Neo-Quickie Sex:

A *Better Sex* Definition: *The Art of the Quickie* is the most comprehensive look at what we think of as "neo-quickie sex" we've read. Neo-quickie sex expands the old definition of quickies in this new age adult sex education book. In the past quickie sex had one goal—to please the man. Neo-quickie sex, according to Dr. Joel D. Block, senior psychologist at the Jewish Medical Center on Long Island, is about creating pleasure for both partners.

## Outercourse:
A *Better Sex* Definition: Outercourse is a form of pleasuring and sexual sharing other than penile-vaginal intercourse. The term is used to give credibility to the many forms of sexual pleasure that are underused because of the common view of having sex as having intercourse.

## Paraphilia:
A *Better Sex* Definition: A paraphilia is a mental health term recently used to indicate sexual arousal in response to sexual objects or situations which may interfere with the capacity for reciprocal affectionate sexual activity.

## Queer:
A *Better Sex* Definition: Original definition is strange or odd. The definition morphed to also include people in a negative connotation, such as sissy or pervert, back in the '50s. It has since been adopted as a term of empowerment by the gay community and has come to be a broader term that signifies anyone who dresses or acts outside societal norms.

## Runway:
A *Better Sex* Definition: Also referred to as the "taint." This is actually medically called the perineum and is the strip of skin between the scrotum and the anus.

## Sybian:
A *Better Sex* Definition: The Sybian is a motorized seat used by women for simulated sex. The Sybian consists of a saddle, which contains an electric motor connected to a rod that protrudes from a hole in the center of the saddle. Various attachments, including dildos, butt plugs,

and clitoral nubs can be attached to the rod. The Sybian vibrates (stimulating the clitoris) when turned on while the attachment rotates (stimulating the g-spot). The intensity can be increase or decreased using the control box attached to the Sybian.

## Tea Bagging:

A *Better Sex* Definition: Tea Bagging is a form of oral sex where a scrotum is stimulated by the other person's mouth or tongue. It is practiced by both heterosexual and homosexual couples. In one variation the male squats over his partner's face while his partner licks his ball sack.

## Uncut:

A *Better Sex* Definition: Slang for an uncircumcised man. Many parents who recognize that there is apparently no medical advantage to circumcision are now choosing not to have their sons circumcised. There is no evidence to suggest that circumcision has any effect on male sexual functioning one way or another. Opponents of routine circumcision argue that removing the foreskin lessens the sexual sensitivity of the glans since it constantly rubs directly against clothing. There is simply no evidence demonstrating that circumcision makes a difference to sexual excitement, erection, and the ability to reach orgasm or the ability to have a pleasing and complete sex life with a partner.

## Vaginismus:

A *Better Sex* Definition: Vaginismus is a purely psychological condition that occurs in women causing the muscles surrounding the vagina to close so tightly that they will not allow anything in. Women with vaginismus believe that they have no control over their vaginal muscles (which is not true). Vaginismus is due to earlier unresolved sexual traumas, fears, or anxieties. Psychological and behavioral therapies are helpful for dealing with this issue.

**Withdrawal:**
A *Better Sex* Definition: Withdrawal is the removal of the penis from the vagina before ejaculation occurs. This is NOT an effective contraceptive method. The pre-ejaculate lubricating fluids contain sperm capable of fertilization. A condom is recommended for safer sex and contraceptive practices.

**X-rated:**
Pynk Definition: Explicit sex acts, mainly used in pornographic movies.

**Yoni:**
Pynk Definition: An ancient Indian term for vagina, often mentioned in the term Yoni massage, aka pussy massage.

**Zoophilia:**
Pynk Definition: Fetish involving sex with animals.

Definitions A–W are provided courtesy of the Adult Education Sex Dictionary terms listed on www.bettersex.com, where you will also find information on various Better Sex categories, including Adult Sex Education, Adult Sex Toys, Adult Movies, and more. You can log on to www.bettersex.com for more information.

# READING GROUP GUIDE

1. Do you feel you understood Miki's need to have as many men as she did? Was it kind of a boomerang effect? What would you say was her biggest character flaw, other than her addiction to sex?

2. As far as Valencia was concerned, should Greg have understood her need for the girls, being that she accepted his chronic need for masturbation? Should he have been more patient, since they had experienced various partners throughout their long relationship and she helped him out as far as his career was concerned?

3. With Teela agreeing to allow Austin to be with other women as long as she could watch, do you think she got what she deserved, or was he the one who crossed the boundaries of their relationship? What would you like to see happen to her?

4. Did you begin to feel some understanding for Brandi's situation toward the end of the story? In the end, did you see her as a victim or as a criminal?

5. Which character would you say had the biggest addiction to sex and why?

6. Have you ever had sex with a stranger, meaning sex with someone you'd known less than a few hours? Did it grow into more or was it a one-time, hit-it-and-quit-it incident?

7. What was the most dysfunctional sexual scene in *Sexaholics*?

8. Which lady would you like to see make an appearance in a future Pynk book? Why?

9. Out of all the male characters in *Sexaholics*, which one do you think was the best lover? What was it about his sex habits that impressed you?

10. Do you personally know of anyone in your life who might be a sexaholic, but perhaps they're unaware of the intensity of their situation? What makes you suspect they could be addicted to sex?

11. If you were to classify yourself as having one addiction, what would it be? Food, gambling, alcohol, surfing the web, porn, cigarettes, shopping, shoes, sex, etc.

12. What would you do if a best friend betrayed you the way Valencia betrayed Miki? Did Valencia get what she had coming to her when all was said and done?